THE RAVEN'S DAUGHTER

PEGGY A. WHEELER

DMP

THE RAVEN'S DAUGHTER

PEGGY A. WHEELER

The Raven's Daughter

ISBN 13 p 978-1-897492-98-7

Printed on acid free paper

www.dragonmoonpress.com

For Steven D. Wheeler, my life partner, best
friend, and greatest love. Without your support
The Raven's Daughter would not exist.

Deepest gratitude goes to my loving husband, Steve, for being there for me above and beyond all reasonable expectation. Thank you so very much to my stellar publisher, Gwen Gades, for not only taking *The Raven's Daughter* for Dragon Moon Press, but for the beautiful cover art. I have so much appreciation for John Kenny from Dublin, Ireland, a terrific pro editor with a keen eye (you helped me so much, John, with those first ten pages), and to his wife, my lovely friend, Susan Caldwell, who put me in contact with John.

I have a bucket load of gratitude for my gem of an editor, Andie Gibson, and for the Hemet Writing Group—first of all big thanks to the wonderful Ray Strait, friend, mentor, and talented writer —and, thank you to my other good friends and teachers in the group, Jim Hitt, Vicki Hitt, JoLynne Buehring, C.J. Hernley, Lucille Hedges, Christine Stabile, Jim Parrish, Lynne Morgan-Spreen, Natalie Flikkema and Harlee Lassiter. (Rest in peace, Harlee. You were a class act).

Many thanks to my wonderful subject-matter expert, David Laffranchini, former Undersheriff in Trinity County, California, and Administration of Justice instructor at Shasta College. A note of thanks, too, to Dan Lambach, retired from the Los Angeles Police Department, and one cool ex-motorcycle cop, for your ideas and direction that night at the holiday party.

Thank you Deb Hoag, my former writing partner, for scanning every line of this manuscript and providing great feedback. Marie E. Berglund, wonderful long-time friend and wonderful attorney, thank you so much (you know why).

Thank you Denise Dumars, my one-time agent and still wonderful friend of more than thirty years. Your constant support means the world to me. Also, a nod of appreciation to the people of Trinity County, California, and Weaverville in particular (known in the book as Wild River County, and Wicklow, California).

And lastly, thank you so very much to my mom who cheered me on every step of the way (I miss you so much, Mom), and to all my good friends who absolutely believed I could write this book even when I absolutely doubted I could.

CHAPTER 1

Canada, Twenty-Eight Years Ago

Three weeks before his sixth birthday, the boy tasted his first human heart. It happened during an elk hunting trip with his father, Noshi, his mother, Chepi, and his twin brother, Sheshebens.

"Uncle Sokamon says the Elk are plentiful on the back side of the La Cloche," Noshi said.

The family packed, Noshi grabbed his rifle, and off they went. The day before, a freak storm, "the worst of the season," the weatherman said, dumped another meter of snow over the already blanketed peaks. But today the sun was blinding orange and the sky, hyacinth blue. The boy shielded his eyes with one hand and squinted at the glinting snow.

Northern California, Present Time

AN UNKINDNESS OF ravens, knocking and cawing, settled into the branches of a gray pine. Maggie squinted at them through the morning glare of the sun, and reached into her coat pocket. "You gluttonous, winged pigs." She withdrew her hand and tossed corn onto the dirt. No matter where Margaret Tall-Bear Sloan was, ravens were certain to be nearby. She always carried corn.

The phone rang. She dropped the kernels remaining in her palm, and sprinted into her cottage. "Hello?"

"I've got bad news," said Jake Lubbock, Wicklow's sheriff.

"Don't tell me. More kids?"

"Six-year-old girls. The O'Malley twins."

"Dammit. God dammit."

"You still thinking about joining the reserves? Your certification is current, and you still have your license to carry. Right? I can expedite this."

9

Silence.

"Maggie, listen to me. We sure could use your help. Two sets of twins in less than eight months.

No clues. We can't get a handle on this."

"You know after what happened in Oakland, I don't deal with child killers. I'm sorry, but I have to say no."

"Can we meet for lunch and talk? At least hear me out."

"What time? I've got an appointment this morning. I can be in town around one if that's not too late."

"One it is," Jake said. "And...Maggie?"

"Yeah?"

"Thanks."

"Don't thank me. I'm not getting involved. This is only lunch, and you're buying."

"Whatever you say. See you at The Dandelion."

She slicked back a few stray hairs. *Not bad for an old broad.* With her bare foot, she stroked Samantha, her blue point Siamese rescue cat with a crooked tail and an attitude. The slinky feline leapt onto the table and butted Maggie's hand in a bid for additional petting.

For 46, Maggie figured she'd held up pretty good, her complexion wrinkle-free except tiny crows' feet at the corners of her eyes when she smiled, which was seldom. Maggie had Yurok features from her mother's side, toasted butter skin and Native hair, glossy stuff of legends she plaited into a thick salt-and-pepper braid that fell to her waist. Her lime green eyes that turned dark olive when she became angry, which was often, she owed to her Northern Irish father.

She pulled on her favorite T-shirt, the one that read, "I'm half white but can't prove it," kicked off fuzzy pink slippers, yanked on her Dan Post boots, and left with her dog following close behind. "See ya later, Samantha. Keep the mice away while we're gone."

She opened the door to her '54 cherry red Chevy pickup. "C'mon, Chester." The old bloodhound leapt into the passenger's seat. As Maggie headed toward town, a raucous cry broke the mid-day stillness. She glanced in her rearview mirror. "Yup, ravens following us, Chester. What a big surprise, eh boy?"

—

"Hi," she said as she entered the café. The screen door slammed behind her.

"You look *really* pretty today," Jake said. "I ordered a cup o' java for you."

"Thanks, and if you hit on me, I'm walking out." Maggie laughed as she slipped into the booth opposite Jake. "Can't stay long anyway. Chester's in the truck."

A waitress with spiky purple hair, an earplug the color and size of a new copper penny and a dragonfly tattoo on her neck set mugs of coffee on the table. "Ready?"

Jake and Maggie put in their orders, but the waitress lingered.

"Yes, Dawn?" Jake asked.

"Sheriff, those little girls, the O'Malley's? Their family lives in my neighborhood. Their mom was planning a party for their seventh birthdays this Saturday, and she'd hired me to help out. I hope you catch that asshole."

"We'll get the guy, I promise. We'll have him by..."

As he spoke to the waitress, Jake raked his fingers through his hair from right above his brow to the nape of his neck. When stressed, he had a disarming habit of combing his fingers over his scalp. Maggie drifted into a memory.

She had first noticed him in 8th grade during a math exam. Jake sat at the desk in front of her raking his fingers through his hair again and again distracting her so much she almost flubbed the test. "Would you knock it off with the hair thing," she whispered. "I can't concentrate."

"Sorry. I didn't mean to bug y...," he said turning in his seat to apologize, but the moment he made eye contact with her, he froze. His last word caught in his throat, and the only other sounds from his gaping mouth were stutters.

That was how their friendship began. Jake became the only person, maybe other than her friend Sally, Maggie could be herself with. But, there was no way she could make herself want him the way he wanted her. Even now as older adults, they jousted, kidded each other, argued, and picked on one another like adolescents. For Maggie, this was her way to demonstrate the only affection for him she could muster. Not known for a stellar sense of humor, Maggie never joked with anyone else like she did with Jake. She took no pleasure in breaking his heart, although she'd done it a hundred times.

"Want a refill?" Dawn said, breaking Maggie's revere.

"Sure. Thanks. "The waitress poured the coffee, and departed, her red Doc Martens clumping against the tile floor.

Jake shook his head and laughed. "Those shoes can't be comfortable to work in."

Maggie grabbed her bag and inched from behind the table. "I really can't handle kid murders. You're going to have to fly solo or hire someone else. Thanks for the coffee, but I have to leave."

"Wait, Maggie. At least have some lunch. Food's already ordered. C'mon. If you don't want to give us a hand, I understand, okay? I'm not going to pressure you."

"You better not be lying."

"Stay put. Please."

She scooted back and said nothing as she stirred a packet of sugar into her mug.

"I thought you liked your coffee black."

"Yeah, I do. But, today, I need something a little sweet." She studied Jake's face.

Although handsome in a rough sort of way, the years had neither been easy nor kind to him. "You say there are no clues?"

"That's what's so goddamn baffling. We can't even find footprints. It's like a ghost is killing these kids, Maggie. Forensics can't find hairs, cloth fibers, or fingerprints."

"Nothing at all we can work with?"

"From what we can tell, it looks as though the son-of-a-bitch keeps the kids for a couple of days. "He leaned across the table, looking around the café to ensure no one was listening, and whispered, "We find the kids face-to-face, arms around one another in an embrace. In each case they were placed...I don't mean dumped... *placed* in graves almost reverently. This is the work of a 100 percent authentic sicko." He leaned back, laced his fingers behind his head, and stretched. His upper back made an audible pop. "Damn, I'm getting to be an old, creaky fart. You don't want to retire, Maggie. C'mon. Get on the reserves. Help us out. We need you. I need you."

"Any sign of sexual assault?" she asked.

"No."

"How old did you say the victims are?"

"No younger than four, no older than eight."

"Babies then."

"Yeah, Mag. Pretty much."

"Shit." With the fingers of both hands she massaged the tops of her shoulders.

A scraping noise outside caught their attention. "Will you look at that?" Jake pointed at the window. "Check out all those crows."

On the ledge, a half dozen ravens perched in a row.

"They aren't crows."

———

Maggie settled into her lounge chair overlooking Wild River. Her lump of a lazy bloodhound stretched out on the grass beside her, and Samantha curled into a snug ball on her chest. She'd put on her favorite Clannad CD, and opened a paperback book, *Learning Irish Gaelic.*

The lunch meeting with Jake wore on her, and Maggie had not slept much the night before.

The placid music lulled her into drowsiness. Her eyes closed, and as she fell asleep, her fingers went limp and the book slid from her lap landing with a soft plop on the ground.

She dreamed she was a raven. She flew through a remote part of the forest deep into the Trinity Alps. Below, elk and bear foraged for food. Maggie cawed a greeting to them, veered west and flew toward the white cliffs of Sunset Mountain. Beneath the shade of an old Douglas fir, alive in spite of being split nearly in two by lightning, she saw a thin human-like figure, only much too tall to be a human, hunched over something. Curious, as ravens are, she flew closer, settled onto the limb of the fir and cocked her head to get a better look.

An emaciated Native man in dirty torn buckskins with strips of rotting flesh hanging from his hands and face busied himself digging a rectangular hole with a spade. The man had long, stringy black hair that appeared plucked out in patches revealing skull the color of coffee stains. The music of unseen whistles and drums echoed off the cliffs.

"Who are you?" she said. The question came out in a series of caws and clicks.

He ceased his digging, tilted his head above to the branch where she perched. With one eye he stared at her. Where his other eye should have been was a foul hole from which dropped, one at a time, glistening maggots.

CHAPTER 2

Canada, Twenty-Eight Years Ago
"Let's get out here," Noshi said as he stopped the old Ford pickup. "If we walk the road, there's a good chance we'll find elk tracks."

The family climbed out of the truck and made their way through the crunchy snow, so deep with each step, the boy sank to his knees. He struggled to keep up with his parents; his brother lagged behind. "Sheshebens, come on. Mommy! Daddy! Wait..."

Northern California, Present Time
AS SHE DRANK her morning coffee, Maggie mulled over the previous day's meeting with Jake. "I'm not going through this again. I want to help, but I really can't," she said to Samantha. The cat arched her back and yawned. "Anything to do with children getting hurt rips me into shreds." Then she remembered the dream.

She'd experienced the raven dream since she was a kid. It used to frighten her, but as the years passed, her sleep-time adventures became familiar, sometimes comforting. Mostly her dreams were benign, or even fun. She'd fly among the white oaks, climbing further into the sky above her A-frame along the river and over the town. She observed the people below going about their business. Sometimes it was day time, other times night. Sometimes she was alone, other times she flew among an unkindness of ravens.

Once, flying solo over Main Street, Maggie saw her best friend, Sally Winters, crossing the street from her store, *Mama Winters Bookstore and Coffee House,* known to locals as *Mama's.* She swooped down. "Hey, Sally. How's business?"

Sally looked up at Maggie, shielding her eyes with her hands against the midday sun.

"Sally, it's me, Maggie," but only caws, rocks and clicks issued from her beak.

The particular dream following her meeting with Jake at The Dandelion Café was different. When image of the one-eyed specter invaded her morning thoughts, her hand shuddered with such violence that coffee splashed over the mug's rim and scalded her. She dropped her cup, shattering it into a dozen pieces against the kitchen floor and sending Samantha skittering out of the room, tail down, ears plastered to her head.

———

"Danny, I don't want to alarm you," Maggie told her brother when he'd called, "but warn your son to keep a closer eye on the girls. I tried to phone him this morning, but he didn't answer."

"He's been out on a job. No cell reception. What's up?"

"I met with Jake yesterday. No leads on that kid-murdering psycho. He got the O'Malley girls. And, Danny, he targets twins between ages four and eight."

Maggie's brother, Daniel Tall Bear Sloan, who she called Danny but everyone else called Bear, looked much like her but stood four inches over her 5-foot-10-inch frame, muscular with darker skin, and a bit more gray in his hair. Although twins, no one ever said they were "two peas in a pod." There wasn't much they agreed on, but they both loved Danny's grandchildren.

"Christ," Danny said. "Those little girls sometimes play with Flower and Bird. Jesus!" He sighed. "Why don't you tell Jimmy in person when you see him? He'll be here all weekend."

"He will?"

For a moment, Danny was silent. "You forgot again, didn't you?"

"Oh, God. The Bear Dance. Is Jake going to be there?"

"He comes every year. You know that."

"I really don't want to talk to Jake about...he wants me to do something that I don't want to...never mind. I'll be there."

Every year the third weekend in September, no matter sunshine or hail, Danny held the traditional event on his property. As much as Maggie was into "all things Irish," Danny was into "all things Native." Bear dancers from everywhere in North America came to Danny's sixteen-acre parcel downriver. There were talking circles, sweat lodges, medicine wheels and tables piled with food. Some local whites and a Natives from different tribes brought meat to share and gifts of tobacco. The Yuroks always brought salmon for the "bears."

The Hoopa, Yurok and Wintu women grouped together at this event, but Maggie sought the company of the white people. Although every year she attended The Bear Dance she identified more with her daddy's people, her Celtic Tribe from Belfast.

She wasn't up for the three day's festivities at Danny's, not so much because of the native ceremonies, but because she'd have to talk to Jake. *I can't avoid him the entire damned weekend.* Also, she'd be missing her favorite Celtic band, The Ulster Boys, scheduled to play that weekend at The Silverado.

The Ulster Boys, a trio of ginger haired brothers from Derry, County Antrim, Northern Ireland, were the Silverado house band. The family settled in Wicklow when the boys were young, and their mother and father, prominent Irish musicians themselves, made certain their children grew up appreciating their Irish heritage. The boys spoke fluent Gaelic and were skilled on all the traditional Irish instruments. One brother played harp, reed, and uillean pipes. Another was adept on tin whistle, fiddle, bodhrain and bones. The third had become accomplished on the concertina and the tiopan. Sometimes, their cousin, Molly, sat in with them. She played Celtic harp and had a honey-toned voice reminding Maggie of a hybrid between Loreena McKennit and Moira Brennan. Although she loved Molly's voice, she avoided the Silverado when Molly sat in. It was because of that one night when Maggie walked in the door, and Molly, stopping mid-song, pointed at Maggie. "Fiach Dubh."

Maggie had just put in her order for a Harp, when Molly stopped singing mid-phrase, and in an unnatural voice, high and tinny like a muted brass whistle, she said something unintelligible into her microphone. Maggie got an eerie feeling, and looked over her shoulder both ways. *She wasn't talking to me, was she?*

"Fiach Dubh." Molly's eyes glazed over, and the mic slipped from her hand to her lap. She pointed at Maggie. The band paused and her siblings gaped at her, their hands frozen on their instruments. "Molly!" Sean, the brother on the bodhrain said. "Snap out of it. We're in the middle of a gig. C'mon!"

"Fiach Dubh."

The bartender handed the Harp to Maggie but she waved him away, and stepped closer to the stage. "Sean, she is talking to me, right? What is she saying?"

"I don't get it, but she's saying, 'Raven.'"

Maggie felt like an ice-cube had lodged in her throat. The room went quiet as a funeral, and all eyes turned on Maggie, who swallowed hard to force down the frigid lump, spun on her foot and pushed her way through the crowd to the door.

The Saturdays when Molly didn't sing, Maggie could be found at the bar drinking beer and listening to the band. "A hand for the Ulster Lass" they'd say as she walked in, and the patrons applauded as though she were a celebrity. Anyone whose family came from Belfast was a friend of the band from Derry. Maggie felt most at home in the company of these musicians who poured their souls out at The Silverado. But, she always called ahead to make certain Molly wasn't going to be there.

This weekend, she would be at the Bear Dance, resenting every minute of it. *I want nothing to do with this case, nothing. And, I don't feel like hanging all weekend at my brother's house with all those people. Is it too much to ask to be left alone on the river with Chester and Samantha, learn Gaelic, and raise a few Araucana chickens?*

Maggie had gotten her fill of child killers a long while back.

CHAPTER 3

Canada, Twenty-Eight Years Ago

They had walked no more than fifty yards from the truck when an explosion came from nowhere. The ground shook, pines toppled like Jenga pieces, and scattered screeching birds into the morning sky.

"Hurry, Sheshebens." the boy said.

"Oh my God," said Noshi.

Another rumble as through the Earth split in two, and the boy turned to see a wall of snow bury the family truck...

Northern California, Present Time

MAGGIE PUT ON her best face, but participated in the Bear Dance weekend without energy or will. Her brother, Danny, however, was in his glory. He'd always said, "No one is invited, but everyone is welcome." It was anyone's guess who might show up. People trickled in throughout the weekend, and this year, it seemed as though the entire population of northern California responded to Danny's welcome.

Sunday evening the bears were scheduled to dance. By late morning, tipis and tents were crammed so close together there was scant space to walk between them. In the afternoon, the property was a chaotic wall-to-wall mass of humanity. Danny greeted attendees as though holding court. "This is great," he whispered to Maggie.

Yes, great. With this crowd, maybe I won't have to talk to Jake at all.

"Something's on your mind. What's wrong?" Danny asked.

"Nothing, really. It's fine."

"Jake's been looking for you."

—

Jake had always been her rock even though he'd endured so much himself during his warped childhood that she marveled at his ability to be so steady, and so available to others. Doctors had diagnosed his mother with schizophrenia, and what then had been called "manic depression," when she was only a kid herself. She'd been in and out of mental wards since her sixteenth birthday. Unable to hold a job or manage a long-term adult relationship, and with her acidic attitude and tenacious paranoia, she had driven her family away. She refused anti-psychotic drugs, making life for her and her only son a challenge. He never knew when he came home from school what to expect. She had a raging temper and would fly into screeching fits over minor infractions, sometimes beating Jake with a belt leaving bruises and welts on his legs and back. Other times, she'd be affectionate and motherly, all cuddles and sugar.

His alcoholic father couldn't take it, and left when Jake was only eight, and afterward...a succession of step-fathers, each worse than the previous.

Later, after Maggie had completed her first university psychology course, she gave Jake a book about bi-polar disorder. "I think this might help you to better understand your mom," she told him.

As a teenager, when he needed a reprieve from his mother, Jake ended up at the Sloans'. Maggie's mother made fry bread with powdered sugar for Danny, Maggie and Jake to take to the garage where they'd hang out for hours listening to 1960s and 70s rock and roll on Danny's tape deck. The Rolling Stones were the boys' favorite. Maggie favored Janis Joplin. Whenever, "Piece of My Heart" came on, Jake asked Maggie to slow dance. She was a willing partner until that one time she felt his erection against her, and then she stopped accepting his invitations to dance.

After his father left, although just a child, Jake assumed the role of caretaker for his mother between her marriages, massaging her neck and shoulders when she had one of her many "sick headaches," doing her laundry, seeing that her bills were paid, and cooking for her. Even as a small boy, he looked out after himself, making his own breakfasts, and packing his own school lunches. Jake told Maggie that he loved his mother and resented her in equal measure.

He was in his thirties when she died of heart failure. He told Maggie, "My mom is the only biological family I have, and I know she did her best." Maggie held him as he cried. The Sloans had long before become his de facto family, a fixture in Maggie's life. And, right now, she was avoiding him...

——

"I don't want to talk to Jake."

"What's up? You two have a fight?"

"No, not that. I'd prefer not to discuss it right now. Let's enjoy the weekend, okay?"

Another group of attendees made their way through the crowd toward Danny.

"Hey, Bear," a Hoopa man in full regalia called out.

Maggie exhaled in relief when Danny turned his attention to his guests.

——

She liked Danny's wife, Catharine Two Tails, a full-blooded Wintu, born and reared on The Chester Valley Reservation. She'd been only seventeen and Danny not quite nineteen when their son, Jimmy, forced himself into the world butt first. The breech birth nearly killed the diminutive Cathy, and she was unable to conceive again.

During weekends of the Bear Dance, Maggie didn't see much of Cathy who spent the majority of her time working in the outdoor kitchen Danny had built and christened "The Longhouse." This year, Maggie spent as much time as she could with her sister-in-law, grateful for the mountain of unpeeled potatoes on the prep table.

"Too bad about them twin girls," Cathy said. "I hear Sheriff Jake is gonna try to get some local help to find that bad killer.

Them little girls was barely older than Flower and Bird."

Maggie snatched up a potato and began peeling with such fury that she nicked her thumb.

"Ouch. Oh, dammit." She dropped the peeler and stuck her wounded thumb into her mouth.

Cathy handed her a damp paper towel. "Are you hurt?"

"I'm fine, thanks. It's a tiny cut."

"I'll get you some peroxide if you want." She reached for Maggie's hand. "Here, let me see that thumb."

Maggie jerked her hand away. "I said it's fine, Cathy. Let's focus on getting these potatoes peeled, if you don't mind."

Cathy stepped back. "I think it's best you leave The Longhouse for a bit. Your mind ain't on potatoes, and I don't want nobody snapping at me when I'm tryin' to help."

"I'm sorry. I just..."

"Why don't you go out and see them Yurok womens? They're talkin' about acorns. I hear them white oaks were plenty good this year. Besides, that peeler you're usin' is dull and you're gonna cut yourself again. I'll take care of them potatoes faster with a knife anyway." Cathy waved to a group of women busy cubing venison and carrots. "Or, one of them can do it. Go on out of here."

"I'm sorry, Cathy, really. I didn't mean to be surly. I guess I'm testy because of those little girls. I'm happy to be in here with you. Let me help," but Maggie had been drinking iced tea all day and her bladder felt like a cheap overfilled balloon ready to explode. She put aside the potato peeler, pulled off her apron, wadded it into a ball and tossed it on the counter. "Cathy, I have to pee. I'll be back in a minute."

The moment she stepped out of The Longhouse, she encountered Jake sitting with a group of men, some brown, some white. She halted, turned on her heels, and took a few brisk steps in the opposite direction before he called to her. "Hey, girl. Where have you been? I've been looking for you. Come on over and take a seat with us."

"Shit," she said under her breath, and spun around to face him, "No, thanks. Lots of people this year. Cathy needs my help in the kitchen."

"Aw, c'mon. Take a break. It's the last day and I haven't seen you at all."

"Gimme a second. I'll be right back." Maggie used the bathroom, washed her hands, and took her time returning to the circle. The men shifted their seats to make room. She plopped on a folding chair next to Jake. "Glad it's not raining like it did last year. I scraped mud off my boots for a week."

"Clouds moving in. We might still get wet," Jake leaned closer to her, slung his arm around the back of her chair, and lowered his voice. "We've got to find some place to talk, or maybe you can meet me at the station tomorrow?"

She didn't hear him because she was distracted by a stranger headed toward them. He was indigenous, tall, maybe 6-foot-4, well-built but thin, with a beautiful face. He looked to be in his late 30s. "Who's that?" she asked Jake.

"Some Algonquin guy, Mingan Metchitehew. Moved here last year from up north. He's a banker."

"Yeah? Never seen him."

"That's because you hardly ever come to town. Everybody knows Mingan. You wouldn't know this, but he hangs around with Bear sometimes."

"He's tall for an Indian, and *really* good looking."

"Stand in line, girl. The women at the Wicklow Christian Church fall all over themselves baking him cookies."

"Christian? I wouldn't have figured that. Not many of those show up at the Bear Dance."

"I'm a Christian, and I'm here."

"Yeah, but you're different."

"How so?" He shifted in his seat.

"You never push it. I think in thirty years, you invited me to your church once maybe. But, this Mingan? He's religious?"

"Oh, yeah. Church goin' full-blown Christian. I hear he's a deacon. Maybe he's here to save you."

Maggie checked out the newcomer as he passed. "Nice ass," she whispered.

Jake looked at Maggie, at Mingan, then back to Maggie. "Forget about it. Not your type. He's not blonde and blue-eyed, and he doesn't drink much." He spit on the ground.

"I think I could *make* him my type...." She paused. "Well, it depends, I suppose." She watched Mingan's receding figure. "Naw, never mind. Too young for me anyway."

Jake's expression relaxed, and he leaned back in his chair.

Maggie was grateful to have Mingan to think about, and something to talk about other than child murders, although it seemed that's the only topic anyone wanted to discuss. *If I hear one more person say, "Isn't it awful about those kids? I hope Sheriff Jake catches that killer soon," I'll pull out my own hair by the roots.* This good looking newcomer gave her a respite, a mental diversion, a solid reason to change the course of Jake's conversation. *Besides, really, Mingan does have a great ass.*

Nearby, Wintu women gathered in their own circle. "Hi, Mingan," one said as he approached.

"Hello, ladies." He waived, then continued toward the river.

Another said, "Hell, I wouldn't kick that one out of my bedroll for eatin' crackers." The women laughed. "I'll cook up fry bread for him *any* time, but he'll have to earn it." She stood up and made lewd bumps and grinds with her hips. The women guffawed.

"He likes them prissy white Christian girls," said another.

"I'll believe in Jesus for a night, and with the lights off, he won't know I'm Indian," said the hip bumper.

⎯

For the event, Danny always built a traditional Yurok sweat house half buried in the soil, and covered with redwood strips.

"Hey, Bear! You gonna sweat?" a man who had joined the circle asked Danny, "I haven't seen you at the lodge."

"I'll be there in a minute. Gotta get Jimmy."

James "Jimmy" Sloan worked with his father in "Bear and Son Construction," and raised his twin daughters on his own. His wife, a buxom half-French, half-Modoc woman, ran away with a wealthy Los Angeles investor when the girls were barely old enough to crawl.

"Mag, would you mind keeping an eye on Bird and Flower while Jimmy and I sweat?" Danny asked.

"No problem."

Tiny identical girls with bobbed hair ran to Maggie. "Hi Auntie!"

Maggie was available to babysit because she would not be sweating. Only men were allowed in the Yurok lodges. Maggie didn't mind. Sometimes there were women sweats or co-ed lodges other natives hosted, but whenever one of the women invited Maggie to go, her response was always the same, "Hell, I sweat enough. You go. I'll wait for you at The Silverado." Right now, Maggie wanted to spend time with the children.

"When I'm old enough, I'm going to change my name to Maggie, like yours, Auntie," said Bird.

The little girls told Maggie they hated their names and often talked about when they were of legal age what they would rename themselves.

"I wanna be Lucy," said Flower.

"Well, gentlemen, I'll see you at dinner. I've got some serious playing to do with my girls," Maggie stood. "C'mon *Lucy* and *Maggie*, let's go." She stood, scooping one child into each arm. "Hide 'n seek?"

"Maggie," Jake called out. "Let's catch up tonight. I need to talk to you about that thing we discussed at The Dandelion. I wouldn't ask if I didn't really need your help."

"Not this weekend." She ran to the river, carrying the giggling girls bouncing against her hips.

Mingan sat alone on a flat rock on the river bank. With his shoes off, and his legs crossed, he tossed pebbles into the water.

"Hi," Maggie said.

He turned to her. His grin warmed his otherwise serious face, and tiny crinkles appeared around his eyes. *Charming.* He wore his thick hair, so black it was almost blue in the sunlight, parted in the middle, loose, informal, and too long for a stuffy banker. *Sexy as hell.*

"Hi," he said. He stood, and with both hands he brushed off his jeans. He leapt off the rock, and extended his hand to Maggie. "I'm Mingan Metchitehew."

"Maggie Sloan."

"These two cuties your daughters?"

"God, no. My grandnieces. Flower, Bird, meet Mr. Metchitehew."

"You must be Bear's sister, then? He's mentioned you." Mingan squatted on his heels, and put his hand out to each of the girls. "How do you do? And, you can call me Mingan, okay? I wouldn't guess you to be old enough to have *grand* anything," Mingan said as he raised to his feet.

"Thanks. I'm old enough; probably could be *your* mother."

"No, I don't think so."

Maggie couldn't help but notice when he eyed her with appreciation. It felt good, like warm cream-and-berry-pie good. "You're new to Wicklow?"

"Been here close to a year. I work at National Bank."

"I bank there. I don't recall seeing you."

"I'm in the back offices. I don't recall seeing you either. I would remember." When he smiled at her again, she felt as though she could dissolve into a quivering mass of warm gelatin. His eyes roved for a split second to her breasts and settled back onto her face. "Next time you're in, ask for me. Maybe we can grab a cup of coffee at Mama's."

"That'd be great."

"Auntie, can we play now, *please*?" said Flower.

"Yeah, I want to find pollywogs in the stream over there," said Bird pointing to a shallow creek.

"Pollywogs?" said Mingan. "In my day, I was a premier pollywog hunter. Can I come?"

"Sure," said Bird. "Let's go."

"Are you certain?" Maggie said to him. "They can be a handful."

"I love kids. It's fine."

"All right girls, but stay where I can see you, listen to Mingan, and take off your shoes before wading."

Maggie climbed on the rock where Mingan had been sitting to watch the little girls and the tall man play. Before long, all three were in the water. The kids giggled and splashed Mingan, who laughed along with them. He slipped on a lichen-covered boulder, and fell butt-down into the creek soaking the back of his jeans. The two little girls piled on top of him, all three in hysterics.

"Hey, I thought you were looking for pollywogs," Maggie said.

"Sorry, I think we frightened them," said Mingan.

"Yup, they all swam away," said Flower. "They were scared we was gonna eat 'em."

"Ew." Bird wrinkled her nose. "We don't eat pollywogs. Gross."

"What?" said Mingan. "You've never tasted delicious pollywog stew?"

"Yuck," said Bird.

"Mingan eats pollywogs, Auntie Maggie," Flower screwed her face and wrinkled her nose.

Maggie had dated plenty of men, but never had any of her romantic partners played with her grandnieces, or showed any interest in them at all. *Maybe this one is a good guy.*

CHAPTER 4

Canada, Twenty-Eight Years Ago

Noshi dropped his rifle. As it plummeted down a cliff, it cracked and splintered against rocks. He ran to his children, snow flying off his boots. The boy's twin brother, still lagging behind, slipped on an ice patch and screamed as he tumbled over a steep embankment. The world became dense and silent. Even the jays fell mute...

Northern California, Present Time

MINGAN SAT WITH Maggie and the girls at the Bear Dance feast. From across the table, Jake fixed a steely eye on the Algonquin. "You're at the bank?"

"Yes. Transferred from Washington late last year. Building a house upriver," Mingan pointed with his fork in the general direction of "upriver."

"You'll be settling long term in Wicklow, then?"

"I think so. I kinda like it here, *especially now*," Mingan turned to Maggie and grinned.

Jake clenched his jaw, and the muscles beneath the skin on his cheeks rippled. "You're Algonquin? Aren't you a little far from home? Where do you come from, anyway?"

"I was born and raised near Ontario."

"Canada?"

"Is there another Ontario?"

"Right here in California. Down south, not far from L.A."

"Is that right?"

"Yeah, *that's right.*"

Maggie blanched in response to Jake's spiky tone. She glared at him with such scalding ferocity she thought if he'd noticed, he would have disintegrated, but Jake wasn't looking at her.

"What's an Algonquin doing here?"

"Came through a few years ago on a driving vacation and stopped in Wicklow. Thought it was a pretty place."

"Wicklow's a little far off the main highway, isn't it?"

Mingan grabbed a handful of napkin into a fist, and he shifted in his seat, looking first to Maggie and then back to Jake. "Look, I heard it was a nice town, so I wanted to check it out, that's all. When I did, I thought it might be a good place to live."

"Is that so?" said Jake.

"Yeah, *that's so*. When the bank opened a branch here, I asked for a transfer because I wanted a change. There's no law against that, is there? You know? I came here this weekend for the Bear Dance. I wasn't expecting the local sheriff to give me the third degree. I'm only..."

"...Mingan had quite a play-date with the girls in that little creek near the river. Isn't that right girls?" Maggie said.

"Mingan and us went pollywog huntin' and got all wet, Uncle Jake," Flower said. "It was fun."

"He eats pollywog soup. Icky," Bird stuck out her tongue in disgust, and shook her head.

"Mingan says he'll take us fishing," said Flower.

"*Well, now, isn't that nice,*" Jake said, pulling his fingers through his hair.

Maggie stood, and grabbed her plate and fork. "If you don't mind, I think I'll finish my dinner where I can better digest it."

"Aw, sit down," Jake said. "I'm only edgy today because of those kids, you know? Sorry, Mingan. Here. Have something to drink." He reached for a pitcher and poured iced-tea into Maggie and Mingan's glasses.

———

When the sun set over the Trinity Alps, the guests headed to the circle for the bear dance. First, there were prayers, then the men threw offerings of whole salmon, local honey, and tobacco into the fire. Jimmy was on the drum with Danny, so the girls stayed with Maggie for the dance. Maggie sandwiched herself a few steps up on the bleachers between Jake and Mingan. The twins balanced on the Algonquin's lap, one on each knee. Drum beats reverberated through the arena. Bear dancers paraded into the circle covered in hides from bears they'd hunted, killed and skinned themselves.

Ruben Yellow Knife, a local healer and Native language teacher, smudged them as they entered. The men danced in intricate steps clockwise around the fire. Bent at the waist, they made lumbering bear-like movements, huffing and growling, shifting their heads side-to-side. The bears' steps matched the rhythm of the drum, the fire providing the only light.

As Maggie watched the dancers and listened to the drums, an exhilarating intoxication overcame her. Her vision slipped out of focus and she lost awareness of the others in the bleachers. Voices and ambient noise disappeared altogether, leaving only the drum beats, the percussion of dancers' footsteps against the compacted dirt, and their bear-like grunting. As the men circled the fire, a cool gray mist descended over them. Wraith-like shapes appeared from the fog and took form. The figures hung mid-air over the dancers. "Bear spirits? Can't be. I have to be hallucinating," she whispered.

"What did you say?" said Jake.

—

This was not the first time Maggie had experienced ghostly apparitions. Although a confirmed skeptic, it seemed everywhere Maggie went things happened she could not explain. Sometimes, she became so frightened by what she saw or heard, like a little girl, she'd sleep with the light on. One time when she was on a profiling case at police headquarters in Chicago, she'd been given a room at a nearby bed and breakfast in an old Victorian with a gingerbread house paint job and lace curtains. Every night she was there, right as she was falling asleep, a figure appeared beside her bed. In his hand, he held a knife over his head and whispered to her, "You're Number Fifteen, girly." As he looked as though he was about to plunge the blade into Maggie's chest she bolted upright, flipped on the light by the bed, and the specter disappeared. As soon as she turned off the light, he'd appear again. After that, for her entire ten-day stay, the lights stayed on. When at the office, she asked some of the cops if they'd seen or heard anything strange.

"Oh, you must have heard talk about Mikey." One old timer said. "I don't believe in any of that woo woo stuff, but the story going around for decades is he's been haunting this neighborhood since he got his in the electric chair in 1933. Kid stuff, really. Don't take those stories seriously or you'll end up with the heebie-jeebies."

"I don't believe in any of that stuff, either, but out of curiosity, what was his M.O.?" Maggie asked.

"All his victims were attractive, single women with dark hair who lived alone, and all resided within a ten-mile radius of the precinct. It was like he was taunting us. No sexual assault. He'd break into their homes, find them sleeping in their beds, and stab them through the heart. He murdered fourteen women before we got him. Of course, that was before my time. Hahaha."

"How many women did you say?"

"Fourteen. According to urban legend he's been looking for victim Number Fifteen since." When kids are in a mean mood and want to scare someone, they'll sneak up behind a pretty, dark-haired woman and say "You're Number Fifteen, girly."

———

But, now, at the Bear Dance, she watched the animal spirits sink into the dancers' pelts one at a time superimposing their hulking forms over the men's smaller bodies until it became impossible to distinguish between the men and ghost-bears. Muzzles, heavy skulls and shiny black eyes obscured the faces of the humans, who now issued grunts and huffs of *ursus americanus* rather than men. Maggie squeezed her eyes tight, then opened them in hopes the apparitions would vanish. They didn't. *Impossible.*

Danny rose from the drum. "Our people believe it's good luck to touch the bears' pelts."

Maggie's spell burst with the cacophony of people chattering, jostling one another on the stands, and shuffling toward the arena. The bears became human again, and Maggie's shoulders dropped in relief. *I knew it. I'm seeing things because I'm tired. That's all it is.*

Mingan held the girls out one at a time so they could reach the pelts on the dancers' backs. Danny invited the crowd to dance, and Ruben smudged the guests as they entered the arena. Maggie took the twins from Mingan, and followed the group to the fire. She placed the girls in front of her. They took small shuffling steps behind the bear dancers, Maggie behind them. As she stepped around the circle, Maggie felt someone move in close to her. *Jake.* But, when she turned, there was Mingan. In spite of the cold night air he'd removed his shirt, and an oversized silver cross bounced against his coppery chest with each of his steps. He was so near she could smell his skin and hear his breathing. "I understand you're a good Christian boy. Dancing half nude around a pagan bonfire? You must have a wild side."

Mingan moved in even closer, almost touching her. "Jesus is in my heart always, but I'm also Indian. You do believe in Jesus Christ, don't you?"

Maggie thought she'd never met a more beautiful man. She'd long given up on the idea of marriage, but she'd had plenty of lovers, some younger than her. Tonight, as she danced with this sexy man behind her, she couldn't dislodge the mental image of what he would look like naked. *It's been a long time, too long.* "No. I'm afraid I'm a non-believer, an atheist." She added the atheist bit to make herself clear on where she stood.

She could no longer hear Mingan's steps, no longer feel his heat. She imagined Mingan had halted, allowing her to step further in front of him to distance himself. *I blew it. He'll not want anything to do with me now that he knows I'm bound for Hell.*

After the dance, Mingan bid his goodbyes. "Sorry, I have to get going." He glanced at his watch. "I've got to be at the bank early tomorrow. It's been a wonderful day, ladies. Hope to see you again soon."

"You really goin'?" Flower asked him.

"Yes, I'm afraid I have to."

"Awwww." Bird grabbed his hand and pulled. "Stay. *Please, please, please.*" Mingan leaned down and kissed the top of her head. "We'll go fishing real soon, okay? Maybe your Aunt Maggie will go with us and we'll have a picnic."

Maggie felt her heart quicken. *Maybe that I don't have a personal relationship with his God doesn't matter after all.*

As he climbed into his truck, the girls waved and blew kisses.

After he left, Maggie headed to the Longhouse to help with dishes.

"Saw that tall boy, Mingan, behind you at the dance," said Cathy. "He stepped right in front of Jake who looked none too happy about it. That boy got pretty close to you there."

"He's almost young enough to be my son, too."

"Point is, he's *not* young enough to be your son. Go for it. I would."

"I'm not into Christians."

"You ain't into Indians either, but there's a first time for everything." Cathy eyed Danny who stood with other men outside the door. "That Mingan is too skinny for my taste. I like my men with a little more meat. But, that boy is way handsome. Do you some good to have a man warm your feet in bed now and again."

"I'm getting a little old for that."

"Who says?"

A squad car pulled into the driveway with its lights flashing.

"Oh, what now?" Maggie said.

"Some idiot goin' too fast probably ran off that steep Columbus Lane in the dark," said Cathy.

Deputy Miguel Ortiz stepped out. Everyone called him "Happy" because of his perpetual upbeat personality and his wide crooked grin. It was a rare moment when Happy wasn't smiling. He was tall compared to most Latinos, with a handsome, boyish face that charmed the knickers off the young women in Wicklow — that is until he met his one and only Rosa. Her family had owned land in California when the state was still part of Mexico. Rosa was raised a proud woman with her aristocratic ancestry. Her noble bearing contrasted against her unsophisticated Mexican-American husband who everyone called "Happy," so "Anglicized" he didn't even speak Spanish. "Rosa and I fit together like yin and yang," Happy always said.

Upbeat and positive, Happy, was almost too Pollyannaish for Maggie, but she liked him anyway. Most people did like him. He was goofy sometimes, a little awkward. He rarely uttered a curse word, and had a habit of saying "by golly," like an adolescent from a corny 1950s sit com. When he first came into town fresh out of college, bright-eyed and eager but naive, Maggie wondered how he would manage. *Maybe because he'd decided to settle in a small town instead of a big city, he did okay for himself. He'd never survive in Oakland or L.A...* No matter what, when Happy walked into a room, she could count on a lopsided smile. Tonight, though, he did not smile.

"Maggie, where's Jake? Still here?"

"Yeah, out back. What's up?"

"I gotta talk to him right away."

Maggie dropped her dishtowel on the counter and followed Happy to where Jake sat in a lawn chair laughing with other men. "Happy, what are you doing here? Little early to be off duty, isn't it?" The sheriff squinted to read the numbers on his watch, then motioned to a chair. "Sit and have a smoke."

"No, thanks, I quit. Besides, this isn't social. We have to talk right away. I've been trying to call you. Is your cell turned off?"

Jake's expression darkened. He stubbed out his cigarette, rose from the lawn chair and the two men walked a distance from the others. Maggie jammed her hands into her jacket pockets and paced as she eyed the two men talking beneath a blue spruce. A few minutes later, Jake and Happy approached her.

"Oh God, no. Don't tell me," Maggie said.

A trio of ravens swooped down and settled on a low branch of a ponderosa pine.

Maggie looked at them, and could swear one of the three was staring back at her. It cocked its head, ruffled his feathers before the three lifted off the branch and flew into the darkness.

Jake shook his head, and scraped the dirt in a wide arc with one boot. "Yeah. Four-year-old boys reported missing. The Sorenson twins."

CHAPTER 5

Canada, Twenty-Eight Years Ago

"Sheshebens!" Chepi shouted.

Noshi scrambled down the cliff and found his small son still breathing but unconscious, the child's head bleeding from a gash on the side of his skull.

"He's alive. I'll bring him up," Noshi said. He packed snow into the child's wound to staunch the bleeding and pulled him into his arms. "I've got you, son."

Noshi scaled the frozen cliff; his boots slipping on glacial rocks, his limp child slumped over his shoulder. Sheshebens' blood spilled in thin rivulets down his father's back. "Stay with me, please," Noshi whispered...

Northern California, Present Time

MAGGIE LIT A half melted lemon-sage candle, poured herself a glass of old vine zinfandel and put on her favorite *Celtic Woman* CD. She eased into her claw-foot tub looking forward to a delicious hot bath. She'd been gardening all day and wanted peaceful time tonight to soak the soreness from her hips, and forget about murdered children. *Now, this is my idea of paradise.* She slipped beneath the bubbles. She'd taken her first sip of wine when someone pounded on the front door. "I'm not answering it. Where's that damn dog? Chester, go bite those sons a' bitches."

The pounding became insistent, louder. "Goddammit!" She lifted herself out of the tub. Bubbles clung to her wet skin. "Give me a second, will ya? I'm in the bathroom."

"What?" Jake said.

"Christ. Is that you, Jake? I'M...IN...THE...BATHROOM. Quit pounding on the door."

"Okay."

She dried, threw on a chenille robe and padded bare footed through the living room leaving wet imprints of her feet on the plank flooring. She opened the door a crack. "Can't a woman take a bath in peace?"

"I have to talk to you. Can I come in?"

"Be careful. Floor's wet." She opened the door. Chester ambled to the sheriff for a scratch. "Well, hello, boy"

"*Really,* what is this about? I want to finish my bath and go to bed."

"Can I sit for a minute?"

"Let me get some clothes on. Beer in the fridge."

"No, thanks. I'm on duty."

"I'll make a pot of java."

"I'll take a rain check on the coffee. Gotta get back to town."

Leaving Jake and Chester on the couch, Maggie padded into her bedroom, changed into a pair of sweats and a black wool sweater, then slipped into a pair of ancient, ripped Vans. Detouring to the bathroom, she drained the bathwater, blew out the candle, grabbed her wine and joined the sheriff in the living room.

"What's up?" She turned down the volume of the music.

"We found another set of twins. Those girls from Redbluff that went missing over two months ago."

"No chance you found them alive?"

"I'm afraid not. Happy and I delivered the bad news to their parents an hour ago."

"Goddamn it all to hell." She swallowed hard in an effort to squelch tears. She picked up her wine and rubbed the rim with her forefinger until the glass sang.

"We've got everyone out looking for the Sorenson kids, too, and we aren't getting anywhere," Jake said.

"No updates since last night?"

"The media is having a field day with this. Reporters are coming into town by the truckload. Can't turn the channel without hearing something about 'The Heartless Monster.'"

"Oh, so the murderer has a name now? Fuckin' media. So what's on the news about the missing boys?"

"This has gone national, Mag. You really should get a television."

"No, thanks. No TV plus no newspapers equal no lies. I don't want to put up with all that sensationalized negative stuff anyway. Gives me nightmares. How long have the kids been missing *exactly*?"

"Reported an hour before Happy delivered the news to us at the bear dance last night. Dolly Sorenson said she'd left them in their PJs watching TV while she went to the back of the house to put a load of laundry in the dryer. Gone maybe five, six minutes. She returned to the living room and found the front door wide open, the kids gone."

"I can't imagine what that poor woman is going through right now."

"I know."

Maggie bit her lip, and struggled to maintain her composure. "More than twenty-four hours. Not good."

"No. Not good. We've canvassed the neighborhood. We're running out of time."

Maggie looked into Jake's blue eyes. He wasn't asking for her help, he was begging. She'd never seen him look so desperate, so frustrated. "No one walking or driving around who shouldn't be there?"

"Dolly's next door neighbor reported she'd seen a transient the day before, a tall guy with shoulder length blond hair, walking the neighborhood. I think I know who he is. Bobby Jenkins. Did time for a convenience store robbery. Portland Police picked him up for possession of meth in 2001 and we know he's on a prescription med, olanzapine."

"Schizophrenia?"

"He's definitely flipped his pancake. Paranoid. He's nervous as a toad in a hot frying pan."

"Where does he live?"

"He hangs out near Douglas Bridge with some other homeless men who call themselves The Bridge People. No idea why he was around the Sorenson's neighborhood. We picked him up for questioning."

"Any history of violence?"

"No."

"What about the kids' father? Where is he?"

"He and Dolly split up a few months back. He's in San Francisco living with some skanky stripper. We contacted him, and he's headed to Wicklow."

"Any chance he kidnapped the boys?"

"Not likely. He's not the 'daddy' type. Too busy being a horn dog. When he gets into town tomorrow, he's coming to the station." Jake made furrows in his scalp with his fingers. "Maggie, can you help with this one? We gotta find those boys before it's too late."

Maggie took a sip of wine, and looked out the window. Ravens cawed. "I have to get some corn when I'm in town. Those damn birds will be bugging the crap out of me if I don't."

"Maggie? Please? I would not ask if we didn't need you."

"Okay, okay, enough. I'm in. But, on my terms. I want to interview the father, and that transient, too. Is he still at the station?"

"He's there." The sheriff raked his fingers through his hair again. "Those kids...we're drawing a blank. Without your help, we..."

"I know, Jake." She rested her hand on his shoulder, and gave a little squeeze. "I know."

Maggie walked the sheriff back to his cruiser. "I'll meet you at the station in a few minutes."

"Bring your paperwork so we get the ball rolling for you to get into the reserves."

"You know it's not legal for me to talk to Bobbie until I'm in?" She looked again into the sheriff's eyes. "Oh, what the hell." She patted the roof of the cruiser. "See you in a bit."

When she entered the cabin, Samantha stretched, jumped off the back of the sofa where she'd been rolled into a ball napping, and rubbed against her legs. Maggie reached down and stroked the cat's back. "I knew from the start I wouldn't be getting out of this one, Sam. Goddammit. Guess I'm joining the reserves."

She sat down at her PC, powered it on and keyed in Child Serial Killers.

CHAPTER 6

Canada, Twenty-Eight Years Ago

Sheshebens' breaths came in shallow, broken rasps that turned into foggy huffs as they made contact with frigid air. With one hand he grasped rocks and tree limbs; the other gripped his son's jacket. Noshi labored upwards over slippery rocks. When he reached the landing he handed his son to his wife who clasped the slight body like a rag doll to her chest. Noshi hoisted himself onto the road, and sat in the snow catching his breath. "We've got to get him to a hospital. He'll die."

Chepi cradled her injured son. "No, no, no."

"Mommy, why won't Sheshebens wake up?" The boy strained to see his brother's face...

Northern California, Present Time

THE MOMENT MAGGIE arrived to the station, the officer at the front desk ushered her into a room where Jake, Happy and a team of other task force investigators gathered around a table.

"Some of you know Maggie Sloan."

Happy gave her his most brilliant lopsided grin. "Glad you decided to come on board."

Jake continued. "What some of you don't know is that Maggie has an undergraduate degree from UCLA, a Masters in Criminology from American University, and worked for over a decade in major cities all over the United States as an investigator and profiler. She's a retired Oakland Police Department Detective and will be on reserves with the Wild River County Sheriff's Department." Jake scanned the men's faces, as did Maggie, for expressions of disapproval, resistance, or doubt.

"All right, then," Jake said. "Maggie helped solve a number of tough cases, and she's agreed to join us. I expect everyone here to give her their full cooperation. Are we clear on that?"

The men nodded.

"Hey, Maggie," one of the deputies said. "Good to see you."

She raised her hand in greeting. "Good to see you, too." She couldn't get a solid read on whether or not the men welcomed her or resented her, but at least they were cordial. "So, what do we have so far?"

The young deputy raised his hand.

"Question?" she asked.

"Why here?"

"Pardon?"

"Why would a serial killer target Wild River County? Wicklow is a little podunk town. Don't these guys usually operate in areas with larger populations?"

Wicklow, California, Maggie's home town, was once a thriving silver mining settlement in remote Wild River County, now famous for Bigfoot sightings and a phenomenal number of twins.

"Our killer targets twin children, Deputy," Maggie said.

"That's even more confusing. I've seen twins here, yeah, but wouldn't some place like New York or San Francisco have more than we have?"

"Wicklow boasts more multiple births per capita than anywhere in the world supplanting the village of Cândido Godói."

"Where?" the young deputy asked.

"Brazil. According to an Argentine journalist, the Angel of Death, Joseph Mengele, posed as a veterinarian and conducted experiments with cattle and women in that area of Brazil. He'd fled to South America after the war and lived there for some years. Died in Brazil in 1979. He was obsessed with twins. Some say that Mengele's experiments were behind the unusual high rate of twin births in the village."

A few of the men leaned forward in their seats. "Was Mengele ever here?" asked one.

"It's a sure bet that Mengele never visited Wicklow. Someone would have shot the prick."

The roomful of men broke into laughter. Maggie relaxed a little. *They're okay with me.*

"So, why do we have so many sets of twins?" the young deputy asked.

"Some say the reason for the town's high concentration of doubles is due to minerals from Wild River that effect the human ovulation cycle. No one knows for certain, and no one has ever paid for a study."

Jake broke in. "High incidents of twin births remains one of the town's many mysteries going back decades. The year they outnumbered those in the Brazilian hamlet Maggie mentioned Wicklow made international news. In fact, our multiple births boost the town's revenue."

"How's that?" asked the deputy.

"Can anyone tell me what the biggest industry is in Wild River County?" Maggie said.

"Logging?" The deputy asked.

"No. Our industry is based on tourism. Anyone here know what's our biggest tourist weekend?"

"4th of July?" he said.

"No," said Maggie. "You really haven't lived here long, have you?"

He shook his head.

"Anyone want to tell our newcomer what weekend of the year is the busiest in Wild River County?" asked Maggie.

"The Twin Festival," Jake said. "Maggie and her brother Danny won the competition for 'Most Attractive Twins' every year they entered."

"And that, of course, has not a damned thing to do with the case, Jake," Maggie gave him a sideways glance and smiled.

He returned her smile with a grin of his own.

"Let's get back to the business at hand," she said. "We know the killer was most likely drawn to Wild River County because of our high twin birth rate. What evidence do we have to work with that might help us find the Sorenson boys?"

"We searched the house," said Happy, "and forensics checked for prints. Nothing. We found a cigarette butt outside the front door beneath a window that looks into the living room. American Spirit, menthol."

"Good. At least it's not a common brand. Tested for DNA?"

"Still at the lab," said Jake.

"Footprints?"

"If there were any, the suspect brushed them away," Happy said.

"Doesn't make sense. Why would he take care to obscure his footsteps but leave a cigarette butt?" said Maggie. "Where's the transient?"

"In the interview room," said Jake.

"I will talk to him. The rest of you go back to Peony Lane and pound on doors. I want to know who was driving or walking within four blocks of the Sorensons' during the past twenty-four hours. Find out who smokes American Spirit menthols."

"It's late," said Happy. "Most folks will be in bed by now."

"Happy, you and Rosa have kids, right?"

"Two boys and a girl..."

"There's a killer on the loose murdering children. If it were your kids missing would you want to wait until tomorrow?"

CHAPTER 7

Canada, Twenty-Eight Years Ago

The narrow service road dead-ended into the remote forest. The avalanche had blocked the only road out. One side of the dirt path abutted a sharp, vertical mountain; the other side dropped off onto an impossible cliff.

"We'll have to climb. There's no other way," Noshi said...

Northern California, Present Time

MAGGIE ENTERED THE interview room. Robert Jenkins paced, deep in profound conversation with himself. He was lanky and looked old for his age, with a mess of blonde hair that fell into his eyes. He smelled of urine, wood ash, and stale perspiration. It had been a long while since he'd bathed or washed his clothes, but he had shaven and his hands were clean.

"Mr. Jenkins, I'm Maggie Sloan. I'm here to ask you a few questions. May I call you Bob?"

"Most people call me Bobby." He sat on the edge of a metal folding chair across from Maggie, and gnawed on his fingernails.

"Okay, Bobby, so what were you doing on Peony Lane day before yesterday?"

"Walking."

"I see. Where were you walking to?"

"Nowhere. Just walking. Every morning, I get up and walk all day and sometimes even late at night."

"Why is that?"

"Makes me feel better. I don't like sitting. I'm the nervous type and it helps to move."

"You happened to take a stroll in a neighborhood you've not been seen in before and where two little boys, four-year-old twins, went missing that same night. You wouldn't know anything about that, would you?"

"No."

"Where do you live?"

"Here and there. I'm homeless. The fuckin' government doesn't do anything to help street people. They're trying to kill us." He leaned over to Maggie, looked both ways as though to ensure no one listened. A dirty strand of wheat-colored hair fell into his eyes. Bobby turned his head away from the mirror and whispered, "Careful. I don't want anyone to understand what I'm saying. They can read lips. You know about the chem trails, right?"

"Any family?"

"You think I'd be living under a bridge like a filthy troll if I had family? I got one cousin in Redding. He has nothing to do with me."

In spite of his tough-guy act, Bobby is one sad looking man. With proper care, and meds, I bet he'd be an all right person, a productive, law-abiding citizen. Maggie tried to read his expression. *He may be mentally ill, but he's no murderer. This is not our guy.*

Bobby ripped a piece of cuticle off his little fingernail, and a drop of deep red blood blossomed. Maggie handed him a tissue from a box on the table. "So, Bobby. Tell me about the chem trails."

"Government employed pilots load jets with toxic substances and release this particular kind of poison over populations of street people. We end up with incurable cancers. When they find us dead on the streets, they pick us up by the truck load in the middle of the night and cremate our remains in a secret place. I've seen photos. This shit is real. No autopsy reports, no investigations, no questions."

"Who is the 'they' you're talking about?"

"The government." He looked at her as though she had three heads. "Who do you think?"

"The government?"

"Shhhh...keep your voice down. They're probably listening." He bent over and looked under the table as though searching for something.

"We're in an interview room in the sheriff's office. *Of course* someone is listening."

"I'm not talking about the police. I'm talking about *them*...they place secondary listening devices, sometimes so small you can't see them with the naked eye, in rooms all over the country so they know who is onto them, who to *kill* next." He leaned into her. "Don't you get it? I bet they hear us talking right now. They could even be monitoring your behavior through that wrist watch you're wearing." His eyes darted to the ceiling, to the walls, to Maggie. His voice moved an octave up the scale, and went tight and shrill. "Your life might be in danger, lady — both of our lives."

"Calm down. We're safe here."

"Yeah, right. We're safe. That's how they get to you, by making you *think* you're safe." Bobby jabbed his finger at Maggie's face. "You better get your head out of the sand before you end up dead."

"Do you believe small children who feel safe can end up dead?"

"Everyone can end up dead if they refuse to face the truth and keep their ignorant heads stuck in the mud."

"Do you personally know any children around here who ended up dead because they felt *too* safe, Bobby?"

"I told you already. I don't know about any kids." He tore at a hangnail on his thumb.

"I understand you are part of the group who call themselves The Bridge People?"

"I told you that already, too. I live under a bridge. Don't you listen? There's lots of homeless guys who hang around under Douglas Bridge. It's out of the way. No one bothers us."

"Is there talk among The Bridge People about the murdered children?"

"Sure. People talk about it. They're afraid the guy is killing street people, too. A serial killer like that...well, maybe that whack job doesn't only rip the hearts out of kids, but no one gives a plug nickel if a homeless guy ends up dead. No one cares about us. No one cares about me."

Maggie struggled to maintain control as she watched his expression change from bravado and arrogance to sorrow and vulnerability, then back again, setting his jaw in defiance.

"You have a record."

"Convicted for participating in a robbery a long time ago. I did my time."

"You have a little meth problem, too, don't you?"

"Been clean for more than eight years." He spit his hangnail out onto the floor.

"When were you diagnosed with schizophrenia?"

He jerked his head up in surprise, and looked her in the eye. "When I was a kid. I'm on meds, okay? I used to attend UCLA Half the fuckin' professors, brilliant PhDs, are schizophrenic. Did you know that? Some of us with so-called 'mental disorders' are a hell of a lot smarter than so called 'normal' people with their mediocre intelligence. What's your IQ? Mine's 155."

"Do voices tell you to do things, Bobby?"

"I said I'm on meds. Don't be a condescending bigot. I might be crazy but I'm not stupid or ignorant. 'Voices' — I suppose you think all us *crazy schizophrenics* have little voices in our heads, right?" He made circles around his ears in the air with both forefingers.

"Do you smoke, Bobby?"

"Cigarettes or pot?"

"Cigarettes."

"Yeah. Got one? I sure could use a smoke right now." He went back to gnawing on his nails. More blood oozed from where he'd bitten nails below the quick.

"Sorry. I don't and, anyway, no smoking allowed here."

"You were screwin' with me, then? Hell. Sure could use a smoke."

"I'll tell you what. You answer all my questions truthfully, and I'll buy you a pack."

"Yeah?" He lifted an eyebrow.

"What brand do you prefer?"

"Whatever kind I can get. Too fuckin' expensive. The government is driving up prices higher on everything to *control* us. Pretty soon we'll have to beg the government for toilet paper. By then they'll dominate everything and everyone on the planet. Complete control is what they're after, and to eradicate all us 'undesirables' so we don't mess up their pretty utopia. It's part of the new world order the Illuminati are creating. If you were open-minded, I could tell you a lot." He leaned closer toward Maggie and whispered again. "There's tons of scary shit happening no one knows about that's been going on for years, secret stuff that the government and Illuminati as a team have been orchestrating since before World War I. You know about the FEMA camps, don't you? We are all in danger. Things aren't the way they seem on the surface, lady. You could even be one of them. Are you?"

"No, I'm not."

He leaned back in his seat and smirked. "How do I know for sure?"

"You have to trust me."

"Do you think I'm stupid? I don't trust anyone."

"Are you sure you're taking your meds?"

"I told you I do. I take them when I need them."

"Bobby, you have to take them every single day, not only when you feel like it." *I knew he was off his meds, poor guy.*

"I know my body. It gives me signals when I need them." He glared at Maggie, then he slapped the table. "And, don't ever tell me what to do. I hate it when anyone tells me what to do."

"I won't tell you what to do. I promise. What kind of cigarettes do you buy?"

"I can't even buy food, so I sure as hell don't have cash for cigarettes. Mostly, I bum smokes when I see someone who looks like he doesn't mind sharing."

"Got a favorite brand?"

Bobby looked at Maggie as though she were an alien. "What do cigarettes have to do with missing kids? I already told everything to the other guy who was in here. Why do I have to keep answering the same friggin' questions? Don't you talk to each other, or are you hoping I'll slip up?"

"Answer the question, Bobby. What brand of cigarettes do you like best?

"You're scorin' 'em for me, right?"

Maggie nodded. "That's our deal. You answer my questions, tell the truth, I buy you a pack."

"Excellent. My favorite?"

She nodded again.

"American Spirit, menthols."

CHAPTER 8

Canada, Twenty-Eight Years Ago

The family began their agonizing ascent up ice-covered rocks. Chepi clasped the hand of the boy. Noshi carried Sheshebens. After a futile hour, the boy's hand slipped out of his mother's. He'd lost his footing and slid on his belly down the steep, snowy slope, arms outstretched, "Mommy, help me..."

Northern California, Present Time

BOBBY'S INTERVIEW TOOK more time than Maggie expected. "What's the word on the lab results for the cigarette?" she asked Jake as she stepped out of the interrogation room.

"Inconclusive."

"That's too bad." She stifled a yawn. "Well, I'm going home, guys. See you tomorrow."

She drove home, fell asleep exhausted, woke up at dawn and drove to the sheriff's office to interview Dolly Sorenson's husband. The interview went as expected. He was an arrogant jerk who fancied himself a lady killer, but he was not a kid killer.

Jake and Happy cornered her for the debriefing. She put her hands up, "I've been here all morning and I didn't even get my cup of coffee, guys. I gotta get something to eat first. Give me an hour."

She looked into Jake's face, which she seldom did because of his eyes. Maggie couldn't help but stare. His eyes always took her by surprise every time she looked into them, even from the first time when he turned around in his chair to apologize in eighth grade, and even now when she had to deal with a crushing headache and an empty stomach. When she was younger, she'd made a trip with one of her lovers to Homer, Alaska. Across the Kachemak Bay the Grewingk Glacier pushed its way through a cleft in the mountains toward the sea. What startled her most was its color, bright luminescent blue, the color of Jake Lubbock's eyes. She knew Jake had a crush on her, and had forever. He'd asked her out dozens of times over the years, and she always turned him down, but those glacier blue eyes drew her in. She averted her gaze.

She couldn't allow herself to think of Jake as anything other than a friend. When Sally asked her, "Why not go out with him? See what happens." Her response was, "Why? I'd only risk losing a great buddy." Once, years before, she entertained the thought, but Jake hooked up with Shelly Johnson. They married, and that was the end of it. Then Shelly died. Once he'd overcome his grief, Jake started pursuing Maggie again.

"Let it go, Jake," she told him. But he never quite did.

"If you didn't act so desperate, I might consider it," she said another time.

"I'm not desperate. I'm persistent. If you can't tell the difference, to hell with you."

Now, Mingan entered the picture, and anything with Jake was out of the picture. *Still...*

———

"You got time for a break?" Maggie asked Sally as she stepped into Mama's. Sally hoisted a full Arrowhead bottle with ease from the floor and upended it into a water dispenser. With her tiny lacewing-like frame, and her delicate features, she didn't look like she could lift a kitten, let alone a full container that size.

"I could have helped you with that."

"Naw, I got it." Sally wiped the back of her hand across her forehead. "Actually, I'm about ready for some real food. Let's go across the street and grab a sandwich. I can close for an hour or so."

"Where's Dawn? Doesn't she come in during the week?"

"Some days here, some days at The Dandelion. I'm by myself today, but it's dead right now." Sally flipped off the espresso machine and wiped her hands on a bar towel. "You need to talk to me about something?"

"Sort of...let's see if we can't get a corner booth when we get to the café."

The two women crossed the street. It was late afternoon and the lunch crowd at The Dandelion had dissipated.

"Good," said Maggie when she saw all but two tables were empty.

The women slid into the booth furthest away from the few remaining customers. Without being asked, Dawn brought a mug of coffee for Maggie and a diet Coke for Sally, took their orders, and left.

"What's up?" Sally said.

"I'm in a hell of a place. I told Jake I'd help with the investigation of that son-of-a-bitch child murderer. I didn't want to, but I've gotten myself dragged in, and now I can't back out."

Sally took a sip of her Coke. "What I'm hearing is this: you've committed yourself to helping, so it looks to me like you're in this for the long haul. I understand being part of this case is something you don't want to do, but you're joining the reserves now anyway, yes? "

Maggie nodded.

"As a reservist, aren't you obligated to help if Jake asks you to?"

"I wanted nothing to do with any of this, but those little boys have only a few days at most before that fucker kills them." Maggie rubbed her temples. "I've been at the sheriff's office all damned morning, and I have to go back to meet Jake after we eat."

"You're totally stressed out over this, aren't you?"

"I feel like someone is slicing my nerves into strips with a razor."

Dawn set a BLT in front of Sally and a French dip in front of Maggie.

"Ketchup?" the waitress asked Maggie.

"No, thanks, Dawn. Bring a side of horseradish, please." She salted her fries.

Dawn lingered tableside. Maggie picked up a French fry and looked up at her. "What is it? Did you hear me ask for horseradish?"

"Yeah, sorry. Coming right up." She made no move toward the kitchen.

"What do you want, Dawn?" Maggie bit the end off of a fry.

"I wondered if the two of you heard about the Sorenson kids. What kind of psycho hurts kids, Maggie?"

"I can't discuss that right now. Bring the horseradish, please."

"People are saying that it's an Indian monster or something."

"I'm not in any mood to hear about monsters. My sandwich is getting cold. Do you mind getting the horseradish?"

"Yeah, whatever," her voice tight, pained, Dawn turned, and walked back to the kitchen with her head down.

After the waitress left, Sally leaned forward to Maggie. "You don't have to be rude to Dawn. I know this is tough on you, but the town needs to process this, Maggie. Don't shut people down like that."

"You know I can't discuss a case I'm working on, and I don't appreciate this bull about monsters."

"Back off a little, Mag. What's really bothering you?"

Maggie looked down at the table, and with her voice soft she said, "You're right. I'm sorry. You know about my work in the bay area, and those little girls?"

Sally reached across the table and laid her hand on Maggie's. "What you went through when you shot that bastard who you thought raped and tortured those children to death...it's perfectly understandable why you'd..."

"...it's not what you think. What happened to those little girls was horrible, but that's only part of why I don't want on this case."

"What is it, then?" Sally withdrew her hand.

Maggie glanced around the café and once satisfied no one was eavesdropping, she leaned forward. "Sally, I'm going to tell you something I've never told anyone. If this gets out, I'm screwed."

"I'm listening."

"I'm sharing this with you because, other than Jake, you are the only person on the planet I trust. I killed not because I had to, but because of something else. I don't know if I understand it myself."

Sally cocked her head and knitted her brows. "What do you mean?"

"He fled the scene. Everyone knew the suspect carried a knife, but he was no threat to me. As soon as I backed the guy into an alley I emptied my Glock into him without warning."

"What are you saying?"

"I'm saying I didn't feel anything when I shot him."

"No, no, no. You were in shock. You thought he'd raped and murdered little girls. You were..."

"Listen to me. I'm trying to tell you I killed a man without a shred of remorse."

Sally stared at Maggie, her face ashen. "Where was your partner through all this?"

"Not far behind. When he caught up, I was still firing. He had to pry the weapon from my hand. He's the one who called it in. He covered for me. I just stood there and stared at this...this corpse, this...man, feeling nothing."

"I really think you were wrapped up in some sort of temporary emotional upheaval and..."

"Sally, that's not it. And, what's worse, it didn't even matter all that much that I'd killed the wrong guy. The man I shot was only a junkie street hustler, and I knew he wasn't the killer. He was a scumbag, sure, but not a child murderer. He simply happened to be in the vicinity when we discovered the body, and when he saw we were cops he bolted. He was at the wrong place at the wrong time, but he didn't deserve to die like that."

"Oh, Mag. I've always known you to be compassionate, not..."

"I've kept this secret for nearly a decade and it's eating me alive."

"I think it was the circumstances, Maggie. Nothing more. Did the cops ever catch the Oakland murderer?"

"He's still out there somewhere, maybe raping and killing other little girls, and that's one reason I decided to help Jake...well, and Flower and Bird. I wasn't able to catch that other killer, and want to make sure this one doesn't slip through the cracks and maybe hurt my nieces."

Sally's eyes went blank. She fiddled with her glass, turning it with one on the table so fast Coke splashed over the rim. She wiped the spill with a napkin, and wadded it into her fist.

Maggie reached out one hand to touch Sally, then withdrew it and put it in her lap. "You are my best friend, Sally. I don't mean to dump on you... to burden you with this, but I had to tell someone."

"You didn't retire early because you saw those little girls' bodies?" Sally looked into Maggie's eyes.

"That was part of it, yes, but there's something inside of me that's really scary. Something that makes me think I could be as much of a monster as the psycho child murderer I'm hunting."

"Don't say that about yourself. What you did was...it wasn't right, no, but you aren't the monster. You *killed* the monster, or that was your intention, anyway. And, of course, there's that other thing, too, with your own..." Sally looked up just as John Winters entered the restaurant. "Oh, no."

He strode to the table where the two women were seated, leaned over and slammed his hands on the table, stuck his head to within six inches of Sally's face and glowered. "Who in hell is minding Mama's?"

Maggie felt the hairs stiffen on the nape of her neck.

Sally put her hand up to halt him. "No one. It was slow, and I locked up for a few minutes to grab a sandwich."

"We can't afford to lose customers. Not in this economy. Get your ass back to the store."

Maggie bolted out of her seat. A glass of water toppled to the floor. "Why don't you crawl back to your couch? Sally will continue working her butt off to support your cheap beer habit after she's done with her sandwich."

"This is family business, Maggie. I don't need you interfering."

"And I don't need you busting in on our lunch and intimidating my best friend in public, you worthless jerk-off."

Sally stood. "Please," she said to Maggie.

Maggie had not realized she'd turned into a shrieking virago, the volume of her voice cranked to a strident pitch. She looked around and noticed the other few diners had ceased eating, some of them mid-bite. Every person from the patrons to the busboy stared, frozen. The manager, Missy, walked toward them.

Maggie lowered her voice. "John, go home. I'll get Sally back to Mama's, all right?" She turned to the customers and restaurant workers. "It's okay folks. Finish your meals."

"Make sure you get back to work soon, Sally," John said. "I'm not happy about you hanging around The Dandelion giving them our money when our own business suffers." He gave Maggie a look that could melt steel before stomping out of the restaurant so hard that loose change jingled in his pockets.

Dawn came by with a dishtowel to mop-up the spilled water.

"Sorry," Maggie said to her. "I'm really sorry, Dawn, for everything I mean."

"No problem," Dawn said. With both hands she carried the soggy towel back to the kitchen, never once making eye-contact with Maggie.

Maggie turned back to Sally. "I'm sorry I blew up like that, but your husband is a first-class prick, and he's mean. I'm really scared he's going to hurt you one day."

"Looks who's talking. You've never had a successful relationship in your life. You're the worst judge of character when it comes to men of any woman I've ever known. You can't even tell a good guy from a bad guy, and you call yourself a criminal investigator, a detective? God, help us."

"I know my relationships with men suck, but don't ever confuse my personal life with my professional life. I'm a good criminologist." Maggie grabbed her sandwich and bit into it. "Dammit. It's cold now." She threw the French dip on her plate splashing au jus over the table, and scattering fries onto the floor.

"Don't be too judgmental about my relationship with John, and don't think I can't stand up for myself if I need to."

Maggie picked up the fries. "I'm sorry, Sally. I can't stomach it when he bullies you like that, especially in public. And, right now, I'm completely on edge."

"I can handle it. All right? I know you think I'm a weak little thing, but I've been dealing with this man for over 20 years."

"I only hope you realize that your spells and witchy rituals aren't going to be enough to stop him if he decides to hurt you."

"Give me a break. I do have other abilities, too, you know. I can take care of myself, thank you." Sally pulled from her purse a light blue leather wallet embossed with a silver pentagram. "Lunch is on me."

She laid a bill on the table. "Let's go back to Mama's, and I'll make you a fresh cup of hot coffee."

"I'll take you up on that. Can I snag a banana muffin, too? I'm still hungry."

"I think I can fix you up with something. By the way, tell me about Mingan? Everyone is talking about the two of you at the Bear Dance. He's devastatingly handsome, successful, and seems over-the-top nice. Maybe this time, you've finally got yourself a winner."

CHAPTER 9

Canada, Twenty-Eight Years Ago

Chepi ran, slipping most of the way to her son. Noshi, bearing Sheshebens in both arms, followed, skittering and slipping over the rocks. "Are you hurt?" He asked his sobbing boy. The trunk of an old growth blue spruce had barely stopped the little body from slipping into an icy cavern. "Jesus!"

"I'm okay, Daddy."

Chepi, pulled the boy to his feet. Turning him one way and then another she inspected him for injuries. She wiped away his tears with her gloved hand, and then hugged him so tight he gasped.

"This isn't going to work." Noshi said. "We'll have to stay put. The tribe will miss us. They'll send a search party soon..."

Northern California, Present Time

THE SHERIFF'S OFFICE felt musky-damp and smelled moldy. "Don't you guys ever clean? It stinks like a bear's ass in here," Maggie said.

"We were going over the Jenkins interrogation," Jake said. "Happy thinks he's our guy."

"No," said Maggie. "I don't think so."

"He fits the witness description. Tall, blonde, smokes American Spirit menthols," Happy said.

"That's not enough to go on," Maggie said. "There's other tall blonde men in Wicklow, and I know Bobby Jenkins isn't the only smoker in town. This town could star in a Cancer Society commercial." Maggie crossed the room to grab another cup of coffee. She found herself stealing looks at Jake, *feeling, what? Lusty? Can't be. Gotta be the stress of the case. It's Jake, for God's sake.*

"So, Maggie," Jake said. "I've been meaning to ask you something."

"What?"

"How do you know what it smells like?" Jake stood in front of an ancient, scratched white board listing details of the case with a black marker. He continued writing as though he'd said nothing. As a kid, and even into his thirties, Jake was awkward. Although not unattractive, he was never what anyone could call great looking. But as he aged, he developed a particular down-home cragginess and brawniness that suited him. He was a little shorter than Maggie liked her men. Nonetheless, she appreciated his well-muscled arms and back, and had been checking him out off and on all day. *What is the matter with me?* "What?" she said.

"When you came in, you said the station smells like a bear's ass. How do you know what a bear's ass smells like?"

Happy guffawed.

"I'm not in the mood, Jake," she said. Generally, she enjoyed their juvenile style of bantering, but not today. "Don't be an adolescent jerk."

"Yeah? Well I can tell by the way you're been staring at my ass all day you're finally beginning to notice that I'm a good lookin' jerk."

"Let's take care of business before that killer cuts out those kids' hearts. Are you okay with that plan, or do you want to waste more time?" *He's right, though. The guy is kinda sexy in his own way.* "I don't need this," she said, but she wasn't thinking about Jake's comment. "Don't confuse me, Jake Lubbock," she whispered, pretending to examine water stains on the ceiling. "You are a friend, nothing more, and I've got my hands full as it is with an attractive Algonquin banker. Besides that, I have to focus on the case. Focus, Maggie, focus."

Jake looked to the ceiling. "What are you staring at?" Jake shrugged his shoulders. "And, I didn't hear a thing you said. What is it?"

"Nothing. Never mind."

CHAPTER 10

Canada, Twenty-Eight Years Ago

The family picked their way down to the road and huddled under a copse of Douglas fir adjacent to the road. Chepi held the unconscious Sheshebens on her lap, and the boy curled into a knot on the snow next to her. Noshi used his hands and a beautiful mule skinner with a red stag handle to dig an adequate ice cave, and they all crowded in...

Northern California, Present Time

SOME SAID A pair of ghosts haunted Mama Winter's Bookstore and Coffee House. In spite of her own unexplained experiences, Maggie wasn't about to buy into the idea of phantoms and spirits. When Sally complained about items mysteriously flying off shelves, spooky disembodied voices, and opening shop some mornings to find all the furniture had been rearranged during the night, Maggie said, "There's no such thing as ghosts. Someone's messing with you."

The ghost story first circulated in the late 19th century when a mysterious fire broke out and gutted Wicklow Mercantile and Apothecary, the building that later housed Mama's. The owners, brothers Caleb and Jedidiah perished in the inferno. According to legend, their ghosts haunted the building, and were responsible for all kinds of mischief. Sally named them "Iggy and Squiggy" and often talked to them. Maggie thought it absurd, but even she was a little unnerved when this morning she arrived as Sally opened shop, and the two women discovered every bistro table and chair in the place piled on top of one another into a wobbly tower that reached to the ceiling.

"Looks like a cartoon magician's balancing act. Who else has a key?" asked Maggie.

"John has one, and so does Dawn."

"Where were they last night after you closed?"

"John, as usual, was passed out drunk." Sally tapped her fingers on the barista bar. "Let see. Dawn's still working at the Dandelion this week...no, no, she's at the Medieval Festival in San Diego, that's right. She's not even in town."

"Has to be some explanation. Maybe kids came in through a window."

"I don't know why you are in such denial," Sally said. "As I recall, you've had an experience or two of your own."

Sally was the only person Maggie told about Mikey, the "Hey Girly Ghost," she called him. Just now, she regretted having said anything. Maggie inspected the interior, found all the doors and windows secure with no evidence of forced entry. "I'm telling you, someone is fuckin' with you, Sally. Don't give in to this ghost story stuff."

Sally looked toward the ceiling. "Iggy and Squiggy, do you mind? You know how challenging it is to run a business around here. I don't need to deal with your B.S. on top of everything else. Cut me a break, will ya? She disappeared behind the bar and retrieved a white pillar candle and a bag of sea salt. She lit the candle, mumbled a few words, and walked clockwise around the coffee shop throwing handfuls of the salt into each the corners.

"What are you doing?" Maggie asked.

"Protection and cleansing spell."

"Really, Sally?" Maggie laughed and shook her head.

"Yes, really. And, don't ridicule what you don't understand."

Sally and Maggie disassembled the tower of tables and chairs and were putting things back to normal when Sam entered the shop. "Is it all right if I leave the door open? It's a little stuffy in here."

"Sure," Sally said.

"I see Iggy and Squiggy have been at it again. Need help?"

"No. We got it. Thanks." She walked behind the counter. "The usual, Sam?"

Sally turned to the espresso machine and tamped grounds into the portafilter. The customer sat at a corner table and opened his laptop.

Bearing two mugs, one filled with coffee the other with chai latte, Sally sat across from Maggie. "You want to talk?" She withdrew a small vial from her purse, and dabbed some of the contents on her neck. The space filled with the scent of jasmine, Sally's signature fragrance. Even when she couldn't see Sally, Maggie always knew when her friend was around because the atmosphere was scented with jasmine.

"I'm now on the investigation team for the serial killings. I'm afraid this is official business."

"I'm happy to cooperate in any way I can."

Maggie took a sip of her coffee. "I'm sorry, but I have to ask you about John. Where was he night before last around eight o'clock?"

"I have poker with the girls on Sunday nights. He was home when I left at six p.m., and he was home when I returned at ten. You don't think he has anything to do with this, do you?"

"You have no idea where he was while you were gone?"

"He'd never do anything like this." Sally stared at Maggie with astonishment.

"John was arrested for indecent exposure to children. We have to consider him a suspect."

"Mother Goddess, that was years ago. He was drunk. It was stupid. But, there've been no incidents since."

"He took out his pecker at a library and showed it to a group of first-grade girls. We'll have to bring him in for questioning."

"I think, *really*, you just don't like John."

"You're right. I don't like John. You're my closest friend, but I don't mind saying you're married to a complete asshole. However, that's not why we are bringing him in, and you know it. Because of our friendship I wanted to give you a heads-up, and I was really hoping for your sake you could provide an alibi. You don't have a clue where he was the night the Sorenson twins went missing, do you?"

Sally leaned back in her chair, her posture stiffened. "Yes, I do have a clue where he was. He drank his usual half-bottle of Scorsby with a 12-pack of Keystone chasers. He was keeled over on the couch dead drunk when I came home. He couldn't have done this."

"Maybe he was faking it. Maybe he poured most of the whisky down the drain. Maybe he left after you did and took a drive to Peony Lane."

"And maybe he didn't. Maybe you just think he's an asshole and want to harass him. You didn't think he was such an asshole when we were at Wicklow High."

"That was, *what*, almost thirty years ago? Half the girls in high school had a crush on 'Super Jock John.'"

"You were so pissed off when I went to Junior Prom with him that you didn't talk to me for almost a year."

Maggie laughed. "You got me on that one." She became serious again. "I'm talking to you now. Sally...listen. I know this is hard on you but we're bringing John in, and if you warn him, even though you're my best friend in the world, I'll have to arrest you for obstruction of justice."

"You know things have been tough for John since he shattered his knee."

"C'mon. That was when he was at USC." Maggie shook her head. "You're kidding yourself if you think it's okay for him to be a jerk now because of a minor injury he received when he was nineteen years old."

"He was on a full-ride scholarship. That's all he ever wanted to do – play football. It ruined him when he destroyed his knee, and with it any hope of going pro. That injury was hardly 'minor.' It devastated him."

"Look, I know he's your husband, and I get that you want to protect him, but John's 'poor me shattered knee/shattered life' excuse wore thin decades ago. When he decided to waste his potential getting drunk, showing his dick to little girls, and hitting you, that's when I lost any remaining patience I might have had with that sorry son-of-a-bitch." Maggie took another sip of coffee, then placed the mug back on the table and turned it in circles leaving damp, round traces of moisture on the wood. "Why do you stay with him? I've got extra space at the A-frame. Come live with me until you get on your feet."

Sally raised her hands in resignation. "I'm all John has. In spite of his issues, I love him. I'm sticking, at least for now."

"Suit yourself. But, if you ever come to believe you deserve respect, my door's open. I care about you, Sally. I don't want to see you hurt."

"I know. Thanks."

The hanging bell on the door tinkled as Happy and the new deputy walked in.

Three Dean Koontz novels flew off a shelf landing on the floor spine-end up in a perfect row. Both women jumped. Maggie spilled her coffee.

"Damn it, Iggy and Squiggy. Not now, please." Sally picked up the books and placed them back on the shelf.

"Oh, c'mon," Maggie said wiping the spill with a napkin. "It's windy outside. I'm sure a gust from the open door blew the books off the shelf."

"A gust of wind can't blow books that heavy off a shelf, and you know it."

Sam lifted his head from his laptop. "Man, those two are active this morning. Can I have another espresso, Sally?"

———

Maggie said her goodbyes, and walked across the street to the National Bank. "Is Mingan Metchitehew available?" she asked the teller.

"I believe so, Maggie."

The teller walked to the back of the bank and knocked on a door.

"Yes?" said Mingan.

"Maggie Sloan here to see you."

"Oh, good. Show her in."

The teller escorted Maggie to Mingan's office. She read the title on the door plaque: President.

"Good morning. Glad you took me up on my invitation to stop by." Mingan stood from behind his desk.

He wore a tailored navy blue suit, crisp white shirt, burgundy silk tie, and his hair was slicked back. He looked the part of a successful big city banker, rather than a small town branch president. So different than the "barefoot Indian on the rock" Maggie and the twins played with at The Bear Dance. The two sat across from one another at Mingan's teak desk. Maggie took note of the cross hanging on the wall behind Mingan's desk.

"President? When you told me you worked in the back offices, I thought you might be a bookkeeper or something. I had no idea you were so high on the food chain."

"Don't be *too* impressed. It's only a title." Mingan adjusted his tie and looked at his watch. "Unfortunately, I've got a meeting in about twenty minutes, so I won't have time for a walk to *Mama's*. By the way, some of our customers swear that place is haunted. I've experienced a few strange things there myself."

"Not you, too. I don't believe in monsters, ghosts and myths."

"I've heard within every myth there is a grain of truth."

"My Yurok mother used to say that."

"Wise woman, your mother. She knows things are not always as they seem."

"The better word is *knew*. She's been gone for a long time now. Cancer."

Mingan gave her a sympathetic look. "And your father?"

"Irish from Belfast. Active in the I.R.A. Blown up in a car bombing. My daddy was the most fascinating man I ever knew."

"Sorry to hear about your father. I lost both my parents, too, when I was seventeen. Murdered. Stabbed to death in their sleep. The authorities never found the weapon and never caught the killer."

"That's a terrible ordeal for a teenager. I'm so sorry."

"It was difficult then, but my uncle raised me and it worked out. He was a good guy, but he's passed on now, too. My faith in Jesus sustained me. Maggie, do you believe in God?"

"What about other family? Siblings?" *Damn, I hope he doesn't get religious on me.*

"No brothers or sisters. And the only other relative I have any contact with is in a locked mental ward in a Toronto Hospital. I used to visit her now and again, but she's so delusional that she has on more than one occasion physically attacked me. She says I'm a 'demon,' a 'monster' who has to be killed to save the world." He laughed, reached over, and took her hand.

Not yet, buddy. A little too early for that. She withdrew her hand and put it in her lap. "I can't imagine anyone thinking of you as a monster."

"Well, I'm glad you don't see me that way," he said staring into her eyes. "So, no *Mama's* this visit, but I can offer you a decent cup of National Bank's best?"

"No, thanks. I'm coffee'd out."

"Besides coming to visit me, what are you up to today?"

"We didn't have a lot of time to really talk at the Bear Dance. You probably don't know this but I'm a retired detective with the Oakland Police Department."

"Oh?" He raised a questioning brow. "Bear said you'd been a cop, but a detective?"

"Twelve years ago I led the investigation into a Bay Area rape, torture and murder of two sisters, ages seven and nine. Those little girls...when I saw their mangled bodies and the expressions of terror on their faces, it hit me hard. I killed a suspect who fled the scene of the murderer. What was worse...I shot the wrong guy. I was put on a leave of absence and opted for an early retirement, and the bastards who did it are still out there." Maggie looked down at her lap then up again. "I failed those girls and their families. After that, I simply couldn't do it anymore." Her expression brightened. "So...here I am back in Wicklow, your friendly ex-detective."

"If it hadn't been for that tragedy, I may have never met you. For what it's worth, I'm glad you retired and are here now."

Maggie tried not to stare at Mingan's face, his eyes so dark that she couldn't tell his irises from the pupil. *Onyx. His eyes are the color of polished onyx. Why was it always the eyes that get to me?*

The sexual tension building between them was strung taut to the breaking point. But, Maggie felt uneasy and broke their gaze. "I'm on the reserves with the sheriff's department. Jake Lubbock asked me to help with the investigation into the serial killings. If the Sorenson boys aren't dead already, they will be soon." Maggie looked out the window. The autumn sun back lit the liquid amber directly outside of Mingan's office. Its leaves had already begun to turn burgundy. "I haven't figured out why he takes their hearts. It's too gruesome, too cruel to imagine. I keep thinking about their parents, how they must feel knowing how their children died."

"You've come out of retirement for good, I gather?" Mingan sunk back into his plush chair.

"I don't know for good, but for now. This is my community. You've met Bird and Flower...I have to do this for them, then I'm back to my quiet life on the river."

"Like that guy in the Bay Area, not all killers get caught, you know. Some are intellectually brilliant and can easily outsmart the police. You heard about 'The Monster of Florence' haven't you?" Mingan crossed his arms.

"I studied the case when I was in school. Some sicko butchered seventeen people, maybe more, in Florence, Italy, between 1974 and 1986. He targeted lovers in parked cars on moonless nights. Carved out the women's sexual organs with precision, Jack-the-Ripper style. Sometimes, he cut off the left breast. There were many suspects, but the Italian cops never actually found the murdering son-of-a-bitch."

"That's my point. He's most likely still alive and probably has an IQ off the charts. The most intelligent killers never get caught, Maggie."

"I read the detailed report on this guy. Special Agents Dunn, Galinda and O'Tool from Quantico issued an investigative analysis that states most likely the killer was of average intelligence."

"You really think he is less than brilliant?"

"He's not exceptionally intelligent, or clever, or special in any way. He's nothing but a twisted, psychotic murderer, exactly like the jerk we are dealing with now. I'm going to do whatever it takes to get this bastard. Bird and Flower fit the killer's victim profile too closely." Her folded her arms were snug across her chest.

Mingan picked up a pen and twisted it between his forefinger and thumb. "I'm telling you, no one who commits that many murders over that long a period without getting caught is of only 'average' intelligence."

CHAPTER 11

Canada, Twenty-Eight Years Ago

The next morning, Sheshebens was no better. Chepi put her hand to the child's forehead. "He's so hot."

"Take off his jacket and pack snow on his head to cool him down," Noshi said. He leaned over and kissed her. "We may be here for several days. I'll try to catch a rabbit."

"Without your rifle?" said Chepi.

"I've got my knife." He held up the mule skinner and traced his finger over the blade...

Northern California, Present Time

MAGGIE GREW UP with the Yurok raven myth of a shape shifter, woman part of the time, bird part of the time. According to the legend, a magical raven fell in love with a beautiful green-eyed maiden. He turned her into a bird so he could mate with her. She laid a silver egg and hatched a tiny black-haired human baby girl with green eyes. The bird, not wanting a human child, intended to kick the baby out of the nest to a hungry raccoon waiting below.

"Please," begged the maiden. "Do not kill my baby. I will stay with you forever if you let her live."

The raven thought and thought, and finally decided he loved the maiden so much he would grant her wish under one condition. "I will agree to this, but she cannot spend all her time as a human."

He turned his daughter into a shape shifter. The daughter could not remain in her human form for more than a day without turning. By spending some hours as a bird, the girl honored her father and her raven heritage.

As a teenager, Maggie heard Yurok kids at school talking about the shape shifter. She asked her mother about the legend. "Mom, it seems some people actually believe this raven stuff."

"Ah, yes, I heard some Yurok and Hoopa women talkin' at a bear dance once. They say the green-eyed raven lives down by the river. The women think it's a good sign, too, 'cause some wohpekumeo, shape shifters, are pukkukwerek."

"What's a puc-uc-were-ek, or whatever you call it?"

"Protectors of the Yurok people, monster killers."

"Fairy tales." Maggie shook her head. "Sorry, Mom, but I'm not buying any of this."

"Not all legends are legends. Grandfather always said, 'Within every myth is the seed of truth.'"

"You mean you actually believe a 'were-raven' could exist? There's no such thing as were-ravens and shape shifters or pucawhatevers, Mom. That's like believing in Sasquatch. C'mon."

"There's plenty folk who believe in Sasquatch, and 'sides our people honor the limitless possibilities of nature. Who are any of us to say that *anything* is impossible?"

—

The raven dream returned. Maggie soared once again over the Trinity Alps, but this time, she flew with an unkindness of ravens who cawed to her in Yurok.

"I don't understand everything you're saying," she cawed back. "My Yurok is rusty. I speak mostly English and Raven."

One turned an eye to her and said in English, "I said you're the pukkukwerek."

"What? My mother told me about that. A 'monster killer.'"

"Your mother knew."

It was midnight, but the waxing moon was bright enough that Maggie could see veins in the leaves of the oaks she skimmed. She turned to fly toward the white cliffs of Sunset Mountain. The other ravens bid her goodbye, and peeled off. Their caws grew so faint that all Maggie could hear was the breeze moving through the conifers blended with the beat of an unseen drum. She flew closer toward the drumming until the ugly man-creature she'd seen there before came into view. She perched in the lightning-scarred Douglas fir to observe him.

This time, there were two little boys with him, both dead and naked, their skin so pale it was nearly transparent. Their clothes were folded into two stacks, shoes on top with their socks rolled and tucked inside. The twins lay on their backs side-by-side in the red dirt, arms at their sides, eyes wide open.

The big native grabbed one boy by an arm, and held him aloft in his left hand. The child's head flopped over to one side in an unnatural angle. Bracing the small body against the fir, the creature plunged his right hand into the child's chest as though his fingertips were made of surgical steel, and with a twist and a jerk he yanked out the heart. Unhinging his jaws, the monster shoved the entire organ into his mouth. He chewed for a long while. Blood, saliva and macerated pieces of heart dripped out a gaping hole in the side of his face where a portion of his cheek was missing. As he swallowed, a lump moved down through an exposed section of his esophagus. The monster cast aside the first boy and picked up the other.

When he had finished his second "meal," the hideous specter cleaned the boys with a soft cloth, dressed them, meticulously brushed their hair, and laid them facing one another in the neat, rectangular hole Maggie had watched him dig in her earlier dream. He wrapped their arms around one another in an embrace, and covered them with dirt, rocks and leaves. In a little boy's voice, he said "Bye bye, Sheshebens," and patted the mound.

He stood. The moonlight illuminated his decayed face. Glistening pieces of heart and blood clung to his tattered deerskin shirt. He raised his arms into the air and sang a plaintive song in an Indian tongue unfamiliar to Maggie. She cawed at him. He stopped singing; looked up into the tree where she perched. He pounded his emaciated chest with both fists and laughed.

———

Maggie awoke with a start, tangled in sweat-drenched sheets. "My God, my God." She looked at the clock on the night stand. Three a.m. With trembling hands she picked up her cell and dialed.

CHAPTER 12

Canada, Twenty-Eight Years Ago

As Noshi left the cave, snow crunched under his boots. The boy counted his father's steps until he could no longer hear them. Hours passed. Chepi tended her injured son, now and again cooing or singing to him.

The caw of a lone raven and the harsh breathing of his injured twin brother were the only sounds the boy could discern. Sheshebens issued faster, more ragged breaths. Blood dribbled in a dark line from his ear down the side of his face and clotted against his neck.

"Mommy, is he gonna be okay? Is he?" the boy cried.

"Don't worry. Come closer."

Chepi cradled Sheshebens on her lap and threw one comforting arm over the boy who curled tight against her sobbing. "Shhhh. Shhhh. It'll be all right," she said to him. "Daddy will be back soon with a fat rabbit, and men will come in a helicopter to save us. It'll be fine, little one..."

Northern California, Near Future

JAKE'S VOICE WAS sleepy. "Do you know what time it is? This better be good."

"I know where the Sorenson kids are. I know what the killer does with their hearts. I don't have time to explain, and I'm pretty sure it's too late, but just in case, we need to get there right away."

"Give me a second to throw on some clothes and I'll pick you up."

"No. You're on the way. I'll pick you up. It'll be faster. I'll be there in ten minutes. Bring an evidence kit."

While Maggie was on her cell with Jake, she'd grabbed a pair of jeans and a heavy sweatshirt. She clicked off her phone, dressed, and pulled back her hair. She called for Chester, and ran for the truck. Ravens flew in a thick mass around her, so close she could feel breeze from their flapping wings. She swatted at them. "Leave me alone, dammit."

Jake was outside waiting for her with two travel mugs of coffee and a flashlight, his service revolver strapped to his belt. He squeezed into the old truck next to Chester, and handed Maggie a cup.

"Thanks." She took a sip of the hot brew and exhaled. "Ahhhh. Exactly what I needed."

"Mag, you're going to have to tell me what this is about."

"I'll make you a deal. If the kids are where I think they'll be, I'll tell you. Otherwise, we'll chalk it up to a bad dream."

Jake stared at her in disbelief, and raked his fingers over his scalp. "Ah, don't tell me. Are you saying that you *dreamed* where the kids are? You're goddamn kidding me."

"Humor me, okay?"

"You call me at three a.m., wake me out of sound sleep on a work night, and drag me along to pursue a lead based on a nightmare, and you want me to humor you? If this doesn't pan out, no more free lunches."

"I know it sounds insane. I can hardly believe it myself."

"I'm getting too old for this puke. After this case, I'm going to step down and let someone younger take over."

"You, retire? Can't imagine that. Besides, who could do the job? Happy?"

"Naw. He's beginning to come around, and he's certainly got more going for him than a typical Barney Fife, but he doesn't have the chops."

"Really? He seems like he'd be up to the job."

"To be a good sheriff requires a heap of political acumen and that boy doesn't have it. Election year coming up. It'll be interesting to see who throws their hat in the ring, but no matter who wins, I'm through."

They pulled onto a service road headed off into the forest. The unpaved road was rutted and the truck bumped and rattled, jostling the three occupants.

"Where the hell are we headed?" Jake said.

"Sunset Mountain. The white cliffs."

"We can't make it all the way to the cliffs in this thing."

"We'll go as far as the Chevy will take us, and then we'll walk in the rest of the way."

"What are you thinking, Mag? That's almost a one-mile one-way hike over a rocky path in the middle of the night. Besides, it's bloody freezing. You *are* nuts." He pulled his jacket around him. "Doesn't the heater work in this thing?"

"Sometimes." She looked over at Jake. "Sorry."

Maggie stopped the truck at the end of the service road. The two climbed out. The dog hopped out behind Jake and lifted his leg on the truck tire.

"Goddamn. Can't you pee on a tree?" said Maggie.

Jake and Maggie, Chester close behind, picked their way on the rocky path through the dense forest. By the time they reached the white cliffs, the first rays of the morning sun crested the peaks.

"Let's stop here," Maggie said.

She scanned the trees in front of the cliff. There it was, the Doug Fir, split nearly in half, scorched by lightning. "This way," she said.

About half way to the tree, making their way over rocks and through bushes, Jake halted. "Wait."

He bent over and probed the ground with a stick. A cigarette butt...American Spirit, menthol. He pulled a pair of latex gloves from his pocket, pulled them on, picked up the stub and stowed it in an evidence bag.

"Crap," said Maggie. "He's been here."

As they approached the fir, ravens flew down and settled in its branches.

"Over here," Maggie said leading man and dog around the tree to the side facing the cliffs. There it was. The mound, exactly as she'd seen it in her dream. "Jesus Christ."

Jake dropped to his knees, and using his flashlight as a digging implement, he gouged at the soft dirt. He dug down about two feet until he uncovered something. Small fingers protruded from the sandy, red clay.

"Oh, God," said Maggie.

She squatted and frantically dug with both hands to help Jake unearth the bodies. The figures of two little boys facing one another in an embrace emerged from the red dirt. "I knew we were too late. I knew it," Maggie said. A wave of acidic vomit ascended from her gut into her esophagus. She swallowed hard to keep from retching. Tears rolled down her cheeks. She wiped her face with the back of her sleeve.

"We gotta call this in right away," Jake said as he reached into his coat pocket.

"No reception out here. You go back to the truck and make the call. Chester and I will have a look around."

Jake took off in a trot toward the truck. Maggie inspected the area for any footprints not belonging to her, Chester or Jake. The morning light was pale, so she moved the flashlight beam over the dirt and bushes looking for scraps of fabric, additional cigarette butts, anything. She circled the grave and the tree. "Let's make sure we don't obliterate any other evidence, Chester. Nothing like trying to catch a murderer by contaminating the crime scene, eh?"

Something caught her eye...a long strand of blonde hair high on the tree trunk stuck in the bark. She didn't have an evidence bag with her, so she left the hair until Jake could return to collect it. She popped open her Swiss Army knife and gouged out the spot above where she discovered the evidence.

She turned back to the grave and kneeled. "I'm so sorry, little guys. We'll find whoever did this to you, I promise." She walked into the forest a few steps, put her hands on her hips, looked into the sky and inhaled the icy night air.

By now, the Douglas fir and other trees were lousy with ravens, none of them making a sound. More ravens descended and landed on branches, rocks, and the ground. Silent ravens were everywhere Maggie looked. "Why the hell are you here?"

—

A team of deputies from the sheriff's department and the medical examiner showed up. The team cordoned off the perimeter, swarmed the grave site and surrounding areas searching for evidence, placing yellow markers, and snapping photos. Jake stood outside the perimeter and observed.

The M.E. approached Jake.

"What's the story?" Jake said.

"These boys died about three hours ago. Necks broken. Hearts missing. Whoever did this knows how to handle a knife. The cuts are perfect, clean. I'd say a very sharp hunting knife, maybe a mule skinner."

"Fits the killer's M.O." said Jake. "When you get 'em back to the morgue, you'll find the remains of a meal and a Hershey bar in their stomachs," Jake said. Then he turned to Maggie. "You say you know what the sicko does with their hearts?"

"He eats them."

"Are you fucking kidding me? That's revolting. How do you know that?" Jake looked like he could vomit.

"I just know it."

Happy recoiled. "Jeez."

"He might not have eaten their hearts here," the examiner said. "Too little blood. These kids were killed elsewhere and brought here. Their hearts were removed post-mortem."

"So, our guy is a tall blonde cannibal who smokes American Spirit menthols," Jake said. He turned to the deputy. "Fits the description of our nut-case transient, doesn't it? Take a man with you and go to Douglas Bridge. Haul Bobby into the station."

"He's not our killer," Maggie said.

"How do you know? Have another dream?"

"I have a feeling."

"That's out of character for you. You don't operate on dreams, hunches and feelings. What's up with you, Mag?"

"I don't know. I can't say why, but I honestly don't think Bobby is our guy."

"I'm bringing him in anyway. We've got evidence. If the DNA on the cigarettes and the hair sample match Bobby's, then we have our killer."

"You know, John Winters is tall with blonde hair, too," Maggie said.

"And the pervert smokes," Jake said.

Happy intervened. "Yeah. During questioning he told us he sometimes likes menthols. Could care less about the brand. He could very well be our guy."

"Got any feelings or hunches about John?" Jake asked Maggie.

"Not really, but I think we ought to check him out one more time."

"Okay, bring him in for a second round of questioning, too, Happy," Jake said.

The deputy nodded. "My pleasure."

"You think Winters did it?" he asked Happy.

"He's the only guy I know around here except Bobby who is as tall as I am with blonde hair. He smokes, and he's got a record with kids. Plus, he's got the means to make the drive out here. Bobby doesn't have a car. I'd put money on Winters."

Jake nodded. "Maybe you're right."

A few ravens cawed. Then the others joined in a raspy cacophony so loud the investigators had to yell over them to be heard.

"Why the hell are all these crows around?" Jake said.

Maggie turned her gaze to the tree branches. "They're ravens."

CHAPTER 13

Canada, Twenty-Eight Years Ago

It wasn't until the sun disappeared over the mountains, and the temperature dropped that Noshi returned to his family empty-handed. He stomped his feet and slapped his gloved hands together, then crawled into the cave. "I'm sorry, Chepi. I'll try again tomorrow at first light. How are the children? I'm certain I can find game tomorrow. In fact, I thought I could..." He took one look at Sheshebens and the light drained from his eyes.

Chepi bent her head over her now lifeless son, and whispered, "Daddy's here. It will be okay now. It's all going to be fine. We'll take you home and get you some hot cocoa..."

Northern California, Present Time

'I THOUGHT THIS weekend you and I could take Jimmy's girls on that fishing trip I promised them. How about a day at Twin Trees Lake?" Mingan said on the phone to Maggie.

"That'd be great. I could use a break from all this tragedy. This business about the Sorenson twins kicked my ass hard."

"I can imagine. What's happening to these children is sickening."

"I need a little time away from it all. A day at the lake would be perfect."

"I couldn't agree more. Besides that, I'd like to get to know Bird and Flower better... I'd like to get to know you better, too."

Maggie's pulse quickened. *And, I would like to get to know you, too, up-close and personal when the time is right.* "What about Sunday?" she said.

"I'm Deacon of my church and after services this week I've got a mandatory meeting that could take a few hours. How 'bout Saturday?"

"I work with Jake on Saturday. With that murdering bastard still out there, I don't know. Sunday is my one day off, and with this investigation, it's sometimes difficult to get away even then," Maggie said.

"Well, maybe we can get together the week after," Mingan's voice became heavy, "or maybe we should shelve it until the case is solved."

Maggie's gut and chest hurt where tiny needles of disappointment pierced her. "Let me check with Jake. Maybe I can get away for a few hours on Saturday morning. Does that work for you?"

After she finished the call, she dialed Jake. Given his open hostility toward the Algonquin, Maggie decided against telling him that she was going anywhere with Mingan. When Jake answered the phone she said, "You think you and Happy can do without me for a few hours on Saturday? I need a little time away with Flower and Bird to relax. I can come in around three."

"No problem," he said. "Get some R & R with your nieces. You've earned it."

Maggie hated lying to Jake, but now had to do something even more difficult...ask her nephew, Jimmy, if she could take the girls for a day. She and Jimmy grappled with long-term issues. In addition to their many other differences, aunt and nephew also had a divergence of opinion on how to raise children. From the time the twins were babies, he gave into anything they wanted, which Maggie thought would cause them to grow up with a sense of entitlement. "I know you are compensating for the fact that their bitch of a mother abandoned all of you," Maggie once said, "but if you keep spoiling those girls, you are going to have one hell of a time when they get to be bratty teenagers."

"Look, Aunt Maggie, they are my daughters, and I'm responsible for them. Once you've raised a few kids of your own, you can tell me how to raise mine, deal?"

That stung. Maggie loved children but knew she'd never have any of her own. She'd given birth to a little girl once, a tiny delicate child with almond shaped eyes and a halo of shiny black hair. Her daughter was born too many weeks premature. She looked perfect, beautiful, but her lungs were undeveloped.

The loss was almost too much for Maggie. She'd never become pregnant again. Jimmy knew it. *The little prick. If I didn't love those girls so much, I'd not have a goddamn thing to do with him.*

She didn't hate Jimmy, but she hated what he'd become. When he was a little boy, the two had been exceptionally fond of one another. But, as he matured into adulthood, aunt and nephew grew apart. He'd lost his joyful buoyancy, and became dark, jaded and sarcastic.

She didn't get him and he didn't get her. He was as conservative politically as she was Green Party liberal. He practiced the Yurok religion with the passion of a Dominican monk. She was atheist to the core. He supported the U.S. military presence overseas. She hated anything to do with war and thought the U.S. dead wrong in its foreign military policies.

Her brother, Danny, was disappointed. "Maggie. He's my only son, and your only nephew. Why don't you cut him some slack and at least try to make things work?"

But whenever the two of them got together, what would begin as a conversation about something as mundane as the weather would devolve into a shouting match. It got so bad that even Danny couldn't take it any longer. "You're both behaving like a couple of first-class jerks, and I won't have you spoiling everyone else's good time with your childish bickering." For several years after, when Danny hosted family dinners, he often did not invite Maggie. It hurt her feelings to be excluded, but she understood.

To make matters worse, like his father, Jimmy was marinated in his native culture and didn't understand Maggie's "Celtic obsession," as he called it. They engaged in many nasty arguments about what he perceived as her turning her back on her own people.

"The Irish are my people, too," said Maggie, "and yours as well. Don't ever forget that your Irish grandfather died on Irish soil fighting for what he believed in, and that you are a Sloan."

"I can't forget it, Aunt Maggie. That's all you ever fuckin' talk about."

At last, Maggie called a truce so the two of them could at least attend family functions together, and so Jimmy wouldn't limit her access to Flower and Bird. When Jimmy's wife had abandoned him with twin toddlers to raise on his own, Maggie stepped in to offer her support. Things got a little better between them, but certain topics were forever taboo. The Native vs. Celtic subject rarely came up between them, and Maggie and Jimmy avoided discussing the subjects of child rearing and politics altogether.

But, these days, the taboo subjects emerged at the most inappropriate times, and in most cases, it was Maggie who threw kerosene on the fire. *I wish I could sew my mouth shut when I'm around him, and not let the little snot provoke me. Maybe I wouldn't live with so many regrets.*

When she called Jimmy to ask him if she and Mingan could take Bird and Flower on Saturday morning, he said, "Are you telling me you're going on a date with that Indian guy everyone saw you flirting with at the Bear Dance?"

"It's not a date. We're just taking the girls fishing and for a picnic. I'll have them home by two."

"Is this guy part white? Irish maybe? I hear he's full blooded Algonquin. Of course, that can't be. You don't date guys unless they are white, preferably Irish with green eyes."

Maggie bristled. "Let's not go there. I already told you this is not a date. I only want to know if it's all right with you if Mingan and I pick up the girls on Saturday morning for a few hours."

"Yeah, sure, Aunt Maggie. I was only yankin' your chain. Come by early and I'll have a cup of coffee waiting."

CHAPTER 14

Canada, Twenty-Eight Years Ago

Noshi removed his gloves. With two fingers, he closed his child's eye lids, and pulled him from his wife's arms. He held his dead son close, burying his face in the child's jacket. He let out a single cry of anguish then carried Sheshebens' body outside. The boy followed and watched Noshi dig a hole and lay his brother to rest, covering him with handfuls of snow, mounding and packing it down hard. Noshi stood, lifted his arms to the sky and sang the Song for the Dead.

The boy remembered the song from when Grandpa Segenan died. Although he didn't understand the words, the boy understood their meaning. The song would help his brother's spirit fly to the afterworld. So the boy sang, too, following the lyrics best he could, his arms stretched overhead like Daddy's. Icy wind gusts slapped his face, startling him...

Northern California, Present Time

THE RAVEN DREAMS were on the increase and grew more terrifying. In nearly every dream she encountered the hideous monster, and each encounter became more ominous. It got so bad that Maggie sometimes drank herself into a stupor before going to sleep to staunch her nighttime images.

One cool evening, she'd arrived home from a grueling day to take a dinner break before returning to the sheriff's office. She eased into her backyard hammock hoping the evening air, and the star-filled darkness would eliminate what was now becoming a daily tension headache. Maggie downed four aspirins with a beer chaser, and covered herself with a comforter. She intended only to take a short siesta. She was scheduled to interview John Winters later that night, and wanted to be well-rested.

Above her, Orion's belt lit the sky between the now bare branches of two white oaks. Her hammock, suspended between them, rocked in the breeze. The hammock's movement and the pale radiance of the stars mesmerized Maggie, and she fell into a deep, sound sleep.

She sprouted glossy blue-black feathers and felt herself flying into the dark sky toward the Orion Nebula. She flew in circles, swooped downwards over the tops of spruce and oak, then upwards. She flew high over the river then veered toward the forest.

In a bare patch of meadow Maggie saw a light, a fire. A figure crouched over stirring the flames with a white branch. No, not a branch. She flew down closer to see. The monster. His stir-stick was a leg bone, maybe that of a deer or coyote, or maybe a small human. The ghoul sang in an unfamiliar language, not Yurok, certainly not Raven. She flew down closer. He smelled like ripe road kill, putrid. Without turning his head away from the fire, in one swift movement he reached overhead and snatched her from the sky. He squeezed. She struggled. Maggie felt and heard the snap as one of her ribs gave way, then another snap as second rib cracked. She couldn't breathe. Maggie pecked and pecked, clawed at him, cawing. Her eyes bulged. She struggled harder, pecking, pecking. He brought her up to his one eye, so close she could nearly reach it with her beak, and examined her, turning her body one way and then another. He squeezed a little harder, and pushed his long yellow fingernails into her side. Panic. "I'm going to die," she cawed.

She felt another rib give way, and another. He laughed again. He squeezed one more time, then opened his fingers and released her. She flapped her wings with mad fury, and managed to make it back to the freedom of the sky, the searing pain in her torso almost unbearable.

Maggie awoke beneath the hammock, the comforter in a messy wad beside her, Chester licking her face. She was lying on sharp rocks the size of baseballs. "Jesus," she said.

She rolled off the rocks, tried to stand, but a horrendous twinge bolted through her sides. She grabbed a tree trunk to steady herself. "Whoa. Ouch. I must have cracked a rib or two, Chester."

She walked in small shuffles to the cabin hugging her sides. Chester followed. It hurt to breathe. It hurt to take a step. It hurt to move at all. Before her bathroom mirror, she stood and gasped for air. Maggie pulled up her shirt. "Oh, no." Long black contusions wrapped around her body terminating in punctures, four on each side in the front, one on each side on her back. Overwhelmed with nausea and dizziness, she sat down hard on the toilet seat. "God, Chester." She hung her head. "I don't believe this. I've gotta get to my cell, and I left it outside by the hammock. Shit."

She crawled back outside, reached her cell and dialed Jake's number.

"Where are you, girl?" Jake said. "We're waiting for you. John's in the interrogation cell. We expected you here an hour ago."

"It's the stupidest thing. I fell out of my hammock. I think I broke some ribs on the rocks beneath it."

"Where are you? Inside?"

"Out back."

"Stay right there. Don't try to walk. I'll get over right away to take you to the urgent care center."

"What the hell are they going to do? Tell me to take two aspirin and call them in the morning?"

"Listen to me! You might have punctured a lung. I should call an ambulance, goddammit, and if you move one goddamn step away from where you are right now, I'll goddamn do just that. I'm on my way."

"But, Jake, I..."

"For once, Maggie, shut up. I'll be there in a goddamn minute."

———

Saturday morning arrived and Mingan rang the doorbell. Maggie walked in halting, slow steps across the living room and opened the door. There stood Mingan with his obsidian eyes and a grin as big as Montana.

"Are you okay?" His smile shifted into an expression of concern. "You look awful. I mean, you look pretty, but are you unwell?"

"It's all right. A few broken ribs. I feel like an idiot, but Monday night I fell from a hammock."

"Would you prefer to reschedule? If you're not up for a..."

"...I'm fine, really. I've got great pain killers. I probably won't do much fishing, but I'm ready to go."

"Are you sure?"

"I'm sure."

Mingan helped Maggie into his truck and they departed to get the girls.

———

"Auntie Maggie! Auntie Maggie! Mingan!" Flower and Bird ran out the door of their house toward the truck.

Maggie opened the door on her side.

"Daddy packed us lunch," said Bird holding aloft a thermal bag.

"Peanut butter 'n grape jelly sandwiches, some oranges, juice boxes, and a whole box of 'Nilla Wafers," Flower said. "We have fishing poles, too, and worms."

Jimmy emerged from his house with a cooler and fishing rods. "I packed a few beers and some sodas and ice, too. How are your ribs?"

"Hurts some. But, I'll be fine. Thanks for the lunch and beers."

"Hey, Mingan," Jimmy waved one hand.

Mingan leaned over Maggie and waved. "We'll have the children home early."

"That's fine. And, girls, don't jump on Aunt Maggie. She fell and hurt her ribs."

Jimmy opened the back door to the cab and the twins scrambled into the seat. "All buckled in?" He kissed them, and closed the door.

The day at the lake was spectacular. Crimson leaves littered the damp ground, the sky was magnetic blue. Maggie sat in a chair next to the cooler watching Mingan and the girls at the shore. Mingan took off his shirt, although the temperature was mid-60s at most. Muscles moved under his skin as he helped the girls position their lines into the water. Maggie became aware of how attracted she was to him. She imagined how their bodies would feel next to one another, flesh against flesh. "Well, I guess with four broken ribs, it'll be a long while before I can do anything about it," she said.

"Did you say something?" Mingan asked.

"No, no. Mumbling to myself. Nice day, isn't it?"

After Mingan set up the giggling girls with fishing poles and juice boxes, he walked back to sit with Maggie. "Those girls are really precocious. It's so much fun spending time with them, and you. I'm glad we could do this today."

Maggie nodded. "Me, too."

"Now, tell me again how you broke your ribs."

"I fell out of a hammock onto rocks."

"How did you manage to break ribs on both sides?"

"I really don't know. It's a mystery."

"You didn't wake up as soon as you fell? I'm such a light sleeper I can't image falling two or three feet and not waking up."

"I guess I was so tired, so out of it, that I didn't even realize I'd fallen. I don't remember anything from the time I went to sleep until I awoke in pain."

"That's bizarre," he shook his head, then he scooted a chair close to her, and put his hand on her knee. She was conflicted. She wanted his hand there, and she didn't want his hand there. "Mingan, I am attracted to you, but let's take things slow. I don't yet know you well enough to..."

"Good enough," He removed his hand. "We'll take it slow."

Flower squealed. "Mingan. Look, look. My pole is bouncing. Look."

"Seems like Flower has caught her first trout. Better go help." Mingan ran to the river's edge. Both girls laughed.

"God, I needed this."

"What? I didn't hear you? Is everything okay?" Mingan called to her.

"Things couldn't be better."

———

"I don't know much about your witchy stuff, and you know I don't believe in wonky stuff about dreams, but I need to pass something by you."

Maggie and Sally talked over a cup of coffee and chai at Mama's.

"Yeah, sure, but first...how did your date on Saturday go with Mingan?"

"Does everyone know about that?"

"Mag, this is Wicklow. A town of 3,000 people. You don't think someone wouldn't have seen you at the lake and spread it around that you two were together?"

Maggie sat upright in her chair and looked into Sally's face. "Let's set the record straight. It wasn't a date. We took the girls fishing because Mingan promised them he would when he met them at the Bear Dance. There's no way Jimmy would let his 6-year-old daughters go by themselves to the lake with some guy he hardly knows. That's all it was."

Sally smiled. "Are you sure that's all it was?"

"That's all it was."

"Why didn't Jimmy go with them instead of you? I'm your best friend. Don't you think I know it when you've got the hots for some guy?"

"Knock it off, Sally. I came here to talk about my dream. My ribs hurt like hell, and I'm not in a good mood." Groaning, Maggie rose from her chair, and reached for her bag.

"Okay, okay. Sit down and tell me about your dream."

With both hands, Maggie braced herself on the table and lowered herself back into the chair. "You know me. I don't put any stock whatsoever into spooky stuff like ghosts, witches and fables, and I...."

"I'm a witch, Maggie. You know that. A hereditary witch. My mother was a witch, my grandmother before her, her mother before her. I have practiced the craft in hiding my entire life, terrified someone would find out. Society just now is beginning to accept witches so we can come out of the broom closet without fear of being stoned or burned to death, so..."

"I didn't mean..."

"...so, whether you put stock in what I am and what I believe is of no consequence, but my religion is valid and important. If you want my help, you have to take me seriously."

Maggie reached across the table for Sally's hand. "I'm sorry. I meant no disrespect. I guess what I was trying to say is that I don't understand what you do, or how you are able to interpret dreams. I need your help on this one."

Maggie felt like an ass. She did know how much Sally's religion meant to her. Sally practiced the craft with sincerity, observing the Sabbaths in great faith, fighting for the rights for witches to practice openly without fear of persecution, and spending time educating others. She was so faithful that she even closed her store on one of the busiest nights of the year in Wicklow, Samhain, the holiest of nights when the veil between the living and dead was at its thinnest, a time known to non-believers as Halloween. She performed rites, rituals and spells to heal the sick, to bring fortune to those less fortunate, and to honor the natural world.

Maggie didn't believe in any of this stuff, and didn't get it, but she admired Sally for her passion, her adherence to her beliefs, for her bravery in coming out even though she knew she'd be pierced by arrows of prejudice. Most of all, she admired Sally for the way she loved others and for her unwavering adherence to the Wiccan Rede, "An Ye Harm None, Do What Ye Will." Sally would rather chew off her own arm than hurt anyone else. And, although Maggie couldn't bring herself to believe in these things, there was something to this business of dream interpretation that Sally had a natural talent for.

Sally took a sip of chai, licked foam off her upper lip, and placed her mug back on the table. "Tell me the exact details, any colors you remember, what you recall hearing or feeling. Tell me everything."

Maggie told her about the recurring raven dreams, about the hideous monster, and how she was terrified he was going to squeeze the life out of her the evening she'd fallen out of the hammock.

"This is not difficult to interpret. I'm surprised you didn't get it right away," Sally said.

"What do you mean?"

"The monster in your dreams is obviously the 'heartless monster,' the child killer. Can't you see that? You're getting close to discovering who it is, and he's warning you. Don't ignore your dreams because they are clearly saying if you get too close, the monster will crush you, Maggie. He'll kill you."

The bells on the door jingled to announce customers. Mingan entered with Happy directly behind. The instant both men stepped inside the door slammed behind them startling the other customers. A hefty ceramic coffee mug flew off the shelf behind the counter. Mingan ducked and the cup shattered against the wall with such velocity it left a substantial dent before it broke into dozens of tiny pieces. The mug narrowly missed crashing into Happy's face.

CHAPTER 15

Canada, Twenty-Eight Years Ago

The boy squatted on his heels next to the mound covering his brother. He patted the snow with both hands. "Bye, bye, Sheshebens." Tears streamed down his face and as they fell on the snow, landing as tiny glistening beads that froze into crystals. He stood, grabbed his father around the waist and squeezed tight. He didn't mind that Daddy's belt buckle dug into his chin. He was sure the warmth of his father's body would absorb his pain, transmute it into something safe and ordinary. Noshi stroked the boy's hair. He dropped down to his knees, and held his son away from him with both arms and looked into his face. "It's fine to cry now, but we have to be brave. We have to take care of Mommy..."

Northern California, Present Time

JIMMY ASKED MAGGIE to keep the girls overnight. "I know you'll find this hard to believe, but I have a date. Mom and dad are at a tribal meeting, and they won't be home until late."

It was a rare and beautiful thing when Maggie got the girls to herself. She planned homemade pizza and chocolate chip cookies. She greeted them at the door with their favorite drinks, Shirley Temples with extra pomegranate syrup and five cherries in each glass.

"Aunt Maggie, we brought our Dora the Explorer game. Can we play?" Bird asked.

"Absolutely, but first, how 'bout we make pizza and cookies?"

"Can we have pineapple on the pizza?" Flower asked.

Maggie plucked a can of diced pineapple off the counter and held it out. "Why do you think I bought this?"

That evening, after three games of Dora, all of which Maggie lost, she pulled the girls with her under a comforter outside on the deck where the three together snuggled and counted shooting stars. When the girls fell asleep against her, Maggie carried them in one at a time and tucked them in together in the guest room bed. Then she changed into her flannel pajamas and robe, poured herself a brandy, and sat on the couch with Chester at her feet and Samantha curled in her lap.

She had no idea what time it was when she dozed off, but she'd only been asleep for maybe an hour when the phone rang. She ran to side of the room where her cell was plugged in to recharge, almost tripping over Chester. She got to the phone on the third ring. "Hello?"

"Maggie?"

"Mom? What...you're dead. I'm dreaming, right? This isn't real."

"The problem is, you are always dreaming, but sometimes, your dreams are not dreams. Sometimes what you think is not real is real."

"It's so good to hear your voice." Maggie choked with emotion. "Mom, I miss you so much. There are so many things I want to ask you, and things I want to tell you. You left so soon."

"I love you, my daughter, and you need to know that, but that's not why I called. I need to tell you to pay attention."

"I don't understand."

"I know you don't. But you must learn to understand. Do not turn your back on signs and the messages. Do not."

———

Maggie awoke with a crick in her neck. She'd fallen asleep with her head on the back of the sofa in an odd angle. Samantha was still on her lap. Chester was still at her feet. The phone was in its charging cradle across the room.

What a bizarre dream. Maggie rubbed her neck, and sat straight. "Sorry, kitty, but I gotta get up." As she rose from the couch, the cat leapt off onto the floor and stretched. Maggie went to the bathroom, brushed her teeth and washed her face, then put on a kettle for hot cocoa. Bird and Flower would be up soon, expecting hot chocolate and banana pancakes. She was mashing ripe bananas in a bowl with a fork, when Bird padded into the kitchen rubbing her eyes.

"Good morning, sweetie. Cocoa will be ready in minute."

"Aunt Maggie?"

"Yes, hon?"

"Who called last night?"

Maggie stopped her mashing, and turned to the little girl. "No one called."

"Yes, someone *did* call. I heard the phone ring, and you answered it and were talking. Flower heard, too."

———

A week later Jake showed up at Maggie's cabin to deliver the news in person that Bird and Flower were missing. She collapsed to her knees. Jake offered his hand to help her, but she pulled away. "No. Leave me alone for a second." She composed herself, and stood, knees shaking. "I'm going to find that fucker and strangle him with my bare hands."

———

News reporters from agencies all over the country had descended in a swarm upon Wild River County. The case of the "Heartless Monster" had become the most talked about criminal investigation in the nation. Someone had shared with the press that the suspect was a cannibal.

"When I find the moron who leaked that info I'll skin him alive for compromising our investigation. If he's one of us, I'm going to shove his badge up his ass," Jake told Maggie.

"I'll hold him down for you. Cannibals jack up TV ratings and sell lots of papers. That's why all these vermin reporters are crawling around Wicklow."

When Maggie heard that Mario Panetti, an Italian writer and journalist, famous in Europe for his gory slasher novels and highly sensationalized articles, showed up in town, she had a conniption. "Why the hell is he here? The last thing we need is some pseudo-big shot in town taking everyone's focus off the missing girls."

Mario made a statement to local reporters that he planned to write a book based on the child murders called, "*Il Mostro Americano*," (The American Monster). That is why he had flown from Rome to this 'quaint little backwards town,' as he referred to Wicklow. Maggie read the article over her morning coffee. She said, "Chester, we've got an authentic asshole in our midst."

Later that day, the authentic asshole burst through the doors of the sheriff's department accompanied by a fawning entourage, like a 1940s Hollywood celebrity. He wore a floor-length coat, black fedora pulled over one eye and an enormous emerald pinkie ring. Maggie thought him cartoonish. *Oh, my God. He's a walking, talking cliché.*

He approached Maggie. "I'm sorry, Signora, about your nieces." She nodded, but was on edge and it felt like the Italian was stepping on her last nerve. When he demanded assistance for his research, Maggie leaned into his face so close she could smell stale garlic and cigar smoke on his breath. "Sir, you are as out of place in Wicklow as a turd on a birthday cake, and about as welcome, too."

Jake and his deputies howled with laughter.

Maggie smiled. "You know, Mr. Panetti, there's a plane out of Redding this afternoon that'll take you directly to LAX. I'm pretty sure you can get back to Rome from there. If I were you, I'd consider going home now."

"I'm only here to help, Signora."

"You mean you're here to help yourself."

Jake laughed. "I'm telling you, Mr. Panetti, I've known this woman for a lot of years, and one thing I know with certainty, you don't want to screw with Maggie Sloan. She doesn't much like newspaper writers, and if you ignore my advice, I'll guarantee you, sir, she'll break your balls into itsy bitsy pieces." Jake rolled his thumb and forefingers together to demonstrate.

Again, the men broke into laughter.

Mario worked up an indignant scowl and his puffy cheeks turned bright pink, which made everyone in the room howl with even more gusto. The swarthy man turned heel, snapped his fingers in the air as though summoning a maître d', and stormed out of the station cursing in Italian. His sycophants, a foppish man and two young women with exaggerated boob jobs, followed behind.

"Good work, everyone," Jake said, "I think we got rid of the asshole and bimbo contingency. Did you all see the look on that jerk's face when Maggie called him a turd? Priceless."

Maggie didn't laugh.

"Mag, go home for a while and get some rest." Jake said. "I'll cover this. You haven't rested since the girls went missing. You're no good to me if your senses are dulled. I've got deputies searching 24/7 for Flower and Bird, and I won't let up until we find them, I promise."

Although reluctant, Maggie was exhausted and she'd developed yet another crippling headache. She sighed, looked at Jake and said, "Oh, what the hell. I'll be back in an hour or two."

The ten mile drive to her A-frame took forever. Her neck felt like it was being squeezed in a vise, and the punishing pain behind her eyes overwhelmed her. She couldn't shake the image of her grandnieces' faces. The more she thought of them, the more her head hurt. The harsh brilliance of the midday sun didn't help.

She arrived home and plopped down on the couch for a nap within the welcomed darkness of her living room. Samantha curled on her abdomen and purred. As Maggie began to doze and dream of ravens, someone knocked on the door. "What the fuck?" She dislodged the cat and struggled to her feet. Chester and Samantha at her heels, hugging her wounded ribs with one arm, she answered the door. Sunlight intruded into the cool darkness of the room. Maggie made out the figure of a female reporter standing on her porch wearing flame red lipstick, teetering on six-inch spiked heels. A cameraman stood behind her with a handheld perched on his shoulder.

"Ms. Sloan? We're from KLAA Los Angeles, and we are here to talk to you about your involvement in the case of The Heartless Monster." The reporter stuck a microphone in Maggie's face. When Maggie glared at her, the reporter withdrew the mic and spoke into it. "I understand you've been investigating the murders, and that your nieces were reported missing yesterday. We'd like to..."

"Get the fuck off of my front porch now, and leave my property pronto or I'll shoot your asses. Oh, and that's off the record, by the way." Maggie slammed the door in the reporter's face.

She watched from her window through a small part in the drapes until she saw the "vermin" climb into the KLAA van and drive away roiling dust in its wake. Maggie settled back down onto the couch. Samantha jumped back onto her stomach, and the two slept for five hours.

When Maggie awoke, it was night. She felt groggy as a drunken farmer and her head still hurt. She stumbled into the kitchen, popped a couple of aspirin, and put on a pot of coffee. "Okay, Chester, coffee, a quick hot shower, and then we'll head back to the sheriff's office. You think everyone did all right today without us, fella?"

Her cell rang. "Hello?"

"Good news," Jake said. "We got a lead on the girls. Found their bikes not far from Bear's property."

"I'll meet you there," she said.

Maggie pushed the off button on the coffee pot. She and Chester almost flew out the front door. She jumped into the Chevy, slammed it into first gear, and sped off toward her brother's house.

—

When she pulled into Danny's driveway, a half dozen other vehicles were already parked in the driveway, including Jake's squad car. Cathy, in tears, ran to greet her. "If they don't find my granddaughters livin', I don't think I can take it."

Maggie wrapped her arms around Cathy and rocked her from side to side, her own unbidden tears sliding down her cheeks. She knew there was nothing she could say to make things better for her sister-in-law or for herself, and she had a sickening knowledge that the girls were gone. It had been some hours since Jimmy had last seen them. By now, the killer would have fed them, given them a Hershey bar, broken their necks, and eaten their hearts. He would have then posed them in a grotesque hug somewhere in a shallow grave or on top of the cold ground where coyotes could tear them into pieces. *Please, let them at least be in a grave.*

For the first time since the girls' disappearance she allowed herself to cry over her grandnieces, and having another woman to share her grief made it somehow okay to give in. Still holding her sister-in-law, Maggie lifted her head and wailed. Above her, ravens circled.

"Glad you're here, Mag," said Jake as he approached her.

Maggie released Cathy wiping away tears with her sleeve. "All right. What's the status? Search party assembled and briefed?"

"We recovered the girl's bikes about a half mile from here on an old logging road. We're using Bear and Cathy's house as a base. Everyone is inside waiting for you."

"What do you mean *waiting*? We don't have time to wait. What's wrong with you? Those girls are probably dead already with their hearts ripped out, and the team is *waiting*?"

Maggie caught site of Cathy's stricken expression. "No, Cathy, I didn't mean that. The girls could be alive, really. I'm sorry, I only..."

"I'll go in and make more coffee." Cathy turned toward the house.

Another truck pulled up behind Maggie's, and Mingan stepped out.

"What's *he* doing here?" Jake said through gritted teeth.

"I heard in town the girls' bikes were found nearby," said Mingan as he walked to Jake and Maggie. "I figured you'd all be here. I came to offer my help."

"We've got enough help, thanks," said Jake. "Why don't you go on back to wherever it is you came from, buddy? This is a touchy situation. We don't have time for amateurs slowing us down."

"Jake!' Maggie said. She extended her hand to Mingan. "Thank you for coming. Of course we are happy to have your help."

"You know how fond I am of Bird and Flower. I want to do something."

"Come into the house and grab a cup of coffee. We'll be headed out in a few minutes to find the girls." She put her hand on Mingan's arm. "Thanks for being here. It means a lot."

"It's the least I could do. I've been sick with worry about the girls. I can't imagine what Jimmy, Bear, Cathy and you are going through right now. I've got my entire church in a prayer circle for all of you, but I wanted to be here personally."

Jake had started back to the house so he could have not caught more of the conversation beyond "Jake," and that was just fine with Maggie.

Sally showed up with a basket of blackberry muffins. "I got here as soon as I could," she said as she set the muffins on the hood of a car. "Ah, honey. I'm so sorry." She folded Maggie into an embrace and the two women clung to one another for a long while.

There were twelve in the search party, deputies and townspeople. In groups of twos and threes, each team claiming a separate direction, carrying flashlights, whistles, cell phones and walkie-talkies. One of the men from town brought his pair of Walker hounds and held the girls' unwashed nightgowns beneath their noses. The man and dogs headed off toward the logging road. Chester remained in the bed of the truck because, as Maggie said, "That hound is as useless as tits on a boar hog."

Jake and Maggie headed toward the river, and cried out, "Flower. Bird."

The sounds of the dogs baying, and the search teams stomping through the brush calling for the girls echoed through the forest.

"I've lost track. How long have they been missing?" Maggie asked Jake.

"More than eleven hours." Jake put his arm around Maggie. "We still have time."

"I'm not so sure."

"He's always kept the kids for at least 24 hours before he...I'm sorry, Mag. We do still have time. We're going to find them."

"You're a good friend, Jake." Maggie leaned into Jake's chest. He put his arms around her. After a moment, Maggie dislodged herself from Jake's embrace. "Let's keep on. We don't have time to waste." She tramped down the hill closer to the river. It was colder than she thought it would be, even for this time of the year. Maggie felt frozen inside and out as though her bones and her skin were made of ice.

Ravens called from the trees. It seemed to Maggie they were talking to her rather than to one another. "If you could just tell me which way to walk," she said to them, "I'd double your corn rations. Please. I want to find my nieces."

"What did you say?" Jake asked as he caught up with her.

"Don't listen to me," she said. "I'm going so crazy that I'm even talking to the birds now."

The further down the hill, the denser the forest.

"It's going to be difficult to see much of anything," Jake said.

Two ravens flew overhead, circled. Maggie looked up. The birds rocked and clicked, then flew north.

"We're going this way," Maggie said, following the ravens.

"Why? It's more likely we'll see them in the clearing this way," Jake said directing the beam of his flashlight in the opposite direction.

"I said, we are going *this* way." Maggie clenched her jaw. "Don't fuck with me, Jake. Please."

The ravens settled in a gray pine right ahead of where Maggie and Jake walked.

Happy's voice crackled over a walkie talkie. "Jake, Maggie, you there?"

Jake pushed the button. "Yeah, Happy. Any sign of the girls?"

"Not yet, but there's someone here who needs to talk to you, so you might want to meet us back at Cathy and Bear's."

"Damn, Jake. We don't have time for this," Maggie said. "The house is nearly half a mile up the hill from us."

"Really. You better come up," Happy said.

"Just tell us who it is, Happy." Maggie said.

"FBI."

CHAPTER 16

Canada, Twenty-Eight Years Ago

Noshi and the boy crawled back into the cave. Chepi, curled into a tight ball holding herself, keened until drained of tears, then cried no more. The boy squeezed between his mother and father to keep warm. No one slept that night...

Northern California, Present Time

"WE DIDN'T CALL you," Maggie said as she and Jake approached the agents, "Why the hell are you here?" She knew, of course, this would become a federal case, but the timing couldn't be worse, and she was in no frame of mind to put up with feds right now.

"I'm Agent Marley, and this is Agent Thompson." Marley talked to the sheriff, and ignored Maggie. He gestured to the man with him. Both agents held out their badges for Jake's inspection.

"Sheriff Lubbock, are you aware there are unsolved twin child killings in Oregon and Washington, even across the Canadian border going back at least two decades?" Marley said. He was slender built, about an inch taller than Maggie, with an imperious demeanor that set her teeth on edge.

"I heard that, yes. I figure our guy is a copycat since there have never been killings this far south, until recently, matching the suspect's M.O."

Maggie sneered at the agent. "Yeah, and are you aware that we are here right now looking for my nieces who have been missing for over eleven hours and we don't have time for your horseshit?"

"We have reason to believe we're dealing with the same killer, so this is now officially a federal investigation. We are part of a special task force, and require your full cooperation as well as immediate access to all your files and evidence in the case. We'll take over from there."

Jake's face reddened. "I don't think so," he said. "This is my town. These are my people. I don't give a rat's ass if you are an FBI task force, or avenging angels sent personally by Jesus damn Christ, you know better than to interrupt a search for missing children like this, and you aren't coming here in your cheap suits and your shiny wingtips to take over anything."

There was no way Maggie was going to back down either. "Gentleman, I'm a retired Oakland detective, a criminologist, with more years' experience than you two whelps combined. I've been working with the Wild River County Sheriff's Department since the beginning of these investigations. If you are here to help us, great, but Jake is the boss and you will respect his position and mine. And, fellas, stay the fuck out of our way. Now, if you excuse us, we have to find my grandnieces before it's too late." She turned back toward the forest, and flipped on her flashlight.

"About that, Ms. Sloan," said Agent Thompson, the shorter of the two, a youngster with a pale cherubic face. "In our opinion, given it's your grandnieces we are looking for now, it's a conflict of interest for you to be on this search, or to even be on the case."

"You little maggot," Maggie said, turning on her heels. She started for the agent who took a step back; his eyes popped open wide. He put his hand on his service revolver. Jake thrust out his arm to restrain Maggie who stopped in her tracks to stare down the smaller man. "Don't get in my way."

"We'll be questioning the remainder of the search party, and we'll be looking around a bit ourselves. We'll meet you at the station first thing tomorrow morning," said Agent Marley. The agents headed back toward the house.

"Those arrogant dickheads," Maggie said.

"We knew they'd be getting involved sooner or later."

"Yeah, well, the time those idiots robbed me of could cost the lives of Flower and Bird. If so, I'll be going to prison for murdering FBI agents. And I swear, if that little snot says one more word about my grandnieces, I'm going to slap the piss out of him."

"You know how it goes, Mag. They will question you about how you knew where the Sorenson kids were buried, too. Neither of them will buy your 'I had a dream' story. I don't quite understand it myself."

"Yeah, I do know." She inhaled then exhaled forcefully as though expelling toxic fumes from her lungs. "I can't abide those dickwads interrogating me, but what's worse, I don't have time for their bullshit. Every second I wasted up here with them I could have spent down by the river looking for the girls. Those sonsabitches." Maggie rubbed her temples with her free hand. "I can't take this, Jake. Let's find Bird and Flower."

———

Maggie stayed the course following the two ravens. She appreciated that Jake didn't push her to go in any other direction. He stepped back and allowed her to take the lead, but he remained close behind. The woods were so dense in some places that Maggie and Jake had to hack their way through the underbrush. It was more like a jungle than a conifer forest. The sounds of the other searchers and the baying of the hounds faded into the far distance.

"This is a bloody nightmare" Maggie said.

The sound of the wind in the trees, the caw of the ravens, and footsteps through the pine needles were the only sounds of the forest. As her panic mounted, Maggie was aware of the persistent thrum of her heart pounding hard. *Those girls are dead, I know it.* Her ears were filled with heartbeats, heavy and dreadful. *They're dead.*

They broke through an opening and Maggie spied something near a creek. *A reclining bear cub? No, smaller. A doe?* She shined her flashlight on two little girls on the ground under a rocky overhang partially buried under a blanket of fall leaves, their skin pale as quartz in the moonlight. They were still, face-to-face, their arms in an embrace.

"Aw shit," said Jake.

"No. No. God, no." Maggie dropped her flashlight and ran through the darkness to Flower and Bird.

CHAPTER 17

Canada, Twenty-Eight Years Ago

For days, the family survived on bits of snow and what few pine nuts they managed to pry from fallen cones.

"Mommy, I'm hungry as a coyote," the boy said, "and I'm cold. Why doesn't Daddy build a fire?"

"I'm sorry. The wood is too wet. We'll stay in our little cave where it's warmer. Snuggle close and I'll keep you toasty."

The boy cuddled next to his mother. "Is Sheshebens flying in heaven with the angels?"

"Yes, he is." ...

Northern California, Present Time

"AUNT MAGGIE, DON'T be mad at us, please," Bird said.

"We got kinda lost, and we were tired and wanted to rest for a minute," Flower said.

Maggie scooped both girls into her arms, sat on the dirt, and folded her coat around them. "Didn't you hear us calling for you?" She held the children on her lap and clutched them to her chest. Their bony knees dug into her thighs and stomach, but she didn't care. "I'm so glad you two are safe. I was worried sick about you. You must be really cold, poor babies."

Jake blew a whistle to signal they had found the twins. Jimmy ran ahead of Happy and Cathy to the river bank. "Christ! Are they all right?" He sprinted to Maggie who was still on the ground with the girls on her lap.

"They're fine. They just fell asleep. Those poor little girls must be exhausted and starving. All that time out here on their own. It's amazing that a mountain lion or..."

"...Daddy, are we in trouble?" Bird said, wriggling free from

Maggie to run with Flower to her father.

"I'm so glad you're okay." Jimmy grabbed his daughters into his arms and kissed their heads. "And, yeah, you two are grounded until your eighteenth birthdays. All these people have been looking for you since yesterday. You scared everyone."

The girls sobbed. "We're sorry, Daddy. Don't be mad," Flower said.

"Why are you out here, anyway? Don't you know that bad things happen to little girls who wander around outside on their own?"

"We went for a ride on our new bikes," Flower said. "We wanted to show Grandpa and Grandma."

"Don't you ever, ever leave the house by yourselves again. Do you understand?"

"Yes, Daddy," said Flower. The girls hiccupped and sniffed back tears.

"How did you get here?" he said. "You know how many miles you are away from home?"

"We turned the wrong way, I guess, so we left our bikes on the road and came down by the river 'cause Grandpa and Grandma live somewhere around here. We didn't mean to get lost, and wanted to lay down for a little bit and cuddle to get warm 'cause it was really, really cold. We didn't mean to fall asleep for so long. Honest," Flower said still sniffling.

Jimmy released his daughters. "We'll talk about this later. Go to the house with Grandma."

Cathy put her arms around the girls and hugged them tight. "Let's get inside for some hot cocoa and Vanilla Wafers, shall we?"

"Grandma, can we have marshmallows in our cocoa?" said Bird.

"And whipped cream and sprinkles, too?" said Flower.

"We better get going because that's a tall order and it's going to take me some time to put all that together."

Cathy and the two girls walked up the hill toward the house with Jimmy close behind.

The search party had gathered by the river. "We are so relieved you found them alive," one of searchers said. The Walker hounds bayed. Their owner called to silence them.

"Where in the hell is the FBI? Left already, eh? Useless bags of rotten dung." Jake spit in the dirt. "Happy, notify everyone at the station that we found the girls safe."

"I'm on it."

Mingan approached Jake and Maggie. "Thank Jesus for finding those girls," he said, then extended his hand to Jake.

"Yeah?" Jake said, ignoring the other man's hand. "Jesus had nothing to do with it, buddy."

He turned his back on Mingan and walked away.

"That guy really doesn't like me, does he?" Mingan said to Maggie.

"Don't take it personally. He's a bit of an old curmudgeon, and he's been under tremendous stress with this case." She brushed a stray hair from her forehead.

Mingan stepped toward her. Too close. *Jeez. Any other time I'd love him moving in to me. But right now? Really?* She stepped back. "Thank you for coming to help find the girls, Mingan. Sally and Cathy will have a fresh pot of coffee brewing. Let's go for a cup."

"Sounds good."

———

Maggie pulled the last of the crook neck squash off the vines and yanked up the plants. "Time to put the garden to bed for the season, Chester. I guess we'll have to settle for that store-bought tasteless junk disguised as vegetables for a while." The panting dog stood from where he'd been stretched out on the dirt and ambled to her.

"Hot, boy?" She scratched the dog's head. "Why in hell do you insist on sleeping for hours directly in the sun?"

A raven cawed at her from the branch of a white oak. She shook her finger at the bird. "Plenty of corn on the ground near the bench, fella. Why don't you go over there to get some and leave me alone?"

A truck pulled up and stopped. Maggie peeled off her garden gloves, and put one hand to her forehead to shield her eyes from the sun's glare. She squinted to better see who was in her driveway. Mingan. He stepped out and strode toward Maggie. "Good morning," he leaned to scratch Chester.

Maggie smiled. "What are you doing out on a Sunday morning? Don't you go to church?"

"Went to the early service and decided to take a drive afterwards. Thought I'd stop by."

"Come on in. I'll make you some eggs. It's the least I can do to thank you for showing up at Danny's to help find the girls."

"I like those little girls and, besides, it is my Christian duty to help."

The two walked into the house with Chester behind. Maggie opened a cupboard and retrieved a box of dry cat food. "Don't you even think about eating Samantha's food, you no-good hound." Maggie poured kibble into a bowl. Samantha rubbed against Maggie's legs and purred as she waited for Maggie to place the bowl on the floor.

"You've got quite a menagerie," Mingan said. "Cat, dog, chickens, ravens."

"Those ravens aren't my pets, trust me. They're a pain in the ass."

"They sure act like your pets. I've never seen so many ravens gathered near anyone's house. Look, they're even lined up on your window sill."

"That's because those birds are smart enough to know I'm a sucker with a bag of corn." Maggie withdrew a container of eggs from the refrigerator and placed it on the counter. "Help yourself to coffee. Cream and sugar are on the table." She handing him a mug. "Eggs and toast with homemade strawberry jam coming right up." With one hand she cracked an egg against the side of a bowl. She cast the shell into her compost bucket, and picked up another egg.

Mingan poured coffee into his mug, sat down and scooted his chair to the table. "It's really nice that you invited me to breakfast. Thanks."

"No problem. I was getting hungry anyway. Hope you don't mind your eggs scrambled."

"That's how I like them best, actually." Mingan took a sip of his coffee. "Good. What is it?"

"French roast, organic. Everyone knows it's the only coffee I drink." She sat, scooted her chair closer to the table, and cradled her mug in both hand. "Tell me a little about yourself."

"Not much to tell. You know I'm Algonquin. You know I was born in Canada. You know I was orphaned as a teenager. You know I'm a banker, and you know I'm a Christian. What else do you want to know?"

"Fair enough. Tell me something I don't know."

Mingan looked down at the table. "Before I accepted Jesus as my savior, I was a troubled kid. I had been picked up for assault a few times. I had an angry streak, a blinding temper, given to outbursts. After my parents were murdered, I became vindictive and hateful."

"I can't imagine that. You seem so peaceful."

"I nearly beat a guy to death. He had insulted my then-girlfriend, called her a whore, and I lost it. He was hospitalized, and if I'd not been a minor, and had he died, I would still be in jail. But that's behind me now. I was in a juvenile facility when a chaplain came to visit."

"And that's when you turned to Christianity?"

"Yes. I'm convinced that chaplain saved my life. I haven't laid a hand on anyone in anger for many years." Mingan took another sip of coffee. "Maggie, would you ever consider coming to church with me?"

"No, thanks."

"You believe in God, don't you?"

Maggie stood and returned to making breakfast. She poured milk into the bowl with the eggs, and retrieved a wire whip from a drawer. "I stopped believing in God about the same time I stopped believing in Santa and the Easter Bunny."

She turned her head to look at him. *Incredibly handsome. If I went to church with him, I wonder if I could get him into my bed after.* She knew she wasn't actually ready for that, not yet anyway, but she blushed at where her mind was taking her. She turned back to the counter and whipped the eggs. *That fanatical religious stuff might be a deal breaker anyway.*

"You know, God does exist, and he judges us based not only on our behavior and our character, but on our faith in Him."

Maggie dropped the whip into the bowl, and exhaled trying not to give away her mounting irritation. "Do yourself a favor and don't try to save me. I'm fine with you believing in God, but you have to be fine with my not believing in your made-up, super-power, invisible daddy figure, okay?"

"I'll never be okay with you not believing in God. I'll pray for you because I'm interested in you not only because you are a beautiful woman and I'd like to get to know you. I care about your soul."

Maggie popped sourdough bread into the toaster, and carried utensils and plates to the table. She smiled. *He thinks I'm beautiful and wants to get to know me, eh?* "God, Mingan. If you want to take me on a date, I'll say a hearty amen to that. But you have to stop this religious stuff. I'm an atheist, and you aren't going to change my mind." She banged the silverware and plates on the table, and took a step back and crossed her arms. "If you are all right with who I am without trying to change me into who you want me to be, fine. If not, eat your eggs and go, please."

"If you don't believe in God, why do you keep saying his name?"

Maggie's back stiffened. "Because 'God' is the strongest curse word I know; even better than fu..." she stopped short when she saw the look on his face. "Never mind...Please, will you leave it alone?"

Maggie was upset, not so much because of his proselytizing, but because she might be falling for him. He was the only man in years that made her weak in the knees. *I can't believe I have the major hots for a fundamentalist Christian Indian.* "I'm sorry. I respect your beliefs," she said. "Really I do. I shouldn't have said what I did."

"It's all right, Maggie. Maybe one day you'll see the truth for yourself. I'll pray for you."

"The truth is I am who I am." She shrugged, stirred the eggs in the pan, and tried to quash another wave of irritation. "Pray all you want but you have to take me or leave me as is." She walked over with the pan in one hand, pushed eggs onto Mingan's plate with a spatula, and sat hard across from him. She took a sip of coffee without looking up. *Oh, no. I hoped this would be a nice romantic little breakfast.* Outside the window, a raven cawed.

Mingan stuck a forkful of fluffy eggs into his mouth. "Good," he said. "Nothing like fresh eggs."

The two made small talk through most of the morning, Maggie poured coffee into their mugs or passed strawberry jam.

"Maggie, I really like you," Mingan said. "I'm sorry we got off to a bad start with this conversation. Sometimes after a passionate sermon I become emotionally worked up. If you talk to anyone from my past, you'll find out that I sometimes go over the top about my faith, and I can be, well, a bit reactive, I'm afraid. I make no apologies for being a Christian, but I don't mean to come across as pushy. How about we start over?"

Maggie smiled and shrugged her shoulders. "Sure. Why not?"

"Will you join me for dinner on Saturday night?"

"Promise not to talk about religion, or to try to convert me?"

"Yes," he said, and with his forefinger, he crossed his heart.

"Then I'd be delighted."

They finished their breakfast and Maggie put the two empty plates on the floor for Chester to lick. She cleared the utensils and napkins off the table. Mingan rose to help her.

"I've got this," she said as she grabbed a sponge to wipe off the counter. I'll make another pot of coffee if you'd..."Someone knocked at the door.

"Oh for Christ damn..." she said, then added, "Sorry, Mingan." She tossed the sponge into the sink, wiped her hands on a dish towel, made her way into the living room and opened the door. Jake stood on the front porch. "Come on in. I was putting on another pot of coffee."

"We picked up..."Jake stopped mid-sentence and stared at Mingan who had walked into the living room. "Did I interrupt something?" Jake said.

"Mingan and I were finishing breakfast. Would you like some eggs?"

Jake kept his eyes on Mingan. "This is official business. Can we talk out on the porch, Maggie? Excuse us...if you don't mind," he said to Mingan. "Some of us have better things to do than sit on our asses drinkin' French roast."

The two men glared at each other.

"I'm sorry, Mingan," Maggie said. "I guess some people can't help being jerks. Excuse me. I'll be right back."

She stepped out onto the landing with Jake, and shut the door behind her. "There is absolutely no reason in hell for you to be so rude to Mingan."

"I don't like him, and I don't trust him. I have no need to be cordial to the bastard. That's the way it is, Maggie. Oh, and sorry if I disturbed your little date."

"That's the way it is, you say? Not that I owe you any explanation, but he stopped by and I made him breakfast, okay? I don't give a rat's ass what you think of him. Furthermore, this isn't a date, but even if it were, it's none of your business. *That's* the way it is."

Jake stood his ground. "I'm telling you, Mingan is bad news. I've heard things about his temper. He's not the great guy you think he is. He's been arrested several times for violent assault, Maggie. I worry about you and..."

"...I know about his past. He told me himself, and you have no right to come to my home and be rude to my guests, no matter what," Maggie said. "Now, what's going on that you had to show up at my house on a Sunday morning, my only real day off? You aren't here to give me a load of shit about Mingan."

Jake smiled, but made no apology. "We picked up Bobby Jenkins on a child molestation charge."

"What? You're kidding me."

"No, I'm not kidding you. A little girl complained to her mother that Bobby 'touched her.'"

"Oh, that's not good."

"No, it's not, and I'm afraid I've got more bad news."

"I don't know if I can handle more bad news." A raven landed on Maggie's mailbox distracting her. The bird ruffled his feathers. "Shoo. Get away," Maggie said, "I don't want you crapping all over my mailbox."

"Mag, listen to me," Jake said.

"What?"

"The little girl is Happy's daughter."

CHAPTER 18

Canada, Twenty-Eight Years Ago

Noshi went every morning in search of food but returned every evening empty-handed. He did his best to care for his family. He expanded the snow cave to make it more comfortable, digging a larger air hole. If the boy tilted his head just so, he could watch the night stars. Sometimes he imagined Sheshebens with big white wings flying over the moon. "I miss you," he'd whisper...

Northern California, Present Time

"GOOD DAY, YOU two." Sally greeted Jake and Maggie as they drew near the counter. "I've got a fall special on pumpkin spice latte. Care to try one?"

"When did you ever know me to drink frou-frou coffee drinks?" Maggie said. "I'll have my usual."

"One French roast in an oversized mug comin' up. What'll it be for you, Sheriff?"

"I'll try that pumpkin thing."

Maggie looked at Jake as though he'd ordered a plate full of flies. "You're kidding me. I never knew you liked that sweet crap." She turned her head to Sally. "Sorry. I didn't mean that. I'm sure it's good."

"If I got my feelings hurt every time you blurted out what was in your head, Mag, I'd have ended our friendship before we even started high school."

"Any spooky shit happen at Mama's since I was last in?" Maggie asked Sally.

"No, actually, Iggy and Squiggy have been quiet these past two weeks."

"Good, I don't want to get my head split open by a coffee cup missile aimed at me by a goblin or whatever."

"I didn't think you believed in ghosts. Have you changed your mind?"

"I'm sure there's some rational explanation for what's happening around here. Sooner or later, it'll come to light." *She thought about the nocturnal call from her dead mother, but decided against telling Sally about it.*

"Don't be too certain about that." Sally turned to the cappuccino machine. "You two find a seat, and I'll bring your coffees."

Maggie and Jake moved to a bistro table near a window.

"What did Happy say when you told him about his daughter and Bobby Jenkins?" Maggie said.

"He's still on his hunting trip in Oregon and Washington. He won't be home for another eight days. We haven't been able to reach him."

"Can't Rosa get him on his cell?"

"Afraid not. She's been trying, but I think he's too deep in the forest to receive cell reception."

"Didn't he file a hiking or hunting plan or whatever those things are you're supposed to lodge with the Forest Service when you go into the wilderness alone? He'll want to know about this."

Sally brought the coffees to the table. Jake took his mug in both hands, licked whipped cream from his latte then looked up at Sally. "Thanks."

"Enjoy." Sally walked back behind the counter.

"Yummy," Jake said under his breath.

"Did you say *yummy*?" Maggie couldn't resist the jab. "First you order a fluffy drink. Then you actually lick the whipped cream, and now you say yummy. Really?"

"C'mon, Mag. Let's enjoy our coffee."

"I simply want to make certain you aren't getting girly on me."

"Why? If I order strong black brew with a double shot of whiskey and belch like a real man, will you go out with me?"

"Knock it off, Jake." Maggie suppressed a smile, and scooted her chair back as though to stand.

"All right, Mag. We've got business to talk over anyway."

Maggie moved her chair forward and took her mug of coffee in both hands. "Okay, so back to Happy. He's gone somewhere deep in the forest out of state, and can't be reached. Isn't that a tad bit irresponsible?"

"I've known Happy since he moved here from Oregon almost fifteen years ago. He goes hunting or fishing by himself up north several times a year, usually two to three weeks at a time. He says it clears his head. Besides, have you ever tasted his elk jerky?"

"Is it *yummy*?"

"As a matter of fact it is." Jake shot a killer look at Maggie.

"What you are saying is he doesn't know that Bobby Jenkins sexually abused his daughter. Excuse me, *allegedly* abused his daughter."

"Right. Rosa told him what happened in her last message to him yesterday morning, but he hasn't phoned her back, and he hasn't checked in at the station, either. I'm guessing he'll phone in the second he picks up her call."

"Might be days before that happens."

"Yup."

"You still have Bobby in lock-up, I assume? After we're done here, I want to talk to him."

"I thought you might. He'll be in the interview room before we get to the station."

Sally approached the table and poured a refill for Maggie. "Are you enjoying your latte, Sheriff?"

"Oh, he thinks it's yummy," said Maggie.

The bell on the door tinkled and Mingan walked in. Jake shoved his nearly finished latte across the table, stood and said, "I'll see you at the station, Maggie." He stormed out of the coffee shop, pushing passed Mingan.

———

"Well, Bobby. Seems you got yourself into some more trouble," Maggie said as she entered the room. "Do you want to tell me about what happened with that little girl?"

Bobby scanned the space around him, his eyes darting here and there like a nervous ferret. "So, who besides you is listening to us? I bet you got microphones stashed all over the place."

"I need you to answer the question."

"No, I don't want to tell you what happened with the little girl, lady. You won't believe me anyway, so I'd be wasting my time. Got a smoke on ya?"

Maggie straddled the chair opposite Bobby. "Sorry, no smoking in here."

He looked at her as though she were the most moronic woman on the planet. "I was thinking if you have one on ya, maybe I could catch a smoke break outside later."

"I already told you I don't smoke, Bobby. Tell me about touching that little girl."

"Last time you bought me a pack of American Spirits for answering your questions."

"Last time you weren't hauled into an interrogation room because of a complaint that you touched the deputy's daughter. Tell me about the little girl."

"Little girl, my ass. They planted her to spy on me."

"Who is 'they'?"

"I told you all this before. Do you not listen, or do you lack basic intelligence?" His left eye twitched in a nervous tic. "I'll spell it for you so maybe you get it this time...that is if you can spell. Got a pen and paper to write this down? T-H-E-G-O-V-E-R-N-M-E-N-T. Got that?"

"I'm trying to help you. I'm the last person you want to alienate, trust me on this. You don't have many friends." Maggie leaned toward Bobby. "So, the government is spying on you, and sent a little girl for you to feel up so they could get intel on you?"

"I'm going to tell you what I already told those other idiots. Read my lips so you can understand. I – did-not-feel-her-up."

"What were you doing at the elementary school, Bobby?"

"Looking through the garbage for cans, bottles, anything I can cash in. I'm out of cigarettes." He chewed his thumb nail, ripping off a piece of cuticle. "Dammit," he said. "I'm bleeding." He stuck the side of his thumb into his mouth and sucked at his nail.

"The little girl said you felt her buttocks."

He jerked his thumb out of his mouth. "What? Oh, hell no. I'm no pervert. I was patting her down to find her wire. I also felt her back and checked her socks and lunch bag. Did she tell you any of that? She's a plant. They could have put a microphone anywhere on her."

"Tell me why the government sent a 6-year-old girl to spy on you?"

"Don't you remember even one thing I told you last time I was in here? I'll tell you one more time, and I'm not saying it again, so pay attention. The government is plotting to wipe out the homeless. They're going to kill us. That's all I'm saying. Why should I tell you more? You'll forget it tomorrow anyway. Got early onset Alzheimer's, or are you plain stupid?"

"For a guy with an IQ of 155, you're the one who is stupid if you don't know by now that I'm trying to help. Please, answer my questions."

Bobby flinched as though Maggie had shot him in the face with a dart gun.

"Why *that* little girl, Bobby?"

"I don't know. You'll have to ask her."

"What I'm saying is why did you pat down that particular girl? Why did you choose her?"

"I didn't choose her. She chose me." He leaned forward, looked one way and then the other, and whispered, "I go to the school every few days right after lunch to check the garbage, and every single time that same little girl is there near the trash cans pretending to play with her friend."

"Pretending?"

"I say 'pretending' because why in the hell would kids choose to play near stinking trash bins with that nice grassy play yard with trees?" Bobby inspected his injured cuticle. "Anyway, when I went there last time, she wasn't with her friend. She was hanging around by herself staring at me, and that's when I knew for sure she was a plant. She was waiting."

"Then what happened?"

"I said, 'Hi there, kid. Come here.' She squeezed through a rip in the chain link and walked right up to me, not afraid or concerned that I could be some sick bum who might rape her. She came to me like I was her buddy."

"And?"

"And, what?"

"Bobby, don't play games with me. I'm not in the mood. When the little girl approached you, what did you do?"

"I asked her if I could see what she had in her lunch bag. She said 'sure.' She even offered me her sandwich. I thought that was a clever touch." Bobby chuckled and shook his head.

"What do you mean by 'clever touch'?"

"Pretending to care if I was hungry. How sweet. Yeah, right. If I'd been stupid enough to fall for it, that would throw me off, wouldn't it?"

"What if the reason she offered you her sandwich is because she thought you were hungry and was genuinely concerned for you?"

"Oh, that's priceless, lady. You think I couldn't see through that shit? She just didn't want to blow her cover."

Maggie rolled her pen between her forefinger and thumb. *Naturally, Bobby would never believe that anyone cared for him.* "A six-year-old undercover agent working for the government?"

"They use everyone and anyone, even babies and house cats. I never trust anybody, human or animal."

"After she opened her lunch bag, what did you do?"

"I searched it. I even took the sandwich apart to see if there was a chip or wire in it. I turned that bag inside out. The little girl stared at me with her mouth opening and closing like a dumb-ass fish." He made a movement with his mouth like a bass out of water. "I don't think she expected I'd be that smart."

"Yeah, Bobby. I imagine she was a bit surprised." Maggie resisted the urge to roll her eyes. "What came next?"

"I walked over and patted her back and sides. I felt around her head, and then checked her socks. She just stood there, but when I moved to search her torso area for a wire, she screamed like I was killing her or something, and took off. I didn't touch her ass. Of course no one will believe that, right?"

"Where did you go?"

I ran back to the Bridge where I was arrested on this bogus child molestation charge. Now I'm here. Is there anything else I can tell you that I haven't already told ten other jerks?" He looked to the ceiling, and raised his voice. "I'm sick of this shit. Do you hear that all you assholes who are listening in? I said, I'm...sick...of...this...shit."

"That's all I need for now." Maggie got up and started for the door.

"When do I get out? You have nothing on me, and I know my rights."

"Bobby, you were picked up on a child molestation charge, and you admitted to touching the girl."

"What the hell? I didn't touch her *that* way."

"It doesn't matter what your intentions were, Bobby. You did touch her. You admitted it."

Bobby slapped his forehead and contorted his face. His hands trembled and beads of sweat blossomed on his forehead. "I'm completely screwed, aren't I?"

"Your arraignment is this afternoon, and if the judge doesn't set bail at a million dollars, maybe someone can get you out tonight." She stepped toward the door. "And, by the way, if by some miracle you have a distant relative who can post bail, whatever you do, don't run."

"Yeah, sure. Where am I gonna go? You think I'll hop on my private Lear Jet to Paris?" He gestured with his hand as though he were sipping on champagne or tea, his pinkie finger sticking out.

Maggie sighed. *This guy's cracked, but I don't figure him for a pedophile. Poor son-of-a-bitch.* "Got any family, Bobby?"

"I told you last time. No family except a single guy, a cousin in Redding."

"If you haven't called him yet, you might want to."

"He doesn't have any money, and even if he did, he doesn't care about me. No one does."

"Sorry to hear that. Really, I am. Goodbye, Bobby."

CHAPTER 19

Canada, Twenty-Eight Years Ago

Chepi and the boy had their job, too. After Noshi left each day, when the sun reached a high point, they walked out into an opening near the snow cave, banged rocks together and shouted for hours in hopes someone might hear. The boy feared mountain lions and bears. "Mommy, what happens if a bear comes?"

"It'll be okay, little one."

But, every morning when Daddy left, the boy's heartbeat quickened with fear...

Northern California, Present Time

MAGGIE DRANK TWO double gin and tonics to forget the day. She opened the living room window to let in the fresh evening air. She fell asleep on the couch with Samantha at her feet, and Chester at her side. As she drifted off, she dreamed she flew through the open window into the night sky. It was dark, overcast. It would rain soon. She could smell it as she soared over Wicklow. Other than a couple of loud drunks stumbling out of The Silverado, the streets were empty. She flew over the men in a tight circular pattern.

"See you later, man," one drunk said to the other. He ducked into an alley and relieved himself against a trash can. The other stumbled toward the trailer park a few blocks down the street. Maggie cawed, and the urinating man tilted his head and turned his eyes toward her. He peed on his own foot.

Humans are idiots.

Drawn by the pale glow of a campfire, she veered off toward Douglas Bridge, and settled on a stack of old tires. Near her were people, men mostly. They were dressed in dirty clothes huddled against the damp air around a meager flame drinking beer from bottles, smoking cigarettes and discussing chem trails. "There are no such things as chem trails," said one older man with a missing leg. "Jets naturally produce contrails."

"When are you going to pull your head out of your ass?" another man said. "The government has been spraying toxins on us for years. Anyone with any knowledge and half a brain can tell you the Illuminati and the government formed a tight alliance." He crossed his fingers to demonstrate the alliance. "They have a secret agenda going back more than a century. You know about the FEMA concentration camps they're building all over the country, don't you? They'll be rounding us up by the thousands and taking us to..." He paused, stubbed out his cigarette and stood. "Shhhh" he said, putting his index finger to his lips.

The others fell silent.

"Who have we got here?" he gestured at Maggie with a dented metal flashlight.

She turned her head sideways to see his face. She recognized him. *Bobby.*

"Aw, shit," he said. "What's a raven doing here this time of night?" He pointed the beam of the flashlight directly into her eyes. The people stood up from the campfire ring and stared at her. She sat still, curious. "That damned bird has green eyes. Ravens don't have green eyes," Bobby said.

"By God, you're right, said a short man with a beard. "I think something's wrong with that bird. Maybe it's got rabies or something. Let's kill it."

Maggie gripped the tires with her talons. *Uh oh.*

"Oh yeah, something's wrong with that bird all right, but it ain't rabies. Trust me. It's not even a raven. It's an automaton, a robot. They sent it to spy on us," Bobby said.

"Bobby, it's me, Maggie. Caw, Caw," she said.

He picked up an empty beer bottle and threw it at her. She flew off the tire in a frenzy of feathers and wings. The beer bottle cracked hard against the rubber right where she had been perched.

"Tell your bosses to try harder next time," Bobby called after her as she flew away.

———

When Maggie awoke, she was belly down on the floor. "I gotta quit drinking, Chester. What a weird-ass nightmare. Let's go to bed." Rain pounded against her roof. She got up to close the window and stopped. She bent to pick up a single black feather resting on the ledge. "Damn birds sitting on the sill again. I'm lucky there isn't shit all over the place." Maggie, Chester and Samantha lumbered off together to the bedroom.

She awoke the next morning feeling refreshed, not hung over in the least. She showered, dressed, toasted a bagel and put on a pot of coffee. The sun was out, and the earth smelled clean. Maggie stepped onto her back deck, full mug in-hand. She looked up into the sky. She'd have a whole hour to herself before leaving to meet Jake at the station. *Nice to have a little time to relax, to greet the new day without bullshit stress for once.*

Her cell phone rang. She fumbled as she retrieved it from her pocket, and in doing so, splashed coffee onto her clothes. *Oh, fuck me. I only bought these pants yesterday.* Caller ID told her it was Jake. "I don't have to meet you for an hour and twenty-five minutes. Can't you let me have a little precious time to myself? Besides, I spilled coffee all over myself when I answered the phone, so now I have to waste more time to change my clothes." She dabbed at the spill with a paper napkin. "I need a few minutes in peace to finish one lousy cup of coffee and get on some clean pants."

"Mag, listen, we got a call."

"More kids missing?"

"No...it's..."

"...since it's not kids, I don't give a rat's ass. I'm hanging up now."

"Wait, wait. Don't hang up. Some of the Bridge People found Bobby Jenkins' body early this morning near a dumpster."

"How'd he get out? What happened?" *Oh God, why Bobby?*

"He was murdered."

"Oh no. You didn't tell me how he got out."

"A cousin from Redding came in and posted bail."

"Well, I guess someone cared after all," she whispered.

"What?"

"Nothing. Never mind." She sipped her coffee. *Damn, tastes like battery acid.* She tossed the remaining contents of the mug over her deck railing. "Was he shot?"

"Someone broke his neck..."

"Christ."

"...and his heart is gone."

CHAPTER 20

Canada, Twenty-Eight Years Ago

Once, the boy and his mother clambered up a white oak when a pack of wolves heard their distress calls and showed up for what promised to be an easy meal. "Hurry. Grab my hand tight," said Chepi. "Use both hands." She hoisted the boy onto a sturdy branch.

Mother and child remained in the tree bunched together against the cold, safe from the wolves who circled below, until Noshi returned. He yelled and threw rocks until the snarling canines at last retreated. A large male yelped when one of Noshi's rocks found its target. "Get away from my family, you goddamn bastards," he yelled.

The boy had never been so frightened in his entire life. He clung to his mother long after the wolves had disappeared, and the two climbed down from the tree, for the time-being, safe...

Northern California, Present Time

"HOW WAS THE hunting trip?" Maggie asked Happy. "Did you bag an elk? I hear you make a mean jerky."

"Came up empty-handed."

"How's your little Katy after her ordeal with Bobby?"

"She's fine, thanks. She's always been a real trooper, and I think she was more scared than anything else. That Bobby was one sick guy. I'm sure he did touch her, and I'm not a bit sorry to say that I'm glad he got what was coming to him."

"If it were Flower or Bird, I'd say the same."

"Got any idea who the killer is — I mean Bobby's killer?" Happy asked, looking from Maggie to Jake.

"Could have been anyone. Jake thinks it's a copycat since the kid murderer doesn't target adults. I'm not sure I agree with that theory. We haven't established a solid motive." Maggie looked through a window the moment a gust of wind blew the last fist full of leaves off a maple tree.

Jake took a long draw from a glass of water. "You know, actually, you are the only guy with motive to kill Bobby."

"I'm not a suspect, am I?"

"Of course we don't think you did it," Maggie said, "but you were also out of touch for nearly three weeks with no one to verify your whereabouts. A lot can happen in that time. I know this, if it were my daughter, I'd want to kill the son-of-a-bitch."

"I was in a rugged part of the mountains, Maggie." Happy was calm, composed. His eyes clear, his hands steady. He relaxed in his chair. No way could he have done this, Maggie thought.

"Took me almost four days to hike in. Does someone think I somehow received Rosa's and Jake's messages even though I was out of cell range? Really? Then, of course, I had time to bust down camp, pack, hike back out, hop a plane with all my gear, rent a car, drive in from the Redding airport to the Bridge, cut out Bobby's heart, clean up, then go back hunting, all without being noticed or leaving any trail? I only returned to Wicklow yesterday, and didn't even know what had happened until I picked up Rosa's messages two days ago."

"We aren't saying you did it," Jake said, "but the FBI might want to question you anyway. Just letting you know, buddy."

A raven cawed. Maggie looked out the window. Ravens stared back at her from a gnarled, bare maple branch. *Where did you all come from? You weren't sitting there a second ago.* She turned back to Happy. He gave her his famous lopsided smile.

———

Maggie couldn't decide which one of the FBI pricks she disliked the most. Agent Marley or Agent Thompson. She decided on Marley, the imperious, high-handed jerk-off. The chubby-faced little guy, Thompson, might be a little dick, but is only doing his job. Yeah, Marley was the one she hated most. As he grilled her, all she could do was imagine what it would feel like burying an axe in his skull. Back in the day, she'd been good friends with an FBI agent, Lacy Cohen. The two women spent a lot of time together drinking beer and shooting pool. Lacy was a true professional, dedicated and smart. The FBI sure doesn't make 'em like Lacy any more, Maggie thought.

"So, explain one more time how you knew where the Sorenson boys were buried."

"Agent Marley, have you ever worked off a hunch?"

"No, the FBI works off facts."

"A lot of bad things go on in that part of the forest. It's not the first time bodies have been dumped or buried there. I simply woke up with a hunch that's where we'd find the boys, and called Jake. Do you have a problem with that?"

"No problem, but doesn't seem likely that you would know exactly where the grave was."

Agent Thompson fidgeted in his seat like a bored teenager. *Maybe he has to pee.* We had clues, Agent, such as cigarette butts, the same brand we'd encountered before in this investigation." Maggie grew impatient. She tapped her fingers on the scratched, gray Formica table top. "Does the FBI use clues in its investigations, or are clues not factual enough to go on?"

"We'll ask the questions, Ms. Sloan."

There was a knock on the door. Jake stuck his head into the room. "Sorry to interrupt, but I have urgent news."

"Come on in, Jake. I think we were about ready to end this overwhelmingly useless line of questioning, aren't we, gentlemen?" Maggie stood and pulled on her jacket.

"We aren't quite finished yet," said Thompson.

"Oh, wow. You mean Marley actually lets you say something on your own now and again?" She moved one quick step toward the shorter man, who took a short step back. *I could easily kick his ass. Poor guy. He's not FBI material. How'd he even get in?* "What is it, Jake?"

"Another set of twins reported missing. The Dalton girls."

"When?" said Maggie.

"The mother said her girls disappeared about thirty minutes ago from the Grange Park.

She was watching them play on the swings, went to the bathroom, and came back to find them gone. There was no one else in the park when she left for the restroom, and she didn't see anyone around when she returned. She looked everywhere before calling it in. No trace of the girls."

"How long was the mother in the bathroom?"

"Under five minutes, she says."

"How long did she search for them after?"

"Another ten. You know that park is only a small lot with a swing set, a bathroom and a few trees. Nothing else around. Wouldn't take more than a few minutes to search every inch. This happened within the last half hour, so if we act fast enough, we might have a chance of saving those little girls." Jake motioned with his hand to the agents. "Sorry to break up your party, but Maggie and I have to get on this."

"Anyway, I couldn't possibly be here talking to you two brainless yahoos, and be snatching twins at the same time, now, could I?" Marley and Thompson looked at her and Jake dumbfounded. "Now if you'll excuse us," she said, "we've got work to do before that murdering bastard kills two more kids." Jake exited the room opened the door wider and stood back. She bolted from the interrogation room, and slammed the door behind her leaving the agents inside.

After searching for hours, Jake called off the search for the evening.

Maggie, objected. "C'mon Jake. We don't have time to waste. By tomorrow, those kids could be dead."

"Nothing more we can do tonight, Mag. Go on home."

"Yeah, whatever you want, Jake, but those kids..." She looked up as the two agents exited their Suburban and approached her and Jake. "Uh, oh."

Leaving Jake to confer with the FBI, an exhausted Maggie climbed into her truck, and drove to her A-frame.

———

Maggie had sucked down her second bourbon and was about to pour a third when she heard the pounding at her door. When she opened it, Jake stood there, his bright blue eyes dark and hollow, his face drained of blood. "Sorry to bother you so late, but I'm afraid I've got bad news."

She knew the little Dalton girls were dead before Jake even showed up at her door. She didn't bother to tell him that she'd had another dream, one where the ravens talked to her as she flew with them over Sasquatch Mountain Dam. *He already thinks I'm a nut case, and, besides, the ravens told me it was too late to do anything about it.* She'd been cursing the sky, the earth, the entire universe a few minutes before Jake's patrol car pulled into her driveway. *Little girls, just little girls.*

CHAPTER 21

Canada, Twenty-Eight Years Ago

After nearly two weeks, the boy, weak from hunger said, "Mommy, I'm tired. I can't bang rocks and yell today. I wanna sleep."

"Sleep, little one. Rest."

When Noshi returned that evening again without game, Chepi said, "You've got to do something. We can't lose our other child, this one to starvation. Please..."

Northern California, Present Time

BESIDES A CARL'S Jr., a Del Taco, and a Quizno's Sub, there were five restaurants in all of Wicklow. A few weren't open on weekends, which everyone thought crazy. "No wonder folks go down to the city and spend their money there instead of here. Nothin' ever open on weekends," people said. There was Martinez' Mexican food, run by the same Thai couple who also owned the only Chinese restaurant in town, The Golden Pagoda. There was The Dandelion Café, a German deli, Otto's, that served the best sausage with red cabbage salad on the planet, and there was Nito's Italian Restaurant, which although short on atmosphere, served surprisingly good northern Italian cuisine and a decent house Chianti. That's where Mingan told Maggie they were going on their first real date.

"Sure. Nito's makes excellent homemade wild mushroom ravioli," Maggie said.

"I'll pick you up at seven."

The latest twin killings, coupled with reading a sensational article printed by Mario Panetti in an Italian newspaper claiming that *Il Mostro Americano* is a "Demon from Hades with wings like a giant bat," put Maggie in a dark place. She wasn't up for a night out. She called Sally. "I have to break this date with Mingan. I'm not in a mood for it."

"Go on. Get out for a few hours. Have a little pasta and a bit of wine. It wouldn't hurt you to get laid, either."

"Given what's going on, I don't feel much like partying."

"Go anyway. You need a break now more than ever."

———

Maggie spent hours getting ready. She'd seen Mingan once after their breakfast. They'd gone to Mama's for coffee. In their hour together he'd kept his promise to refrain from proselytizing. She figured Sally might be right, that it wouldn't hurt to get laid. *Tonight, then.* "What do you think, Samantha, my sexy skinny black jeans, and a white sweater, or a dress?" She pulled a dark blue knit dress over her head and examined herself. The dress fit like an upscale designer had custom made it for her, snug enough to show off her curves, and a few inches above her knees to show off her legs. "No," she said. "I'll save this one for another time." She yanked it off and left it in a pile on the floor next to the bed. She pulled on her black jeans and sweater instead, and put on a pair of bright red Tony Lama's she'd bought in Wyoming during an investigation years before. She'd worn them so seldom they looked brand new. She weaved tiny dried white flowers into her braid. "Oh no. I look like a hippie now," she said to the cat, then she snatched the flowers out of the braid and tossed them on the blue dress. She applied a slick of apple red lipstick, brushed on a coat of black mascara, and announced to Chester and Samantha, "This is as good as it gets."

Mingan knocked on the door, and when she opened it, he eyed her from her forehead to her toes, "You are so pretty tonight."

"Thanks. You look great, too." Maggie's cheeks turned warm.

Nito's was crowded, and as a hostess led them to a corner booth, Maggie felt certain every person in the restaurant had fixed their eyes on the two of them. She didn't mind. In fact, she felt privileged to be seen in public on a date with the hunky Mingan Metchitehew. *This might be fun.*

By the time she had finished her second glass of Chianti, Maggie allowed herself to relax. Dinner was delightful. Old man Nito approached their table as they were finishing their veal and ravioli. He talked fast, not giving either an opportunity to respond. "It's good to see you," he said to Maggie. "It's been a long while, and here you are with our banker?" he nodded to Mingan. "How are you this evening, Signore? I trust you both enjoyed your dinner?"

"It was delicious, Nito." Maggie said.

"Please allow me the pleasure of serving you a homemade panna cotta for dessert and cappuccino on the house."

Mingan reached across the table to stroke Maggie's hand. This time, she didn't pull back.

A few moments later, a busty waitress with her black hair in a thick bun and dewy eyes for Mingan, appeared with a pair of foamy cappuccinos and two Pana Cotta's. Maggie picked a raspberry off her dessert with her fingers and popped it into her mouth. "Thanks for inviting me tonight. It's been tough lately, and it's nice to have dinner out for a change."

"I'm surprised you don't have dates every night. You really are an extraordinary woman."

Maggie smiled. "I'm not as extraordinary as you think."

"No, you are different, Maggie. Unique. I don't think I've ever met anyone like you."

Maggie wondered why he didn't say something like "I find you intoxicatingly sexy," or "You are drop-dead gorgeous," but unique? Extraordinary? She refocused their conversation. "I don't know if you're up for this, but after dinner, The Ulster Boys are playing at The Silverado, no cover. We have to buy a couple of drinks, but that's all. You do like traditional Irish music, don't you?"

"I don't think so. I've never really listened to it. But, sure, we can stop by. Why not?"

———

After the Silverado, Maggie and Mingan took their time driving home. He avoided the main highway, detouring through a winding mountain pass. It was dark, but the sky smelled of fresh pumpkin pie and burning leaves. Autumn was Maggie's favorite time of year. It was when she felt the most energized, the most alive. Mingan switched on the radio. It was set to a Christian station so quickly turned to an oldies station and Maggie found herself humming along to Joni Mitchell's, "Court and Spark." It was the first time in weeks she felt like singing. By the time they reached Maggie's driveway, both Mingan and she were harmonizing on Neil Young's "Harvest Moon."

"What did you think of The Ulster Boys?" Maggie asked.

"Interesting."

"Interesting? Is that all you have to say? I love them, and if you are going to hang around me, you'll have to get used to traditional Irish music. It's part of my heritage, and it's the only music I listen to with regularity."

"Well, then, I suppose I should listen to it more and develop a keener appreciation."

"I suppose so."

Mingan pulled some kindling and a log from the bin on the rock hearth and lit a fire. Maggie retreated into the kitchen to put on a pot of coffee. She brought out a tray with a bottle of Remy Martin, and two partially filled steaming mugs of coffee. They sat side-by-side on her overstuffed couch in front of the flame, mugs in hand, thighs touching, Samantha and Chester curled at their feet. The conversation was about much of nothing but before she knew it, Mingan took her mug and his, set them on the coffee table and kissed her. She snuggled into his arms and inhaled his scent, slightly spicy, musky, lovely. Maggie kissed him back and as they embraced, he reached under her sweater, sliding his hand over her rib cage to her chest to caress her breasts. When he worked a finger under her bra and touched her nipple she inhaled sharply. *My God, it's been a long time, such a long time.* The glow of firelight and the feel of Mingan's hand on her breast intoxicated her more than the wine, more than the brandy. She felt like a stupid, giddy teenager. She stood, smiled, and put out her hand with the intention of leading Mingan to her bedroom.

Mingan halted and pulled away from her. "Not now," he said. "Not yet."

"What do you mean?"

"You are lovely, and I want you, but like you said, let's take it slow."

"You kissed me. You…I don't understand. Are you actually saying you don't want to have sex with me?" Maggie stepped back, flushed with raw embarrassment. *He's been trying to move in since the day we met, and now he doesn't want me? What the hell is his problem?* This had never happened to her, never.

"Oh, I do. I want to make love to you in the worst way. But… not yet. I hope you understand but as deacon, I…"

Her face burned with the heat of rage. "This is about your damned religion? Fine." She threw her hands into the air. "Thanks for dinner, but let's call it a night. Go now, please."

———

"Did you have fun on your date last night with Mingan," Jake asked over coffee at Mama's. "Or, did he just happen to stop by unexpectedly, and instead of making him eggs you decided to go out for Italian?"

"It's none of your business."

"You're right. And as long as it doesn't interfere with the investigation, I don't really care who you fuck."

Maggie felt fire rising like magma from the base of her spine to her throat. "You don't care who I fuck? In that case, *fuck you*, Jake."

CHAPTER 22

Canada, Twenty-Eight Years Ago

The next morning, before the sun's rays broke over the sharp-toothed peaks, Noshi arose. The boy pushed himself onto one elbow. "Where are you going, Daddy?"

"Don't wake your mother," Noshi whispered. "Go to sleep. I'll be back soon."

When he returned, Chepi was awake, the boy, too, was awake but still in a tight ball at her side. He kept his eyes closed. "Where have you been?" she asked.

"Oh, I thought I'd try something new. I went out earlier, and guess what?"

"You killed a rabbit?"

"Yes, a big jack with plenty of good flesh on its bones."

"Oh, thank God," said Chepi. "Thank Holy God..."

Northern California, Present Time

AS AN UNDERGRADUATE at UCLA, Maggie took an English lit class. She was surprised how much she enjoyed it, especially when studying James Joyce's *Ulysses* with its rich descriptions of Dublin, Ireland. She identified with the sexy, feisty character of Molly.

Her professor, Donald O'Shea, a handsome man, who'd earned his doctorate from Trinity College, had lime green eyes like Maggie's. There was an immediate attraction-spark between teacher and student. Early in the quarter, he'd called her into his office under the pretext of discussing her paper on 'The Function of Greek Myth in James Joyce's *The Artist as a Young Man*.'

In the midst of delving into the character of Stephen Daedelus, Professor O'Shea leaned over and kissed Maggie. In a heated frenzy both stripped off their clothes from the waist down, and on the wooden floor of his Royce Hall office, they had the best sex of Maggie's life. Afterwards, he said, "You're good enough for me to consider leaving my wife." Although taken aback that he was married, and why she'd not considered it before she allowed him to kiss her, was beyond her own comprehension. She excused his marriage away.

Mary Gail O'Shea, a good Catholic girl, who bore Professor O'Shea two fine sons, Darrell and Donnie Jr., sat home on Thursdays and Saturday nights either alone eating Cheetos and watching classic movies, or playing Bunko with her girlfriends, while Maggie and Donald screwed for hours like rutting ferrets in every conceivable direction, position and way.

Their delicious affair lasted for over five years. He took her to B&Bs at Morro Bay, and to Big Bear Lake, helped her cultivate an appreciation of Irish literature and music, and taught her a few Gaelic words, of which only póg mo thóin, translated as 'kiss my ass,' she remembered. The knowledge that, in turn, she gave him pleasure made her feel sexy and powerful. *If he loved his wife, he wouldn't spend his weekends with me. The little mouse of a woman must not give him what he needs.* He told her often how much he delighted in her fine mind, her spunky character and her adventuresome spirit, as well as her eagerness in the boudoir. "You are a lovely tumescent pool of pudding flesh, the most beautiful woman I've ever known," he told Maggie.

Being young, dumb and dreamy, she ate his words like coconut cream pie. Maggie was in love. She bought the old line that he would leave his wife for her, so when she became pregnant with their daughter, she delighted in imagining a blissful family life. Instead, he abandoned her. He hung up on her when she called, and walked the other way when he saw her on campus. He wasn't there when their daughter was born and then died. He never even knew that she'd named their little girl Bridget. The experience gutted her, and once healed enough to get on with life, she swore to never allow a man to hurt her again. Never. Her father abandoned her, then her brother Danny turned away from her. And then the passion of her life, Donald O'Shea? *Enough.*

During that same quarter where Maggie had fallen in love with both James Joyce and Professor O'Shea, she also studied the florid purple prose Victorians, whom she didn't love quite so much. Victorian novelist Edward Bulwer-Lytton once started a novel with the infamous line, "It was a dark and stormy night." The literary world tagged it the worst beginning of a novel ever, and English professors world-wide held it up as a prime example of hack writing. When Maggie was in angry mood, instead of calling her "Sweet Maggie Green Eyes," Professor O'Shea used to refer to her as his "Dark and Stormy Night."

———

By the time she opened the door into the sheriff's office, Maggie was the dark and stormy night. Angry, cold and scary, she didn't care even a little if she came across as hack-ish. She was furious with Jake Lubbock, more than ever during the course of her relationship. She'd prepared a litany of unoriginal obscenities and intended to shove them down his throat until he suffocated. She was almost disappointed when he greeted her with a sincere and contrite face that stopped her short from calling him a goddamnedmotherfuckingsonofabitchcocksuckingprickhead.

"I was out of line with that crack about Mingan and you," he said to her. "I behaved like a real ass."

She softened but pretended to still be angry. "You weren't only out of line, you crossed so far there's no way back."

"Look, I'm trying to apologize. Cut me a break."

"Fine. Let's get some work done, then. What's this about a witness?"

"We received a call from a mail carrier. While on her route she remembers seeing a tall, blonde man smoking near the park where our latest victims played a few minutes before they went missing. She's coming in to look through some photos."

Maggie sat on an ancient wood swivel chair and with one foot pushed herself around 360 degrees. "Obviously it's not Bobby, poor slob. Maybe John Winters?"

"Mail carrier isn't sure. She wasn't close enough for a positive ID but doesn't think it was anyone she knew. Says he didn't look like a local." Jake paused, and then cleared his throat. "Knowin' how sensitive you are about Mingan, I kinda hate to bring this up, Mag, but you do know that the child killings in our county didn't start until after he moved to town."

"Yes, I do know that. But there were almost forty people who moved here last year. Could be anyone. Maybe someone we haven't even considered yet. I'm not buyin' that he has anything to do with this."

"Why? Because you can't stand the thought that you may be having sex with a psycho child murderer?"

Maggie bolted out of her chair and thrust her face within four inches of Jake's. He set his jaw and stood firm. She was prepared to deliver her obscenity thread but instead, through clinched teeth said, "What exactly is your problem? You're acting like a jealous fifteen year-old. I don't have time for your juvenile bullshit."

She stormed out of the office, slammed the door, ran across busy Main Street, and escaped colliding with a speeding Harley by a fraction of an inch. "Asshole!" she shouted at the biker as he sped over Hyde Mountain Pass. When he crested the hill, he held one arm over his head, and without looking backwards, he flipped off Maggie, who returned the gesture with a two-handed flip-off of her own, even though she knew he couldn't see it. A couple of teenagers watching the scene whooped. Maggie flipped them off, too, then stepped through the door to Mama's and looked for Sally. "Where is she?" Maggie asked Dawn. "I'm having a crappy morning and I need to talk to her."

"Migraine. She went home."

"Sorry to hear it."

"French roast?"

"Yeah, put it in the biggest mug you've got." She looked around the coffee bar as though searching for something. "I'm going to buy Sally a bottle of hooch to stash under the counter for emergencies."

———

Mama's had only two power outlets for customers. Sally put in wifi, but some patrons wanted to plug-in. Her response remained solid. "No. I don't have money for that stuff. Use the library if you need electricity. If customers start draining additional utility dollars, I'll have to charge more for java or start serving the cheap stuff." To please her clientele, she caved and put in two funky side-by-side thrift store desks in front of the new outlets. Sally never increased the price for a cup of brew or compromised on quality, so her coffee retained its title as the best in the county.

Mingan sat at one of the desks charging his notebook battery. Happy sat at a bistro table near the window working on his laptop. There were three other customers that afternoon — Sam with his usual double-shot of espresso and a paunchy middle-aged couple in matching bright green "Wild River County" sweatshirts nursed mocha lattes. *Tourists.*

Maggie, still hurt by Mingan's rejection, turned away when he attempted to acknowledge her. As she was about to address Happy, who sat as far away from Mingan as he could get, he said "Damn battery!"

He hauled his laptop to the only space to plug in next to Mingan. Maggie, seated at the counter, kept her back to the two men.

"God, I really wish Sally were here," she said to Dawn. "... but I feel for her. She's had these migraines since she was a kid. The only thing that really helps her is to sit in a darkened room for a while. I'm sure she's appreciative you're here to look after things so she can be home right now."

"I'd do anything for Sally. She's a good person."

"That she is. We all love her and I..."*Crash*. A hardback Roget's Thesaurus flew off a bookshelf and smashed into the mirror behind the counter, shattering the glass into hundreds of brilliant splinters.

"Get out from behind there!" Maggie motioned for Dawn to move to the other side of the counter.

Dawn's eyes and mouth gaped. "Oh, no." She scuttled from behind the counter, keeping her head low.

A trio of coffee mugs lifted themselves off their shelf, floated into the air, then smashed to the floor.

"What the hell?!" Maggie said. "Get out, everyone, get out."

Startled customers bolted for the front door. As they approached the exit, an oversized antique armoire slid by itself in front of the door.

"Back door," Maggie shouted, "Now!"

"The customers, with Dawn and Maggie close behind, rushed toward the rear exit. An enormous display case loaded with CDs, gift items and kitschy bric-a-brac toppled blocking the only other exit. Happy ducked under a table and dialed. "Get someone over to Mama's," he ordered the dispatcher.

Forks and knives flew through the air as though shot from a bow. Mingan crawled on the floor toward Maggie. He looked mesmerized, trapped in a bizarre hypnotic trance.

He's gotta be in shock. "Take cover," she ordered Mingan.

"I...I want to help."

A fork flew across the room and imbedded itself in Mingan's thigh. Without uttering even a murmur of pain, he withdrew the fork from his flesh, and flung it aside. With blood trailing from his leg, he scrambled on all fours until he hunkered down near Dawn. She had ducked down behind an overstuffed couch near Maggie. She shuffled from knee-to-knee. In one hand she held a paper napkin and brushed pieces of broken mirror under the couch.

"Careful," Dawn said to Mingan, "or that glass will rip your skin to shreds." When he stared at her, his eyes blank and glassy. She cocked her head and said, "You don't even hear me, do you?"

"No, I don't think he does," Maggie said. "He's flipped."

"Jake's on his way," Happy called to Maggie, who now crouched behind an overturned table.

Townspeople gathered outside the plate glass window punched digits on their cell phones. A burly trucker attempted to break the window with a 2 x 4, swinging repeated blows. The glass held.

Jake showed up, ordered the bystanders and the customers to back away, and rammed the window with his patrol car, a black SUV with "Wild River County Sheriff's Department" on the side. The window erupted into shattered glass crystals glittering in the sunlight. Everything inside Mama's went silent, numb. Jake climbed out of his vehicle, and ran to Maggie, his boots crunching broken pieces of pottery, glass and mirror. "What the hell happened here? Is anyone injured? How about you?" he asked.

"I don't know what happened. Felt like an explosion or something," Maggie said. She stood brushing her slacks with both hands. "I'm fine, but let's check on the others."

Maggie and Jake were in process of ensuring no one was hurt when Mingan, still huddled behind the couch, issued a wail that sounded like a cross between a coyote in heat and a banshee. "It's a demon, a satanic entity." He fell to one side, oblivious to the stray pieces of glass digging into his flesh. He rose to his knees, and then lifting his arms overhead he prayed aloud. "Oh Father, deliver us from this hellish demon. Most glorious Prince of the Heaven defend us in our battle against the ruler of this world of darkness, against the spirit of wickedness."

"Shut up," Maggie shouted. "Shut the fuck up."

Mingan ignored her. "Come to the assistance of men whom you created in your image and likeness, and whom your only begotten son redeemed at a great price from the tyranny of the devil."

"What a moron," Maggie said.

"Told you so," Jake said.

"You shut up, too."

"...and dearest Jesus, expel Satan, that he may no longer retain us captive so that without delay we may draw your mercy down upon us. Take hold of the dragon, the serpent, the devil. Bind Satan, and cast him into the bottomless pit, in your name." Blood pooled around Mingan's knees and trickled from the wound on his thigh.

Jake pulled the dazed man to his feet. "Happy, get Mingan to the medical center. We'll take his statement later. I'm going to question witnesses."

Maggie stepped over piles of rubble, making her way out of Mama's. "I'm headed to Sally's before she gets this news from some insensitive jerk who doesn't care that she's dealing with a migraine. See you back at the station,"

"We got a lot of paperwork to complete. Don't be long or we'll be at it all night." Jake shook his head. "I'm getting way too old for this crap."

CHAPTER 23

Canada, Twenty-Eight Years Ago

Noshi brought small chunks of partially frozen meat into the snow cave and offered them to his wife and son.

"You caught, killed, skinned and butchered the rabbit that quickly?" Chepi examined her piece of meat, turning it over in her hand. "It doesn't look like rabbit meat. Are you sure it wasn't some dead squirrel you found and skinned in the dark?"...

Northern California, Present Time

"YOU'RE UPSET ABOUT something. What is it?" Maggie said to Sally the next day when she answered the phone.

"It's John. He's gotten worse."

"Meaning what? If that man hurt you, I'll kill him."

"He blames me for what happened at Mama's."

"What the hell? You weren't even there."

"He doesn't care. He's convinced the whole thing is my fault somehow. He thinks if I'd been there instead of home, it wouldn't have happened. It's getting ugly."

"Where is he?"

"Passed out on the sofa drunk. At least, I suppose he's still there."

"Get out of the house right now. Don't wake him. Grab your purse. I'm on my way to get you. You're coming here."

"No need."

"Oh, yes there is. Don't give me any shit about this, Sally, I mean it."

"There is no need because I'm on my way to your house. I called to let you know I'm taking you up on your offer. I'll be using that spare room."

—

"What's your plan?" Maggie asked Sally once both women were seated at the dining table nursing their gin and tonics.

"Sell Mama's, move away, divorce John, and start over."

"You need a restraining order. I'll help you take care of that."

"I don't think so. John's a pathetic alcoholic who wants to blame me for everything wrong in his life, but he'll never really hurt me. He's mean when he gets his drunk on, but he prefers to drink at home these days, and doesn't leave the house when he's wasted. When he's not blasted off his ass, he's a gutless wonder who wouldn't hurt a gnat."

"The dickhead hit you before, Sally. What makes you think he won't do worse next time? Does he know you're here?"

"He hit me one time, Maggie. I hit him back, and told him I'd tear off his balls if he did it again."

Maggie chuckled. "Really? You hit him?"

"Split his lip. He was so embarrassed that he told his pool buddies at The Silverado he'd slipped on an ice patch and hit his mouth on a parking berm. I told you I could handle him."

"Oh, that's priceless. I never knew you popped him in the mouth. Good for you, girl. Still, does he know where you are?"

"I didn't tell him I was coming here, if that's what you mean, but he'll probably guess where I am. I don't have a whole lot of friends around here other than you."

"I'd like you to stay here. I mean, I don't want you going out for a while. I'll arrange with Jake to put a protective detail on you. Get Dawn to cover for you for a few days. She can supervise the cleanup. You don't know how John will react once he wakes up and realizes you're gone."

"No, I don't think so. I'm not going to be a prisoner no matter how good your gin is," Sally smiled, lifted her glass in a toast to Maggie, and threw down the rest of her drink.

———

This particular raven dream was less ordered, more fragmented than those of the past. She was inside Mama's flapping her wings, disoriented, trying to find her way out. Two men dressed in 19th century garb floated around the room with her. They wore striped trousers, dress brogans, crisp white shirts with detachable collars, bowler hats, and checkered vests with gold pocket watches. Maggie wondered how they could fly without wings or even feathers. The men looked human but were translucent, pale, yet not quite invisible.

One withdrew his watch fob, turned his time piece over in his hand and examined it, then tucked it back into his vest pocket. "It's high time you found this fella and took care of things," he said to her.

"Who are you?" she cawed, "I want to get to the sky. Which way is out?"

She flew behind the counter and looked down. In the mirror shards, she saw herself, but not as a raven or as a human, but as something in between. A woman's head on a raven's body. "Oh, God, what am I?" She perched on the counter and clawed at her human head. The scratch stung and bled. A clump of long hair fell to the ground and morphed into a glossy black feather as it settled among the broken mirror pieces.

Sally woke that morning to find Maggie dabbing a cotton ball dipped in peroxide on her scalp. "What are you doing? Did you scratch yourself?" she asked Maggie.

"Samantha got me. She heard a bird or squirrel or something outside when she was sleeping on my pillow and launched off my head to get to the window. That cat's a furry menace."

———

Clean up at Mama's was underway. Maggie stopped by and found Dawn working alongside the cleaning crew. She wore a checkered red bandana tied around her head like a babushka and a pair of bright pink latex gloves, too big for her small hands.

"How's it going?" Maggie asked.

"Slow. Everything's a total mess."

"Where's Sally?"

"At a realtor's office. She's selling Mama's. Did you know that?"

"Business is sluggish and with this thing that happened, we can hardly blame her. How are you holding up?"

Dawn hugged herself and shivered. "I was scared shitless. I couldn't sleep last night I was so spooked. This place is haunted by some bad-assed ghosts."

"Dawn, there are no ghosts. Maybe there was an earthquake, or something, but no ghosts."

"You think it was an earthquake that nearly destroyed Mama's but no one else in town even felt it. Really?"

"This old town is undercut by all kinds of ancient tunnels. Maybe one of them collapsed, or maybe a pocket of gas exploded. I'm sure the investigators will get to the bottom of it."

"I don't think so. It's an evil wraith, or maybe several, and they are uber mischievous." Dawn lowered her voice. "And, you know what else is really weird? A crew came in and boarded up the whole place afterwards...doors, windows, sealed tight."

"That's standard procedure, Dawn. Nothing weird about that."

"Yeah? Well, how'd the blackbird get in?"

"How do you know a blackbird was here?"

"Because right in the middle of the broken mirror pieces, I found this." Dawn reached over to the counter and picked up a solitary black feather. She held it aloft like a trophy.

"Could have been here already and you didn't notice it, or maybe a bird flew in before the guys sealed the windows and doors."

Dawn gazed at the feather and shook her head. "I scrubbed this place from top to bottom before we opened yesterday. And, I was right here when the guys started pounding nails into the plywood. There were no birds anywhere near Mama's." Dawn whispered, "I think this is from a ghost blackbird or some scary supernatural flying thing." She held the feather close to Maggie's face.

"Oh for Christ sakes, Dawn. Don't be so melodramatic. There's no goddamn ghosts, human or animal, and that's not from a blackbird anyway."

CHAPTER 24

Canada, Twenty–Eight Years Ago

"It's rabbit, Chepi. Eat it. Wake up the boy and make sure he gets some, too. It's all we have to keep us alive."

She jostled her son. "Daddy got us a rabbit to eat."

"Yay!" The little boy clapped his hands.

Chepi held out a piece of the flesh to her son.

The boy recoiled and screwed up his face. "It's raw, Mommy. Icky. I don't want it."

"Remember when we went fishing with Uncle Sokamon and Grandpa Segenan, and Grandpa caught that great big salmon?"

"Yup."

"Remember when Uncle carved up the fish and gave us little pieces of it raw? It was good wasn't it? This rabbit is yummy like the raw salmon. Show me how brave you are and eat some."

With expressionless eyes fixed directly on his mother's face, he stuck out a small hand, palm up. Chepi pressed a piece of the meat into his glove. He took a bite and chewed. The boy's eyes widened. "Good, Mommy. Best meat I ever ate. More..."

Northern California, Present Time

THE POT OF split pea soup had come to a boil when Maggie's phone rang. Stirring the pot with one hand, she picked up her cell with the other and depressed the talk button. If she'd read the display, she would not have answered.

"I thought we were great together," Mingan said. "Now you don't even want talk to me? I've left you at least a half dozen messages."

Maggie turned the fire down under the peas. "I'm right in the middle of something, Mingan. Can this wait?"

"Let me talk to you for one minute. That's all I ask."

"Wait a second." Maggie turned off the heat under the soup and pulled a chair to the kitchen table. "I'm listening."

"I don't know why you don't want to have anything to do with me now, and I..."

"...look, Mingan, you're a good guy. You're handsome, you're great with my nieces, and you can be a lot of fun. But, I don't see this thing working out between us."

"Is it because of what happened the other day at Mama's? I was really rattled, and I know I overreacted...look, I really care about you and I thought you felt the same way about me."

"Frankly, the way you acted at Mama's was really weird, but that's not the only reason why. It's because..."

"...because I respected you enough to not want to fuck you on our first date?" Mingan's voice was dark, angry.

"Fine talk for a nice Christian boy, a church deacon. You sure know how to impress a lady."

Mingan's voice softened. "I want another chance. Let's give it one more try, shall we?"

"Thank you. That's nice, but it's not..."

"...it's because I'm a Christian, right?"

"It's not that you are a Christian that concerns me. Jake's a Christian. I have many friends and family who are devout Christians. My father was a Christian. It is the *kind* of fanatic that you are. Don't get me wrong. I respect your choice to believe, but your brand of Christianity is over-the-top for me. I'm an atheist. I'm not going to change, and you'll never accept that about me. You'll continue trying to recruit me, so sooner or later all this religious stuff would end us anyway. I'd rather it be now before we get in deeper."

The only sound was his breathing.

"Mingan, are you there? Do you hear what I'm saying?"

"I'm here."

"I gave it a go with you. We had some fun times together, but this whole hardcore fundamentalist thing is too much for me. Let's be friends and call it good."

"Bitch."

"What did you say?"

"You led me on. You let me believe you wanted something with me, and now you are using my religion as an excuse to kick me to the curb. You know how many women in this town would cut off one of their tits to have one night with me?"

Maggie held the phone away from her ear, and looked at it as though a lump of rat feces stuck to the earpiece. She put the phone back to her ear and in a slow, controlled voice said, "I'm done. Don't ever call me again. Don't ever show up at my house. Don't acknowledge me on the street. Don't even nod your head in my general direction if we accidentally run into one another at the mini-mart, you unstable, self-righteous prick."

Maggie clicked off her cell and threw it against the wall. It broke into two neat pieces. "Dammit all to hell. I'm not looking for someone to marry, but I'd so much enjoy a normal relationship with a normal man. Is that too much to expect?"

She drew a bubble bath, lit her sage-lemon candle and opened a bottle of pinot noir. She put on a *Lughnasa* CD and stepped into the bath. The cat settled in on the bathroom rug next to the tub. "Samantha, that arrogant jerk doesn't even like Celtic music. We had nothing in common. Nothing. I'm glad we're rid of him, aren't you?"

That night, Maggie slept the sleep of angels. For the first time in a long while, no ravens or monsters haunted her dreams.

———

Maggie stepped up to National Bank's service counter. "I need to close my account," she said to the teller.

"Oh my. Is there a problem with our customer service? Mr. Metchitehew is in if you'd like to talk to him. I'm sure he'll be pleased to clear up any problem you may be experiencing."

"No, thank you. I do not want to talk to Mr. Metchitehew. My decision has nothing to do with your level of service. You've all been great." Maggie gave the teller a look to relay the message that she didn't care to discuss the matter further.

As she turned to leave the bank, Mingan peeked around the corner of his office at her. For the first time, instead of seeing him as good looking and sexy, he was creepy. She resisted the urge to tell him once again what she thought of him. Maggie walked a block down the street and opened an account with Umpqua Bank, whose motto is "Welcome to the World's Greatest Bank."

CHAPTER 25

Canada, Twenty-Eight Years Ago

That night, the boy dreamed. He heard drums and a bird whistle. His mother held him in her lap, her arms wrapped around him. It felt good and warm until he heard a deep scary laugh and then he smelled it. Something really bad, nasty. Something dead. He became frightened, worse than when the wolves came...

Northern California, Present Time

JAKE'S FEET WERE propped on his desk, arms crossed against his chest. He looked very much like an archetypal law man from a bad made-for-TV western.

"Don't be so smug," Maggie said to him. "I've heard about a thousand times I'm a lousy judge of character when it comes to men. I don't need to hear it again."

"I only said I wasn't surprised that things between you and Mingan didn't work out." He put his hands up in the air and waved them about as though he were a tent revival preacher. "I'm glad you finally saw the light, sister."

"Wipe that grin off your face. Because I broke it off with Mingan doesn't mean you've got a chance in hell with me, okay?"

"Did I say something to imply that I want anything with you? What makes you think I'm not interested in someone else?"

"Good to hear it, Jake. I'm getting sick and tired of you staring at my ass and hitting on me." Maggie felt a pang...of what? *Jealousy? Can't be. Fine, he can go out with whomever he wants. I've had enough of men and their bullshit.*

The door swung open, and Happy entered. "I hear Mingan broke up with you, Maggie. I'm sorry."

"Is that what that arrogant jerk is telling everyone?" Maggie's

151

back arched. "Let's just say I'm relieved to be rid of the lying, rotten piece of trash."

As she prepared to spew more venom, Jake intervened. "Now that Happy finally showed up, we've got everyone here. Let's get this meeting going."

Maggie, Happy, Jake and the other deputies assembled in the conference room. Marley and Thompson took seats at the back of the room.

"I've worked out a decent profile on our killer," Maggie said.

"Are you with anyone from Quantico?" asked Agent Marley.

"I work directly with Dr. Stone."

"I'm impressed," said Marley, raising an eyebrow.

Dr. Max Stone, a leading profiler, was a famous forensic psychologist and a professor at American University. At one time, he'd been on the faculty of the National FBI Academy. He encouraged Maggie to apply. "You'd make a fine agent."

"The world doesn't need more FBI," she said.

He'd taken Maggie under his wing partly because she was one of his brightest graduate students with her insatiable curiosity and her bullish determination, and partly because she had incredible legs. He was a handsome older gent, and a notorious ladies man who'd had affairs with a number of his students, Maggie among them. She broke off their sexual relationship, much to his chagrin, but through the years, the two remained in contact. She often consulted him.

"I've had a professional relationship with Max Stone that goes back a few decades, gentleman. Now can I get on with this?"

One of the FBI agents raised his hand.

"Yes, Agent Marley?"

"You worked on the *Oakland Kiddie Killer* case in the bay area."

"Yeah?"

"Case was never solved."

"And your point is? The Jack the Ripper case remains unsolved, too. We aren't here to discuss the past. I'm here to present a profile of the child killer who operates in Wild River County right now. Do you mind if I get back to the business at hand so we can catch this prick?"

Maggie picked up a glass of water, took a sip. It was warm in the room for October, and the solitary ceiling fan provided little relief from the stuffiness. The glass of ice water trickled sweat down its sides and dampened Maggie's hand, which she wiped on her slacks. She noticed Jake's eyes following her hand as she rubbed her palm against her thigh. She felt a sense of satisfaction after that crack he made about her not being the only woman he had any interest in.

"Profiling is not an exact science by any means, but can be accurate, and has been helpful in apprehending serial killers. We are going to go over a few basics so you all understand the anatomy of a profile, what I think we need to look for, and hopefully you'll take away some valuable info to help find this sonofabitch. Any comments or questions so far?"

Neither of the FBI agents, busy on their laptops, looked up. *Either they are taking great notes, or the useless bastards aren't even listening.* Maggie turned her attention to the other investigators.

"What we have to go on is witnesses reporting a tall, blonde male, smoker, in the general vicinity of where children have gone missing. We have ruled out one of our suspects, Bobby Jenkins..."

A deputy snickered, stopping Maggie short. "You think it's funny that an innocent man was found with his neck broken and his heart cut out? What the hell is the matter with you?" The deputy screwed up his face, and cast his eyes down

"It's okay, Maggie. Please go on," Jake said.

"As I was saying," she gave the deputy a withering look, "we have witness reports of an unidentified tall man, over six feet, blonde, and who smokes American Spirit menthols. Am I missing anything?"

A few men shook their heads. One raised his hand. "How detailed do most of these profiles get, or are they mostly generalities?"

"Good question. One of the best examples of detailed profiling was in the New York City 'Mad Bomber' case back in the 1950s. After close examination of all the available data, Dr. James A. Brussel, who assisted local law enforcement, deduced the criminal wore a double breasted suit, tightly buttoned, and was an unmarried, clinically paranoid, Roman Catholic living in Connecticut with immediate family, and was of Eastern European descent. George Metesky who was captured and convicted fit the description exactly, right down to his diamond pinky ring."

"Holy shit," said Jake.

"Holy shit is right," said Maggie. "Let's look at categories of serial killers." She turned to a white board and drew a line across the top. "Who are they? How do we know someone is a serial murderer? Any guesses?" The men remained silent. "It's difficult to know because most of these killers usually blend right into the general population, and are often a community's most upstanding citizens." She turned motioning to the men and said, "Even one of you could be our guy."

"A law enforcement officer?" Happy smiled. "Not likely."

"Serhiy Tkach from the Ukraine, who suffocated a number of girls between ages eight and eighteen and after, had sex with their dead bodies. He been a well-respected police criminal investigator."

"So, if the killer can be anyone, how do we know what to look for?" Jake asked.

"I'm getting to that. There are three primary categories of serial killers." She wrote the words 'organized,' 'disorganized' and 'mixed' on the board, and drew three vertical columns. "The organized serial murderer plans his crimes methodically, and usually has some knowledge of forensics because he rarely leaves evidence, or when he does, it's deliberate. From what we have so far, I think our guy is an organized killer, who...'

"Go screw yourselves, you Bible thumping jerks," a man yelled from outside.

A woman called out, her voice shrill above the sound of glass exploding against the cement walkway. "Get off our streets, or I'm going to the sheriff,"

"What's going on?" Maggie said. "Let's check this out."

The men rose from their seats and followed her through the door. The woman ran to Jake. "Those idiots are causing trouble. When we walked out of Mama's and crossed the street, one of them threw a bottle of coke at my husband and me."

"Settle down," said Jake. "We'll get to the bottom of this. Did you see who threw the bottle?"

"No, but it was one of them," she pointed.

Across the street picketers with signs marched back and forth in front of Mama's. Jake, Happy and Maggie approached the protesters.

"Any of you throw a soda bottle at that couple?" Jake indicated the man and woman standing in front of the sheriff's office.

"We're from Wicklow Christian Church," said Mingan. "No one here threw anything. We are assembled here in a peaceful demonstration."

"Those people claim someone on this side of the street threw a bottle at them. If so, we'll find out who did it."

The picketers bore signs that read "Do Not Suffer A Witch To Live, Exodus 22:18." "Sally Winters Is An Evil Witch." "Sally Winters Is In League With Satan." "Mama's is a Satanic Cult Hangout." "Sally Murders Children."

Mingan, in a dark blue Wicklow Christian Church t-shirt, led the charge. He turned away from Jake, and through a bullhorn, preached to those who passed by, "Leviticus 19:26 tells us that we are not to practice divination or sorcery. Leviticus 20:27 tells us that 'a man or woman who is a medium or spirits among you must be put to death. You are to stone them; their blood will be on their own head.' Brothers and sisters, I have seen with my own eyes the demon's work right here in Mama's. Sally Winters practices witchcraft. She invited the demons into her place of business, and into our town of Wicklow. Let's pray to cast out the demons along with their satanic leader, Sally."

"Oh my God. We have to stop this right now," Maggie said.

"You know the law, Maggie." Jake said. "Citizens have a right to assemble. We'll find out who threw the bottle and make an arrest. And, we'll stick around for a bit to make sure things don't get further out of hand."

"That bastard. I hope Sally sues him and his church for slander, or libel, or both."

Mingan turned toward Maggie, extended his arm and pointed his forefinger at her. "And there is another she-devil, one of Satan's bitches. Maggie Sloan is Sally's friend, ardent follower, and is covering for Sally's wicked deeds. If you are wondering why the children of Wicklow are being murdered, look to the demonic cult operating right here under your noses. Maggie, tell us, what does Sally do with the children's hearts after her ritual sacrifices? You know, don't you?" He yelled through his bullhorn, "Sinner, repent."

"You sanctimonious pig," Maggie shouted back. She began a fiery tirade aimed at Mingan, but was drowned out by the crowd's chant of, "Sinner, repent. Sinner, repent. Sinner, repent."

"Get back to the station, Maggie." Jake put a restraining hand on her shoulder. "Happy and I'll handle this. We'll call for backup if necessary, but we don't need you here. I want you out of the line of fire."

"That vindictive dickwad." Maggie's face turned purple. She put her hand on her Glock and started toward Mingan and the protesters.

Jake grabbed her harder and pulled her back "What are you going to do, Maggie? Shoot him? You're wound way too tight. Leave until you cool off. I mean it."

Maggie relaxed and took her hand off her holster. "You better get their asses off the street now."

As she walked back to the station she heard Jake say, "Mingan, we are going to find out who threw that bottle, and after, if you don't disburse this crowd I'll arrest the lot of you for disturbing the peace."

A reporter from *The Wicklow Daily* pulled over to the curb.

—

"You're kidding me," Sally said to Maggie. "Mingan actually accused me of having something to do with the murder of those children? I always liked that guy, too. What an incredible prick he turned out to be."

"If I were you, Sally, I'd sue his ass. He's slandering you, and look at what he's trying to do to your business."

"Obviously, he has no idea I plan to sell and move out of Wild River County."

"And when you do, he'll take credit for having driven out the evil witch."

The two women sat on the edge of Maggie's back deck, dangling their feet. The evening had turned cold and they both wore UGGS, leather gloves and heavy sweaters. The friends sat close together wrapped in a thick wool blanket.

Maggie looked at her watch. "Well imagine that, it's wine time," she said. "Wanna glass?"

"Bring the bottle."

"Maybe we should go inside, light a fire."

"No, let's stay out here for a little longer. I need the feel of the cool air. The wine will keep us warm."

Sally didn't drink nearly as much as Maggie, but once in a great while, she could put away a substantial amount of alcohol.

"You bet. We both can use a little buzz right now," Maggie said. "I never figured Mingan to be vengeful. I knew he had a past, and he was furious when I broke it off with him. Still, I didn't see this coming. Clearly, he's going after me through you."

For a moment, in silence, the two women basked in the glow of their wine. Maggie took a deep breath of cleansing autumn air. "The bastard had better never get near Flower or Bird or I'll kick him in the crotch so hard he'll choke to death on his own testicles." A raven perched on the deck railing. Maggie reached into her pocket, pulled out a handful of corn and tossed it at the bird. "I'm sorry, Sally. I know you don't need this crap on top of everything else."

"Speaking of crap...John called me here earlier today."

"Uh oh."

"We had quite an argument."

"Don't answer the phone when I'm gone. You don't need the aggravation." Maggie rose and headed toward the cabin.

"He was drunk of course, so I know he didn't mean it," Sally called after Maggie, "but he said if I don't come home, he'll kill me."

CHAPTER 26

Canada, Twenty-Eight Years Ago

The boy opened his eyes a crack and saw that it was not his mother who held him, but a monster. A skinny monster, way taller than a man, in dirty, torn buckskins. Strips of rotting flesh hung in thin tatters from its arms and neck. Face bones jutted from sunken cheeks. Cracked grey lips drawn back taut exposed brown, jagged teeth and a section of yellowed jawbone. Patches of bare skull appeared through its black, coarse long hair. Too horrified to move or call out, the boy laid in the monster's arms still as a rock. "Please, Jesus, please, please, make the monster go away." The little boy squeezed his eyes shut and prayed as hard as he could...

Northern California, Present Time

YELLOW HAD ALWAYS been Cathy's favorite color. When she needed dining space to seat eight, Danny made a table of scrap lumber painting it the color of fresh Meyer lemons. It was so heavy it took four grown men to haul it from the back yard to the kitchen. Thereafter, the lemon colored table became the social center of Danny's home. Maggie, Danny, Sally, and Jimmy sat around it snacking on Smokehouse almonds and drinking Fat Tire Ale from the bottle. When not on duty, Jake would join them for these dinners, but today, he was at the office. Bird and Flower played outside, piling up the last of the fall leaves and diving into them. Jimmy sat close to the window keeping a close eye on his girls. After their disappearance, he rarely let them out of his sight.

Cathy stood over a blue enamel pot of venison stew stirring its contents in a wide clockwise circle. She tapped the side of the pot with a charred wooden spoon, then dipped a teaspoon into the savory stuff and brought it to Danny. "Give it taste and tell me if it needs more salt." She stuck the spoon into her husband's open mouth.

"This is perfect as is, darlin'. Don't add a thing." When she turned back toward the stove, he patted her rump.

She whipped her head around toward him, and threatened him with the spoon. "Don't try that again, mister."

"You love it when I touch your butt. Admit it."

"Shut up. I do not." Cathy blushed. "Some Hoopa women came by with some nice white oak acorns processed already," she said changing the subject, "So, we have muffins, too, and I'm makin' fry bread later. Can't get more Indian than venison, acorn muffins, and fry bread."

"Sounds great," Maggie said. She loved acorns. One year at a Bear Dance a Yurok woman taught her how to process them.

"*Everyone knows white oak is best for acorns,*" the Yurok said. "*You gotta shell 'em, crack 'em open and break 'em up a little. Then they gotta go in fast running water for a long time to get out all the acid. The old way is to put them in a sack in the river, but the new way works plenty good, too.*"

"*What's the new way?*" Maggie asked.

"*Put 'em in pantyhose and stick 'em in the toilet tank. Ever' time the toilet flushes, those acorns get rinsed good. Didn't your mama teach you 'bout that?*" Yes, she had, but most of the time, Maggie didn't listen to her mother, and when she was finally ready to learn more about some of the Yurok ways, it was too late. Mom was gone. *The phone call from "the other side" that night when Flower and Bird stayed over, though — what was that about? And, why, after all these years would Mom...Naw. It couldn't have been real. I imagined it in a dream, and the girls probably heard wind chimes outside and thought it was the phone.*

"Don't you prefer Irish stew and soda bread?" Jimmy said to her.

"Give it a rest, Jimmy," Maggie got up, opened the refrigerator and grabbed another beer. "How 'bout you, Cathy? I'd offer one to your son, but he's being a jerk. He can get his own."

"In a minute. The muffins take some time, and I want to get 'em in the oven before I sit down with ever' one."

"Whose truck is coming up the driveway?" Jimmy said, looking out the window.

"Uncle Mingan's here!" said Bird.

Maggie leapt out of her seat, nearly upending her beer bottle, and sprinted for the door, "That bastard. He knows I don't want him around these kids."

By the time Maggie opened the door and stepped onto the porch, Mingan had already turned his truck around and was headed out full speed, kicking mud from his tires.

"That's right, you prick. You better get the hell out of here," she said under her breath.

Bird and Flower ran to Maggie. "Why is Uncle Mingan leaving?"

"Oh, he probably forgot he had something important to do."

"He's comin' back?" asked Flower.

"I don't think so, sweetie." Maggie stroked the little girl's head. "I think Grandma has some cold juice in the fridge. How about we all go in so you can watch cartoons and have a glass. Lunch will be ready in a little bit."

Maggie herded the girls back into the house, looking over her shoulder to make sure Mingan had not returned. She locked the door, looked out the window, and closed the curtain.

"Fucker," she said.

Jimmy gestured to the twins. "You've got a mouth like a truck driver, and my daughters don't need to hear this kind of language."

"Sorry," said Maggie. "You know what, girls? I think Grandma bought you a new Dora the Explorer movie. Let's set you up on the couch with your orange juice and I'll put it on for you."

"Yay," said Flower. "Bird and me like Dora."

Once the twins were snuggled under a worn plaid comforter with jelly jars of orange juice in their hands, Maggie started the movie, and returned to the kitchen table.

Cathy popped the muffin tin into the oven, rinsed her hands off in the sink, dried them on her apron and returned to the table with a beer. "I was real sorry to hear about you and Mingan," she said to Maggie. "I guess he turned out to be a stinker. So handsome, that boy, too."

Maggie took a swig of her beer. "He's a total jerk, and I'm glad he's out of my life."

"I hear him and them Christian people came after you with their signs and Bible curses," Cathy said to Sally.

"No problem. It backfired. He's made quite a few enemies."

"That's right," said Danny. "No one better mess with the woman who makes the best coffee in the county." Danny balled his hand into a fist and shook it in the air.

Everyone laughed.

"But, really, too bad for you about Mingan," Cathy said to Maggie. "I was surprised the two of you didn't get along too good and had to stop."

"Mom, everyone knows Maggie is the worst judge of men in the world," Jimmy said. "Why are you surprised that it didn't work? Why would *anyone* be surprised?"

Maggie slammed her hands on the table. "Look who's goddamn talking," she said. "How many successful relationships have you been in since that whore you married fucked around behind your back then abandoned you and her own daughters?"

Jimmy's gaze shifted to the entrance to the living room.

"Grandma, can I have more juice?" Bird said holding her glass out to Cathy with one hand, but staring Maggie straight in the eye.

"Oh God," Maggie said. "Sorry...I..."

"Maggie, come out on the porch with me. I need to talk to you right now," Danny said.

Sally patted Maggie's arm and whispered, "It's okay."

"Oh no, Sally, it's not okay," Jimmy said.

Maggie and Danny rose and walked out on to the porch closing the door behind them.

"I'm really sorry, Danny. I didn't mean to lose my temper. Jimmy's been goading me since I got here and I..."

"I want you to leave right now. Sally can stay. We'll bring her by later, and Cathy will package some stew for you, with some leftovers for Jake."

"Please, Danny. I've been under a lot of pressure lately. I didn't mean to say that in front of Bird. I wasn't thinking."

"That's the problem, Maggie. You never think." He pointed at his temple with his forefinger. "You say whatever comes into your head with no regard for anyone else. I've had enough. Until you can find a way to get along with my son, learn to show a little more respect in my house, and think before you open your mouth, you are not welcome at my table."

Maggie walked inside, grabbed her purse, and without saying a word to anyone ran out the door and jumped into her truck. She drove so fast she didn't see the raven. The bird struck the windshield head-on leaving a smear of blood and feathers. Maggie slammed on her brakes, jumped out of truck to find the bird. The raven was dead, neck broken. Maggie burst into tears.

She arrived home, worn, head hurting again. Chester ran to greet her swinging his tail in robust circles. She scratched the dog's head as they both entered the cottage. "At least it's Saturday," she said. "I'm working with Jake this afternoon, then I'm headed off to see the Ulster Boys at The Silverado, then I'm home to get good and drunk to forget this horrible day. Tomorrow I might spend all day in bed. What have you got planned for this afternoon, Chester? A nap perhaps, or chasing a squirrel?"

I'm such an ass. How could I say what I did about the girls' mother when they were in the house? I'm an ass, a big ass, the biggest ass in the world. Then on top of it, I kill a raven?

"Might as well meet Jake early. Wanna come with me to the office?" The dog wagged his tail. "The way I see it, old boy, with the evening starting off this shitty, things can only get better, right?"

CHAPTER 27

Canada, Twenty–Eight Years Ago

The dark figure lowered his head toward the boy. Maggots writhed, dropping several at a time from one empty eye socket. The other eye, lidless and lifeless, stared at the boy, leaking a thin stream of vile fluid down its decayed face. The monster leaned down further. When the ugly thing unhinged its jaws as though to devour him, the stench overwhelmed the boy. He gagged and squeezed his eyes shut to block out what would certainly happen next. "Daddy! Mommy! Help me!..."

Northern California, Present Time

THE MORE TIME Maggie spent at the sheriff's office, the more she felt at home. The musky smell, the old windows that stuck when she tried to open them, and the drip, drip, drip of the faucet in the restroom were comforting and familiar to her. The floors were ancient green linoleum, scratched and lifted at the corners. The furniture was a mish mash of old wood chairs, warped metal desks, and outdated computers. The air conditioning didn't work, and the ancient wall heaters made sounds like howling cats. Now and again, a mouse scuttled across the floor and disappeared behind a row of dented gray metal filing cabinets. Maggie liked it all.

"Did anyone happen to notify you we are well into the 21st century?" She said to Jake. "You don't have one piece of equipment that's less than twenty years old. Jesus, that printer is about to fall apart." She pointed to a large printer on the floor in a corner that rattled and whined as it cranked out about a page a minute of a report.

"Hell, Maggie. We just got rid of our IBM Selectrics a few years ago," he said. "Get me a decent budget, and we'll buy any technology you want."

"Whatever you say. Let's get everyone together so we can finish up our suspect profile. We need to pull every trick we have up our sleeves to find this guy."

A courier showed up with a package and handed it to Jake. He opened it with a letter opener. A book. Although curious, Maggie didn't ask about it. Ten minutes later, everyone had taken their seats. Jake brought the book in with him. The FBI agents sat next to one another at the back of the room, flipped open their laptops and fired them up.

"Shut off your laptops and listen, or get out," Maggie said. "I don't want you wasting my time or Sheriff Lubbock's. Christ help the people of the United States if this is how the FBI conducts business." The deputies snickered. The men closed their laptops and sat straight, humorless.

Maggie nodded to them. "Thank you, gentleman." She turned to the whiteboard. "We need to be on the lookout for a 'pre-crime stressor.' This means most serial killers were victims of physical or emotional abuse as children, extreme sexual abuse, or may have suffered some heinous emotional trauma, such as witnessing the murder of a parent or sibling. When interviewing suspects and witnesses, pay attention to anything they might tell you about their lives as children. Sometimes suspects slip in sad stories about their childhood to get a sympathy vote."

Jake opened the book and flipped through the pages.

"Lots of bad things happen to kids that don't turn them into killers," Happy said.

"You're right, but in many cases there is a pre-crime stressor hooked into a reason why a person turns to killing. Ending lives becomes for some a form of release. We are pretty sure that's what's going on here.

Now, most of our serial killers are white males in their late 20s. In this case, although our witnesses report a blonde man, I'm not convinced he's white, and he's not blonde. The crime lab confirms our hair sample is human but definitely Asian hair, dyed blonde."

"A wig?" Jake asked.

"Possibly. Unless our killer is an Asian who dyes his hair."

"Aren't most serial killers loners? Shouldn't we be looking for someone who is anti-social?" Happy asked.

"That's a myth. Consider the BTK killer who murdered ten people in Kansas. He was a local government official, married, two kids, well-liked, and president of his church congregation. Or the Green River killer who operated in the Seattle area. He confessed to killing forty-eight women. He held the same job for over thirty years, was a regular church guy, attended services every Sunday. Even read his Bible at work."

Jake thumbed through the book.

"What have you got there?" Maggie asked. "Do you mind paying attention to what I'm saying? That is unless what you are reading is relevant to the case in some way."

"It's relevant. Keep talking. I can hear you."

"So, these killers believe in God? They're religious?" asked a deputy.

"Some, not all. These are only a few examples." Maggie looked around the room. *I'm wasting time. These guys need to get out and find that psycho.* "I'm going to have to dispense with some of this explanation for now, and get to the core. Without going into minute detail as to how we reached our conclusions, this is what Max Stone and I came up with." Maggie distributed a handout of the profile to each of the attendees. "We are looking for a male resident of Wild River County. Most likely lives right here in Wicklow. He may be older than the standard serial killer, too. We believe he's somewhere between thirty and forty-five. He's an upstanding citizen, probably well-liked."

Jake ceased reading his book, and put his finger on a page to keep his place. "I've lived here since I was three years old," he said. "None of our upstanding citizens would have done this. I think he's an outsider, or a copycat who came into town recently."

"Jake, you never know who might kill. Some of these guys live their entire lives under the radar, never hurting anyone, and then something sets them off. They are psychopaths adept at hiding their true nature. You don't know, okay?" She took a sip of now tepid coffee, made a face and dumped the remainder into a half dead potted geranium.

She looked to Jake, but he was again lost in whatever he was reading. "We don't think our guy is a loner, either. He's got an active social life, may even be married with kids of his own. We think he's tall, Caucasian, Native American or Hispanic." She halted. "Jake are you getting any of this? Must be a damned good book."

"Yeah, social guy, married, tall, got it all. Go on."

"We are ruling out African American or Asian at this juncture only because there are very few men in those racial categories that meet our profile. He's someone with an ego, who thinks of himself as smarter than most people, although we think he's most likely of average intelligence. We are reasonably certain there's a pre-crime stressor involved that occurred sometime before his 8th birthday."

Happy raised his hand.

"Yes?"

"How do you know the pre-crime stressor occurred before his 8th birthday?"

"Because none of the twins he kills are over eight years old."

"Why does he target twins?"

"That's another piece of the profile...we think our guy is a twin, and as small children something traumatic happened to his sibling. He most likely witnessed the event. Does that answer your question?"

"Yeah, thanks."

"This guy is tidy. He keeps his car clean, his tools organized, and is meticulous in his dress and grooming habits. We think he definitely falls into the category of the organized killer."

"What about the American Spirit cigarettes? Is our guy a smoker?" Jake asked.

"We don't know that he smokes for certain. Since the lab found no DNA on the butts, it means he probably never even had the cigarettes in his mouth or did a fantastic job of cleaning them before discarding them at each scene. He deliberately left cigarette butts as a clue, or to throw us off. Oh, and he believes his killing is justified, or at the very least he has a clearly defined reason for his actions that go beyond blood lust, or the desire to murder children. We know he targets very young twins, but with Bobby Jenkins' death, he's now become dangerous to adults who do not have a twin sibling. Anyone could be in danger."

"Unless Bobby's killer is a copycat," said Jake.

"He's not a copycat."

"How do you know?"

"Jake, we've gone over this before. The killer's M.O. in Wild River County is an exact match to the cases in Washington, Oregon and Canada. Since not all the details of the murders were released to the public there is no way that a copycat would…"

Jake held up the book. "Every detail of each killing up to Bobby Jenkins is right in here in *Il Mostro Americano*, by Mario Panetti".

CHAPTER 28

Canada, Twenty-Eight Years Ago

Instead of biting, the ghoul clamped its jaws over the boy's nose and mouth silencing his cries. The monster forcefully exhaled into the child's lungs. The thing's breath smelled like the dead vole Mommy found behind the shed, bloated and covered in crawling worms and flies. The boy gagged, but frozen in terror, he didn't struggle...

Northern California, Present Time

MAGGIE ADJOURNED THE meeting. She, Jake, and Happy reconvened in the reception area. "Damn it," she said. "Someone has been leaking info about our cases to the press, and when I find out who it is, I'm going to personally stomp a lung out of him. But first, I'm going after that prick, Mario. This piece of garbage book just might have compromised our investigation. I'll have his balls on my pasta." She rubbed the back of her neck. "I'm leaving for the afternoon, guys. I'm getting a nasty headache."

As she was headed out, the door swung open and in barged Mingan. Maggie backed up a step. "What the hell are you doing here?"

"You, you, and you" Mingan said, pointing at Maggie, Happy and Jake in turn, "are incompetent. You're bungling this case. Our kids are dying and you're all sitting in the office here on your asses? I've got my own leads and I'm going to find this child killer myself."

"Yeah? What leads do you have?" Happy said.

"Let's say I'm closer to finding this guy than any of you ever will be. And you," he pointed to Happy's face, "are nothing but a second-rate deputy with the I.Q. of a hamburger patty, Mr. 'by golly.' You aren't going to ever get anywhere, or amount to anything. It's because the sheriff's department hires weak, brainless losers like you that you are nowhere near finding the man who is murdering all these children."

Happy's color turned from brown to scarlet, from scarlet to plum.

Jake stepped in front of the deputy and faced Mingan square on. "You stay away from this investigation, Mingan, or I'll arrest you for obstruction of justice. Do you understand?"

"Get out now," Maggie said. "Don't come back or I'll shoot off both your knee caps." She took a step toward him with her fingers on the handle of her Glock.

"You and I have unfinished business. You'll be seeing me soon, sweetie." Mingan winked at Maggie, and stormed out slamming the door behind him.

"What did he mean by that?" Jake said to Maggie.

"I don't have a clue."

"I don't like the sound of it. I'm putting some protection on you."

"I've got all the protection I need, Jake," she patted her Glock.

"I wonder if he really does have any real evidence?" Happy said.

"If he's got anything, he'd better give it up. If he withholds any information, or goes within 100 feet of Maggie, I'll lock up that bastard," Jake said.

"I'd like nothing more than to see that guy slip on ice and break his neck," Maggie said.

CHAPTER 29

Canada, Twenty-Eight Years Ago

When the boy awoke between his mother and father the next morning, for the first time in many days, he felt good. He wasn't cold, or afraid, or sad. But, he was hungry. Ravenous. The boy wanted more meat. When he got up and looked around, the world seemed different, better somehow. He felt strong...

Northern California, Present Time

WHEN SHE ARRIVED at the A-Frame, Maggie found Sally standing in the kitchen in a green checked apron tasting pasta sauce from a spoon.

"You look like a regular Betty Crocker," Maggie said. "Whatcha cooking?"

"Thought I'd come home early and make a little dinner for us. I was in the mood for old fashioned spaghetti and meatballs."

"Oh, no, not Italian. Please, anything but that."

"I thought you loved pasta."

"I do. I had a bad day involving that slimy Italian writer, and then something else happened...I don't want to go into it right now. Got any wine opened? "

"That I do," Sally said as she reached for a bottle of Chianti. She poured some into a large stemless glass.

"How's the cleanup going at Mama's?" Maggie asked.

"Faster than I thought, and I might have a buyer, too."

"No kidding? Great."

Sally untied her apron and put it on the counter. "I want to talk to you for a minute. Let's have a seat."

The two friends sat opposite one another at the kitchen table. Maggie took the wine glass from Sally. "What's up?"

"You have to make things right with your family, Mag. I have no kids, no siblings, no parents, no one. Family is the most important thing any of us has in life."

"I can't handle my jerk nephew."

"Sure you can. First of all, he's not as much of a jerk as you think. He cares about you, but he gets a major kick out of baiting you because you're so reactive. He pushes your buttons for the fun of watching you blow up. Stop reacting to him, and he'll stop baiting you. It's up to *you* to be the adult here."

"I guess I am a horse's ass sometime."

"Yes, you are, and you way overdid it that afternoon at Danny's. What you said in front of the twins about their mother was not in any way okay. But, if you were to apologize for your behavior, and mean it, you can fix things. They all love you, Maggie. You don't want to leave things messed up like this."

"Family isn't always about biology. We can't help who we are related to by blood, and my closest family members are chosen. You, Jake, you're my family, and I'm yours." She reached across the table to grip Sally's hand. "I don't know what I'd do without you."

"I love you, too, but fix things with Danny, Jimmy and Cathy. Please?"

"All right, I will."

"Promise?"

"I promise, but right now I could use more wine in this glass." She extended her glass to Sally.

After their substantial dinner, the women cleaned the kitchen, enjoyed a cup of decaf together, then Sally yawned. "Gotta be at Mama's to open up since Dawn has the day off. I'm going to bed. Night, sweetie."

"Pleasant dreams. Hope you get a great night's sleep."

"I've taken a double Lunesta. A bomb could drop on the house and I wouldn't wake up."

"You shouldn't drink alcohol when you take sleeping pills. I don't think you're supposed to double up on the dose, either. Are you okay?"

"I've done it before. I have a hard time getting a decent night sleep since that violent episode at Mama's with Iggy and Squiggy, and the split up with John. I'm fine. I'll be out of it for a while, though." She gave Maggie a hug and disappeared into the guest room closing the door after her. Within a few minutes Sally snored almost hard enough to rattle the mugs in the cupboard.

Maggie remained in the kitchen awhile before heading off to the bathroom. She decided on a long hot shower. She allowed the water to pour down her back, and inhaled the steam.

She stepped out of the water, dried herself, wrapped her favorite fluffy blue robe around her, poured herself a coffee and added a generous shot of brandy. Maggie stepped outside on the back deck to feel the cold against her skin. The rough wood under her bare feet soothed her. She always loved the feel of wood grain. She rubbed one foot over the boards of the deck, stopping at the coldness of a screw. The stars were brilliant and the air crisp. A shooting star grazed the sky. She heard a caw and a click. From a bare oak branch, a pair of glistening black eyes stared at her.

"Aren't you supposed to be sleeping?" she said to the raven. The bird ruffled its feathers and cawed again. "Look, I don't know what you want but it's too freezing cold out here so I'm going in. You can sit there all night for all I care."

She went back inside locking the door behind her. Maggie had a couple of hours to herself, at least until midnight accounting for the nine hour time difference between California and Rome, Italy. She'd call at midnight, 9 a.m. Italian time as the offices of *La Gazzetta di Parma*, the oldest newspaper in Italy, opened for business. "I'm going to have that idiot's head impaled on a post," she said to Samantha who rubbed against her legs.

She carried her cup to her desk and powered on her PC. The cat leaped onto her desk and snuggled into a ball. Chester curled up under, his usual spot when she worked online. She input "Cannibals." She skipped articles on the Donner Party, Albert Fish, Ed Gein and Jeffrey Dahmer. Then something caught her eye, "Wendigo Psychosis." She clicked on the link and pushed the cat off her desk "Sorry, Samantha." She scooted her chair in slightly, took another sip from her cup, and read.

...the mental illness known as 'Wendigo Psychosis' is a 'culture bound' syndrome, meaning it is not recognized outside of a specific culture. This particular psychosis generally develops in the winter months when a family, isolated by heavy snow and is starving, is forced to eat another family member to survive."

"Christ," Maggie said, picking up her coffee and brandy. Without averting her eyes from the computer screen, she took a sip and set it back down. She missed the desk entirely, dropping the cup and splashing her brandied coffee all over the floor. The startled dog jumped up and bumped his huge head on the bottom side of her desk. "Did you hurt your noggin, Chester? Hell...I need a straight brandy anyway." She walked into the kitchen to throw away the now cracked cup and to fetch a paper towel. She opened the door to let Chester out for his evening pee. Through the window, she saw the raven still perched on the limb staring in at her. He cawed and cawed. "What is your problem, fella?" she said to the bird. She poured herself a double, wiped up the mess, and sat down to read the remaining text on the screen.

In some cases, when a family member eats another, he or she develops an insatiable taste for human flesh, convinced that he is possessed by a Wendigo (also known as a Manitou), a monster who takes control over the sufferer's will. The afflicted person becomes homicidal, violent, kills without remorse, then eats his victims, or part of his victims, such as the brain or heart. Some myths say the affected person actually turns into the Wendigo monster.

Maggie sipped her brandy. It felt good as it burned its way down her throat.

In the 1980s, psychologists, anthropologists, and ethnographers debated the legitimacy of the phenomenon. They reached the conclusion that the psychosis is authentic, and is generally manifested under stress in isolated conditions. This particular psychosis is directly linked to the nomadic and hunting lifestyle of the Cree, Ojibwa, Chippewa, and Inuit — all the Algonquin people.

"Algonquin? It *has* to be him." Maggie shook her head. "Why couldn't I see it? Oh God." She took a breath and continued reading.

Those afflicted with Wendigo Psychosis often suffer from delusions of...

Someone knocked at the door. Maggie glanced at the wall clock. *Who in hell is pounding at my door at nearly 10:30 at night?* She padded across the floor and opened the door. Mingan. Her intestines turned to ice. To conceal her fear she put on her stern face and said in a voice a little too loud, "What are you doing here? Get off my porch now."

"I told you we've got some unfinished business. I thought now would be a good time to end what we started on our date, honey." He reached in through the entry and grabbed her breast, and squeezed it hard.

She wrenched free and tried to slam the door but his foot blocked the way. He pushed against the wood. Maggie screamed, "Sally!" She knew her cries were futile. In spite of his slender frame, Mingan outweighed Maggie by more than 40 lbs. and stood six inches over her with a powerful back and arms that she had so often admired. Now, as she strained to hold the flimsy barrier closed against him, she wished she'd been attracted to smaller men. He slammed his body against the door, broke in and grabbed Maggie around the waist. She flailed at him.

Chester bayed and clawed at the door to get in. Raven's furiously pecked on the window panes.

Mingan's face was so close to hers she could feel the fog of his breath on her cheek. "Why are you fighting me, darlin'? You wanted me since the first time you laid your sexy green eyes on me at the Bear Dance. Now you'll get to finally know what my big Algonquin dick feels like shoved up your half-breed pussy."

"You're drunk. Get out now."

"I've had a few drinks, but everything works fine. I've got a huge hard-on for you, atheist whore." He slammed her against a wall, and pressed so hard against her she could barely breathe, pinning her legs and arms. He rubbed his erection against her. She felt his hardness through his jeans.

"Feel that, sweetie?" he said. He had one forearm over her throat, pressing hard.

He shoved his other hand through the folds of her robe, "Oooh, nice, nothing underneath." He moved his hand down to her pubis jabbing his fingers into her. She tightened her thighs together, but he forced his way. He withdrew his fingers, clutched her pubic hair and yanked. He crushed his mouth against hers so hard her lips bruised against her clenched teeth. His breath smelled of putrid whiskey. She turned her head and cried out in pain and fury. She managed to wriggle one arm free and struck out at him with her fist. She aimed for his throat and nose, but he evaded every blow.

"Does it hurt?" he said, yanking at her pubic hairs even harder. "That's nothing, sweetie. Actually, I think you probably would like it if I hurt you a little." His voice was raspy, husky.

As she still punched and kicked at him, he pulled his forearm away from her throat. She coughed. He knotted her braid into his fist and jerked her head sideways and back forcing her chin up. She reached up grasping at his hand to prevent him from snapping her neck. He tore her robe open exposing her breasts. Maggie kicked and jabbed at him with her feet and knees, but he crushed himself harder against her body making it difficult for her to land a solid blow.

"Nice tits. Are they real?" he said, before he bit into one breaking the skin.

Maggie screamed, released her grip on his hand. He wrenched her braid even harder. She twisted her head to the side, wriggled an arm free, brought her hand down and plunged her thumb into his eye. She dug in until he let go. He faced her, blood smearing his mouth from where he'd bitten her. He yelled out. "You dirty slut!" As he rubbed at his eye, she twisted free and ran toward the bedroom for her Glock on the bedside table. As he was about to catch up, he reached for her. She spun and kicked hitting him in the solar plexus with her heel. He made an "umph" sound and crumpled, giving her the split second she needed to grab her gun. She wheeled around and turned it on him.

"Stay right there. You take one step toward me and I'll shoot you between the eyes."

He backed away, hands up. "Okay, okay. Settle down. I thought we were having a little fun. As feisty as you are, I figured you might like it rough."

"Don't you tell me to settle down, you rotten lump of horseshit. Lock your hands together behind your head, turn around and stick your nose to the wall. Now." With one hand, she closed her robe. Blood trickled from the bite wound on her breast. A ragged purple patch spread where blood soaked the blue fabric. "Please, move a tiny bit so I have an excuse to blow a hole through your spine." Keeping the gun pointed at the middle of the Algonquin's back, she used her free hand to pick up her cell, and punched the buttons with her thumb.

CHAPTER 30

Canada, Twenty-Eight Years Ago

For days the family ate well. When the muscle meat was gone, Noshi brought in the liver.

Chepi said, "That liver is way too big to be a rabbit's. What is this meat?"

"Don't ask. It's saving our life and the life of our only remaining son. Please, eat it."

She extended her hand to accept the meat, and asked no more questions...

Northern California, Present Time

MAGGIE WAS IN love with her truck, a 1954 Chevy pickup that had belonged to her father. When Daddy died in Belfast, the old truck sat in the family garage for years, dirty, no tires, faded green paint scratched down to the primer in large patches. The rusted body had so many dents there wasn't a square foot that was not marred by at least one ding. The windshield was so cracked and pitted there was no way to see through it. The missing passenger side window created an easy entrance for families of spiders and mice. The cab smelled of decades-old dust, and mold. The ripped seats, their rusty coils poking through ancient upholstery with stuffing spilling out of ragged gashes, was smothered in cobwebs. The nests and feces of rodents littered the dashboard, beneath and on tops of the seats, on the decayed floor mats front and back.

The plucky Irishman, who admired vintage American cars, intended to restore the truck, a prize he'd bought from a neighbor for $300. Everyone thought his son would take up the restoration cause, but when it was time to decide, Maggie and Danny, high school sophomores, had only a few days before received their driver's permits. Danny had his heart set on a used Camaro with a "rad" stereo system, he called it. He'd been working since the summer before his freshman year as a box boy at Tippy Top Foods, the only supermarket in Wicklow, and saved every penny of his salary to buy his Camaro, or one like it. He had almost five grand stashed away and needed another two grand or so. Maggie, who worked busing tables at The Dandelion, had stowed away her earnings for a car, too. She made Danny a deal. "I'll buy that old truck from you for a thousand dollars. It isn't worth half that."

"Why would you want that piece of junk, Maggie? It doesn't even run. How 'bout we sell it for whatever we can get for it and split the money, then you'll have more for a better car, and I can put my share against the Camaro."

"I want Dad's truck. I can get it running."

"You don't know squat about cars, Maggie, and it'll cost you a ton of cash to even get it street safe. You don't want that old thing."

"Yes, I do. I'm offering you a thousand dollars cash, Danny. That way, you only have to work a little while longer, and you'll have enough to buy your Camaro. What about it?"

"If you really want it, but, I would..."

"...I do want it. So, it's a deal?"

"It's a deal."

Maggie sprinted into her bedroom, pulled a wad of cash out of her sock drawer and counted the money into Danny's hand, and then she whooped. "Yes! Daddy's truck is mine."

"I don't want that beat up looking thing anyway. You're welcome to it, and good luck getting it running."

Danny and Maggie celebrated their 18th birthdays. Danny had finally saved enough for a trip to the Redding Auto Mall to buy a shiny almost new Camaro when Cathy ended up pregnant and they needed his car money for a baby. He ended up buying an old truck that, even though road worthy, looked more beat up than the Chevy he'd sold to his sister.

Maggie was a looker who wore her jeans a little too tight and her skirts a little too short. She knew about the rumor that she put out. Boys gathered around her like rutting hogs hoping that if they helped her to fix her truck they might get laid or a blow job or at least she might let them feel her up. "I'm going to milk this for as long as I can. Maybe I'll even get my truck fixed for free," she told Sally.

At the time, John Winters was a clean cut boy, a tall, muscular, blond with sharp blue eyes, and a rakish grin. He was a popular student with a promising career in football, and there wasn't a girl at Wicklow High, including Maggie, who didn't have at least a little crush on him. She was delighted that he jumped into the truck restoration with both feet. His father showed up some Sundays to help. John Winter's father owned an auto repair shop so he was able to get parts cheap, sometimes free. Most weekends, you'd find Maggie, John, his dad, and sometimes one or two other boys crowded under the hood of the old truck. Jealous of Maggie's obvious attraction to John, Jake kept his distance.

Maggie asked for more hours at The Dandelion and put every dime of her earnings into buying truck parts. It took over a year to earn enough money to drop in the 327 cubic inch engine, replace the windows, put on tires, rebuild the transmission, and take care of everything else mechanical and electrical required to get the old Chevy on the road.

John spent every possible moment with her under the pretense of working on the truck. He took abundant opportunities to cop a feel of Maggie's breast or to touch her butt. She let him. It was a small price to pay to get her daddy's truck running, and besides that, she liked it when John touched her. When John invited Sally to the Junior Prom, Maggie was furious.

"I thought you liked me," she said to him.

"I do, really, but I thought you weren't into school dances."

"You're right. But that's not the point. You should have asked me anyway. Sally's my best friend. You know that, you dickhead."

One Sunday, John showed up early and led her into a dark recess of the garage. He kissed her, pushing his tongue into her mouth. She didn't like the way he kissed. He was sloppy, harsh, lacking the skill and finesse of the older boys she dated from nearby Saint Domingo Community College. He pressed his hard-on against her. She was neither impressed nor turned on, but since he'd worked so diligently for such a long time on the truck, she felt she owed him a little something. She let him feel her up. He squeezed her naked breasts under her t-shirt. As he was wriggling his hand under the waist band of her shorts to get into her panties, Danny walked in. "What the hell are you doing with my sister, you sonofabitch? Get your hands off her now or I'll kill you."

John recoiled like he'd been hit in the face with a hammer. "We were only messin' around. Besides that, she's legal."

"Yeah, well, you're messing around with the wrong girl. Get out, and if you touch my sister again, or ever step one foot on our property, I'll break your neck."

John scuttled out of the garage.

"Thanks, Danny," she said. "He was getting a little out of hand."

"From where I was standing, looked like you were enjoying it."

"Maybe a little. Although, he's not nearly as experienced as the Saint Domingo boys."

"You're such a whore. You embarrass the shit out of me."

Good thing the truck was ready for the road, and she wouldn't need more help for a while because after John ran out of the garage like a lame deer chased by a pack of ravenous lions, he never returned. He paid Maggie little attention afterwards. By that time, Maggie's hot crush had cooled, and John was full-on dating Sally. When it looked like it was getting serious between John and Sally, Maggie was relieved.

On the day of her 19th birthday, she registered the truck, and drove it with its ripped interior, springs still poking through the seat in some places, and its rusted, dented exterior. The townspeople made fun of her. "Hey, Maggie, how's that old piece of junk holding up?" some idiot or another would say. Or, "When are you going to get a real truck?" Maggie flipped them off.

When she moved from busing tables to serving, Maggie earned good tips, and soon saved enough to take the truck down to Jacob and Son's Auto Body Shop where she had all the dings knocked out. Then came new chrome, custom cream leather interior, whitewall tires, sporty rims, and a brilliant cherry red paint job. No one made fun of her after that. She had the coolest ride in Wild River County.

She worked full time and attended classes part-time at the local community college. When she was accepted into UCLA as a transfer student, with Sally's help, she crammed the bed of the truck with cardboard boxes and plastic trash bags stuffed with her belongings and took off alone for Los Angeles. The Chevy overheated when she drove it over The Grapevine, and she had to spend a few hours at the side of a road. She didn't mind. She was off to a new life, and her daddy's truck was taking her there.

———

The sky was so dark it seemed more like 8 p.m. than 1 p.m. when Maggie pulled up at The Dandelion to meet Sally. The rain poured from the sky dumping an inch an hour over Wicklow. "We can always use the moisture around here. Rain is good," she said to Chester as they pulled in. She parked in her usual spot at the far end of the lot to lessen any chance that some brainless idiot might pull in too close and leave a scratch in the red paint, or open their door too hard and put a dent in her beloved Chevy. "You wait here, boy. Guard the truck. I'll be out before you know it." The dog whined as she stepped out, closed and locked the door.

The Dandelion was packed. It seemed as though every time it rained the entire town showed up at the restaurant for a bowl of homemade soup de jour, or the café's famous chili dog. There were a few people outside huddled beneath umbrellas waiting for a table.

Sally, seated at a booth toward the back, waved when Maggie walked in. "Over here."

As Maggie made her way through the crowded restaurant, she was aware that everyone stared at her. News had gotten out that Mingan had been picked up for battery and attempted rape. The bruises around her mouth were livid purple. Her lips and cheek were swollen. She ignored everyone, fixing her eyes on Sally seated at the bright blue vinyl booth.

As she walked toward Sally, two women Maggie did not recognize caught her eye. They sat on the aisle side-by-side. The pudgy one in her early fifties wore her garish dyed red hair in an outdated bouffant style, her prim gray dress buttoned to the collar bone. She put her hand out and stopped Maggie.

"Excuse me, are you Maggie Sloan?"

"Yes, I am."

"We are truly sorry about what happened to you."

"Thank you. That's kind of you to..."

"...and we at Wicklow Christian Church know that Mingan is a good man and would never do what you accused him of to anyone. It was someone else who hurt you, and now you are trying to blame it on him. We want to know why."

"What?"

The other woman seated at the table had cotton colored hair she wore in a bubble cut. Her hair was so thin her scalp showed through in places, and it reflected the light from the overhead pendant lamp. She was about seventy-five years old, scrawny with black rimmed glasses, her lips pursed so tight that it looked as through the nasty nag might hurt herself. The woman unpursed her lips and joined in. "Mingan Metchitehew is a righteous, God-fearing man, an important part of our community and our church. Because of your vicious lies, his life is ruined. You need to pray about that and ask the Lord for forgiveness, Ms. Sloan."

"What the hell are you talking about?"

"You went out on dates with him. You tempted him," she said. "If you two shared any physical intimacy at all, which we don't believe because he is not a fornicator, and he knows you are a sinner who consorts with that Satan-loving witch over there," she said pointing to Sally, "it was because you seduced him with your vile ways."

"Look, you dried up old bitch," she paused, looking from one to the other. "Both of you, shut the hell up. You don't have a clue as to what and who Mingan is. The sonofabitch attacked me, tried to rape me, and..."

"Liar!" said the bouffant woman, her face distorted in disgust.

Maggie leaned in close. The woman blanched. Missy, the restaurant manager stepped in between. "Ladies, I'm going to have to ask you to leave," she said to the seated women. "I uphold a zero tolerance policy against harassment."

The women stood, snatched their purses, and the hag with the dark rimmed glasses said to Missy, "We'll not be coming back here again."

The other customers broke into applause.

Without paying, the indignant women stomped toward the exit of the café. Two burly men stood near the door wearing Wicklow Christian Church shirts. The thin one with a handlebar moustache appeared to be in his forties. The other, a corpulent man in sagging pants and heavy scuffed work boots, looked younger and meaner. The heavier man opened the door to permit the women to pass. "Good work, ladies," he said in an overbearing voice. "That slut will pay for the evil she's committed against our beloved deacon."

The restaurant patrons broke out in a chorus of boos.

Maggie sat down across from Sally. "Dammit," she said.

"It's okay. They're gone now."

Missy approached their table. "I'm sorry about that, Maggie. Lunch is on me today."

Sally ordered a chili dog and a diet Coke.

Maggie said, "Just bring me a cup of coffee, please. I'm not hungry."

"I feel so bad that Mingan did that to you, and I was so out of it I couldn't even help," Sally said. "I didn't hear a thing."

"I know you would have done something if you could have." She reached over and held Sally's hand.

"I should have been there for you. Look at your mouth. He hurt you, and the entire time I was sound asleep in a drugged stupor."

"Really, it's okay. Doc says I'm fine. The best thing in all this is that Mingan will spend many long years in jail where he belongs. With that cute butt of his, he better not drop anything in the shower."

Sally laughed, and Maggie laughed with her. The two women sat together talking for a while. The lunch crowd disbursed until only a few tables remained occupied. After lunch, Maggie hugged Sally, and walked out to the now almost empty parking lot to her Chevy.

Ravens circled over the truck like vultures eying bloated carrion. Maggie looked up at them. "What the hell?" she said. As she approached the truck, Chester appeared nervous. He paced, stopping to press his nose against the glass. As she walked nearer the Chevy, she understood why. All four tires were flat, slashed. Someone had repeatedly kicked the truck with what appeared to be a heavy boot, leaving deep dents in the fender. On the driver's side door, scratched through the cherry red paint, was the word WHORE.

CHAPTER 31

Canada, Twenty-Eight Years Ago

"Gimme," said the boy, his hand palm up. He chewed and swallowed the raw liver with so much gusto Chepi was afraid he might choke. "Don't eat so fast. Chew carefully."

"Gimme more," the boy stared at his mother, his eyes empty as a ghost's. "I'm hungry. Gimme meat."

"No," said Chepi. "We have to save some for later."

"I'm hungry. Gimme more. Now!"

"You can have some tomorrow..."

Northern California, Present Time

MONDAY CAME FAR too fast for Maggie. The swelling around her mouth and cheek subsided, her bruises turned from purple to green, and she felt human again, but she wasn't in the mood to hunt a killer today. She would have loved nothing more than to remain buried to her chin under her down comforter with a good book, a mug filled to the brim with coffee and brandy, and a *Claddagh's Choice* CD playing on the stereo. Instead she kicked off the covers, stood and pulled on her new robe. After that thing with Mingan, she'd cut her old favorite blue one into shreds, and burned it in her fireplace, one piece at a time. She took a rare trip to Redding to buy a plush burgundy dressing gown, so soft and abundant she could disappear forever into its folds. She spent a fortune on it, but it was worth every cent. The only bit of cheer in her life this morning, besides her new cuddly robe, was knowing Mingan Metchitehew was locked up tight.

After coffee, she showered, dressed, and braided her hair twisting a thick rubber band around the end. She grabbed a piece of peanut butter toast and put down bowls of food for the dog and cat. "You two be good while I'm gone, and no hassling the hens, Chester. If you stress them, we won't get any eggs."

She stepped out onto the front porch as Happy pulled into the driveway. Her truck was in the body shop. Insurance covered most of the damage, but the cost of the custom paint job was astronomical, and would take additional time.

"Hi," she said as she climbed into his car. "How are Rosa and the kids?"

"Good. Thanks for asking. So, Jake tells me you found out something interesting about our killer that points to Mingan?"

"Sort of. It's a psychosis specific to the Algonquin people. Has to do with cannibalism."

A raucous noise interrupted their conversation. Dozens of ravens descended from the sky in a dark mass towards Happy's car, diving again and again making knocking and cawing noises. By a scant inch, a few missed crashing head on into the windshield, veering off at the last second.

"Why do they do that?" Happy said.

"I don't know. Maybe ravens are territorial and think they're protecting their land. It's weird."

"What's weird is your thing with the ravens. Why not sparrows? Or jays? What's with the ravens?"

"I think it's because I feed them. Maybe they think I'm their mama."

Happy tapped the steering wheel. "So tell me about this cannibal Algonquin stuff."

"Let's wait until we get into the office. I want Jake to hear about this, too."

"Mingan's our guy."

"I don't know, Happy. There's something not right about this...I mean, there is a possibility that Mingan is who we are looking for, sure, but I've got a feeling..."

"It's Mingan."

"You don't know that. We have lots of pieces to pull together still. I'm not convinced it's him."

"He's Algonquin. He's tall. He fits the profile in other ways, too. We already know he can be violent. And now you've discovered something about cannibals relating specifically to his culture. Besides, look at what he did to you. Don't you hate that guy, anyway?"

"Yes, I do. That doesn't mean he's a serial killer, and there are many native people in Wild River County. Who says that Mingan is the only Algonquin?"

Happy did not smile this morning. He gripped the steering wheel with such force the color of his knuckles drained to white.

"What's up? You aren't yourself. Did you and Rosa have a fight this morning?" she asked.

"No, dammit. It's that I think we've got our murderer in jail right now and you're so stubborn, so dense, you can't see what's right under your nose."

"Whoa, Happy. What the hell is wrong with you? Has the entire human race gone crazy lately?"

Happy's face reddened, and looked out the driver's side window. A driver approaching the other way leaned into his horn. In the split second that Happy had taken his eyes off the road, he'd veered over the double yellow line directly into the path of oncoming traffic. He jerked his wheel to avoid getting them both turned into meat pudding by a logging truck. His pickup spun 180 degrees on the wet asphalt, and when they came to rest, both Happy and Maggie hyperventilated. "Damn, that was close," Happy said.

As he passed them, the driver of the logging truck extending his middle finger out the window. Happy took a deep breath, turned his car around, and drove on. "Maggie, are you okay? I'm sorry about that."

"Keep your eyes on the road. We are lucky we didn't go off the cliff, or get hit from behind. If you want to risk your own life, fine, but don't risk mine." Maggie struggled to catch her breath.

"Sorry, Mag. I hate Mingan for what he did to you, and I guess this whole thing with this kid killer is starting to get to me. I'm worried about my family, and if Mingan is not our guy we aren't any closer to catching this psycho than we were when we started looking."

"You don't have twins. I don't think you need to worry."

"I just want all this over with. Forgive me?"

———

When Maggie had driven to the station the day before to report the vandalism, Jake promised her he'd find out who damaged her truck.

"We'll get to the bottom of this," he said. "You've got my word on it."

A day later Jake arrested the two church bumpkins who were hanging around The Dandelion the afternoon Maggie's truck had been vandalized. They confessed.

"I told them that ruining your truck wasn't very Christian of them, and that's when the guys started in on the fire and brimstone garbage. I told them if they didn't stop spouting Bible passages at me, I was going to lock 'em up for good," Jake said.

"Thanks for keeping your promise to find them." Maggie loved that Jake was always there for her when things weren't going well, and she felt bad that she sometimes was snappish and bristly with him.

Happy offered her rides until her truck was repaired so she wouldn't have to rent a car. "It'll give us time to talk about the case."

———

That night, Maggie, tired to the marrow, walked into the cabin and headed for the booze cabinet, not even greeting Sally.

"Bad day?" Sally asked.

"Actually, other than being a bit wiped, and Happy nearly killing us with some bad driving this morning, my day was decent, but after a little fortification..." she opened a brandy, poured two fingers worth into a water glass and downed it in one swallow, "...I've got a phone call to make to my brother. She picked up her cell and dialed Danny's number.

Sally smiled at Maggie. "That's my girl."

"Is there any way I can meet with you, Cathy and Jimmy?" she said to her brother.

Danny sighed into the mouthpiece. "C'mon, Maggie."

"I need to talk. I'm doing my best to make things right. Please, Danny. I miss you and everybody. It's been weeks. I want to see Flower and Bird."

"You'll have to talk to Jimmy about that. It's up to him if he wants you around the girls."

"Please. Can you get everyone together as a family? Sally says she'll drive me over."

"Oh, that's right...I heard about the Chevy. Sorry about that." Danny was quiet for a moment. "You're okay after what Mingan did to you? We were all concerned. You know we called the hospital. Cathy and I wanted to see you, but..."

"Thanks for asking. I'm good. Can we make this happen, I mean...with the family? Sally will entertain the kids while we talk. Give me a chance, please?"

"Let me check with Cathy." Danny called to his wife. "Maggie wants to come over to talk with us and Jimmy. Do you have any objections?"

"Of course not, Danny. She's your sister, and I don't want no bad blood with family. I'll make us some dinner."

"Okay, sis. Tomorrow night, then. I'll call Jimmy. What time can you be here?"

———

Maggie bid good night to Sally, and climbed under her comforter so spent she hadn't even bothered to brush her teeth. Chester curled into a dog ball on the comforter next to her,

Samantha stretched herself across a pillow. Tomorrow, after work she'd make things right with Danny and Jimmy. Maggie scratched the hound between the ears. "Hey, Chester. We'll get to see Bird and Flower again. How 'bout that, boy?"

She drifted off to sleep, and then the phone rang. "Hello."

Silence.

"Who's there? If that's you Mingan, I'm getting a..."

"It's me, daughter."

"Mom? Oh, shit. I have to be dreaming. What the hell..."

"You know I don't like that kinda talk. I taught you respect. You listen to me, girl. You have to pay attention. You have to know who you are. No more foolin' around."

CHAPTER 32

Canada, Twenty-Eight Years Ago

The boy screamed in rage and grabbed for the liver. Noshi snatched it away and carried it outside. Chepi reached to comfort the boy. He bit her finger so viciously it bled. "Damn!" she said, jerking her hand back.

"I hate you. I will kill you," he said.

Noshi entered the cave. "Don't ever talk to your mother like that." He raised his hand to strike the boy.

Instead of cowering as he had in the past when his father threatened to hit him, the boy straightened to make himself taller and glared at his father. When the boy bared his teeth and growled like a rabid dog, Noshi hesitated then dropped his hand...

Northern California, Present Time

TONIGHT SHE'D SLEEP well. Maggie turned off the ringer to her cell. *No interruptions, thank you very much. No calls from my dead mother.* With three gin and tonics in her, the last one a double, she wouldn't dream, or so she hoped. But, while still in that sweet dozy state, right before drifting into oblivion, she felt the unwanted transformation, the shifting from woman to bird. She flew over the Trinity Alps calling a greeting to a bull elk, an aging Royal bearing the scars of many battles with younger bulls over multiple rutting seasons. The old guy bugled his 'hello' to Maggie, who cawed back. Some of his cows sleeping nearby were pregnant. Within a few months, the bull's herd would expand with several healthy calves on wobbly legs pulling at their mother's teats. *I wonder how many more seasons he'll survive before a younger, stronger guy, maybe even one of his own sons will drive him away or kill him then claim the old boy's cows? Not many. I'll miss him.*

At the base of the white cliffs, the monster sat crossed legged in front of a fire picking his teeth with a small bone. Maggie flew close enough to smell his rotting flesh, to see his tattered clothes, and the patches of skull where chunks of hair were missing and scalp exposed. Viscous foul liquid ran down his cheek from his eye socket. She was careful to remain out of his reach circling overhead. She perched on a branch of a blue spruce, deep under cover of the tree's thick needle bundles.

The monster pulled the bone out of his mouth and pointed it at her. He spoke first in his own strange language, then in flawless, formal Raven he said, "I see you, little bird, hiding there in the spruce. You think you are safe, do you? The rumor is you are the pukkukwerek, and I am to be the monster you are destined to kill. I do not think so. I will eat your heart while you are still alive, then I shall pick my teeth with your bones like I pick my teeth now with the bones of your sister raven. She did not die quickly. You shall not die quickly either." He aimed the bone toward the ground in front of him. "You can see fear in her eyes, assuredly the same fear your eyes will reflect when I kill you, little bird."

On a patch of dirt between his folded legs and the fire lay a bloody pile of glossy black wings and delicate white bones with bits of gristle and meat clinging to them. The detached head of a beautiful raven stared with empty eyes into the sky.

The monster turned away from Maggie, dismissing her as though she were no more significant than a fruit bat, stuck the tiny bone back into his mouth and made a loud sucking noise.

———

The following morning, Maggie drug herself out of bed, groomed, and climbed into Happy's car, travel mug in hand. She covered her mouth, yawned and mumbled a drowsy greeting.

"Are you not feeling well?" Happy asked her.

"Bad night. I didn't sleep well and I had a nasty dream. I'm afraid I'm not up for chit chat this morning. I might try to doze for a few minutes on the way in, if you don't mind."

"The seat reclines. Pull the lever on the side." He grinned at her.

"I know how to recline a damned seat."

His grin faded.

"Happy, I'm sorry. I know you are only trying to help. Thanks, really. I guess I'm a little out of sorts because I'm so exhausted. I just need some sleep." She reclined the seat, closed her eyes and drifted off.

"So, I guess you don't want to hear that Mingan made bail?"

Maggie snapped awake. "What? He battered and sexually assaulted a law enforcement officer. How in the hell did he manage to get together that much cash so quickly?"

"The people from his church pulled the money together, and the preacher came in last night for him."

"Why didn't anyone call me?"

"We tried, Maggie. Your cell was off, and Sally didn't answer hers."

Maggie fished into her coat pocket for her cell. *Oh, no. I never turned it back on.* She pressed the 'on' button and shoved it back into her pocket. "Great. That bastard is running loose in the county."

———

It was good to sit at the yellow table in Danny's kitchen with everyone again. In the living room, Flower and Bird played the *Where the Wild Things Are* board game with Sally. The sound of their laughter brought a smile to Maggie. The kitchen was filled with the fragrance of a baking tuna casserole and buttermilk biscuits. Danny, Jimmy, and Cathy sat on one side of the table. Maggie sat opposite them by herself. She held a mug of coffee in both hands. "Look, Jimmy, I'm really sorry I lost my temper. I should have never said what I did with Bird and Flower in the house. That was bad form."

"It's partly my fault," Jimmy said to her. "I was baiting you. I know it. I'm sorry, too."

"That's no excuse," Danny said. His crossed his arms across his chest, his face hard. "Maggie, you need to control yourself. It doesn't matter what Jimmy did or said, or didn't do or say. You need to think of those little girls before you open your mouth."

"I know. I was wrong...it won't happen again."

"That's what you said last time. I can't have this in my house."

"I understand, Danny. I know I need to..."A thud like something heavy falling against the window diverted everyone's attention.

Jimmy got up to pull the drapes away from the window.

"No, Jimmy. Sit. Keep the drapes drawn. Let me check this out." Maggie withdrew her Glock from its shoulder holster concealed under her jacket, and put one in the chamber.

"You brought your gun into my house?" Danny said. "Are you kidding me?"

Weapon drawn, Maggie cracked opened the door. She stepped onto the front porch, eased around the corner inching her way to the outside of the kitchen window. No one there. She spied a cigarette butt, American Spirit menthol. *It's him.* She crept around the perimeter of the house, her body flat against the cedar siding snagging the fabric of her coat as she scooted against it. A movement caught her attention. She swung around. A doe leapt over the fence into an open field. She relaxed and moved to holster her weapon when she heard something else, footsteps, someone running. She swiveled and dropped down on one knee, Glock aimed. A tall hooded figure, looked to be male, disappeared into the forest adjacent to Danny's property. "Stop!" She called after him. "I'll shoot." She ran toward the spot where she'd seen the man disappear. No sight of him anywhere.

CHAPTER 33

Canada, Twenty-Eight Years Ago

"Noshi. Please. It's okay," Chepi said. "Let's go outside for a minute." She turned to the boy. "You stay here until we get back..."

Northern California, Present Time

AFTER PULLING HER Glock in Danny's house, Maggie was unsure she'd ever be welcome in his home again. Cathy's call inviting her to the Pow Wow in Southern California came as a pleasant surprise.

"Jimmy is putting those girls in the tots dancing competition. We all want you with us there if you can get away from work for a day or two. Besides that, Jimmy and Danny want the girls to know more Indians outside the northern tribes."

"I'd love to attend, Cathy, but it's a long drive. I may be needed here for the investigation, and besides, I don't know if Jimmy and Danny really want..."

"You come. It's important you do something more to mend the family."

"All right. I'll be there, and thanks for including me. I'd love to see Flower and Bird dance."

The day of the event, Bird and Flower dressed in full Yurok regalia, twirled and spun around the room on their toes. "Look at us, Aunt Maggie," Bird said. Both girls turned one way and then the other to show off.

"I hope we win a prize," Flower said. "We have been practicing. Grandpa is on the drums."

"You both look beautiful," Maggie said. "I can't wait to see you out there. You'll be the prettiest girls in the competition."

While Danny and Cathy browsed the booths, Maggie and

Jimmy took the girls to a story circle to hear some of the legends. A Soboba elder in beautiful regalia sat on a stump in the middle of the arena. Children gathered close around him.

"I'm going to tell you a scary Pauma Luiseño story about Dakwish, a bad medicine man who roasts and eats people," he said.

"You sure you want the girls to hear this?" Maggie said to Jimmy.

"It's good for them to learn Indian lore. They're old enough."

There was a great chief named Tukupar, which in our language means 'sky.' Tukupar had an obedient son named Naukit. One day, Naukit went to hunt rabbits. In the forest he met up with Dakwish, a bad medicine man, who killed him, roasted him on a spit over a fire and ate him.

"Ew," Bird and Flower said in unison.

When Naukit did not come home, Tukupar was worried. 'Where has my son gone to?' Tukupar looked and looked everywhere for Naukit but could not find him. He returned and told his people that Naukit was lost. The next day, he went again to look for his son, and on a big hill in the San Jacintos he found the burned remains of Naukit's body, most of it eaten, his hair cut off. He knew Dakwish had killed him.

Tukupar was also a medicine man, a powerful magician, and he had a good plan. He called all his people together and said 'Dakwish killed my son. I am going to Dakwish's house. I will trick him to come here, and we will kill him.' The villagers cried because everyone loved Naukit.

The storyteller lowered his voice and leaned into the children. He looked into the faces of each as if he were telling the story directly to only those whose eyes he caught with his own.

There was no ordinary way to enter Dakwish's house because the door was a huge boulder that men could not open. Only a strong medicine man would know how. Tukupar made himself into a raven and with his beak and claws dug a hole big enough under the rock to get into Dakwish's house. He carried with him two dead rabbits.

Maggie watched Bird and Flower. The girls were wide-eyed, focused on the elder with rapt attention.

Inside he found Dakwish's mother who was very much afraid. 'What are you doing here?'

'I'm here to see Dakwish.'

'He will kill you if he finds you here.'

'I will see him anyway. Tell him I am his cousin.'

'I warn you.'

Tukupar turned back into a man and sat down away from the door, hiding the rabbits.

Late that night, there was a big storm. The thunder clapped, and a big rain came. Rocks tumbled down the mountain. Tukupar waited for a long time. Dakwish came home and his mother met him at the door. 'There is someone here to see you, one named Tukupar.'

'I will roast him and eat him.'

'No, don't,' Dakwish's mother said. 'He is your cousin.'

'Then I will eat my cousin.'

Neither of the girls moved until Bird reached over and grasped Flower's hand.

Dakwish ordered his mother to be quiet and found Tukupar in his house. He tried to grab Tukupar, but being a powerful magician, Tukupar disappeared into thin air and reappeared. Dakwish was impressed.

Dakwish went outside and brought in meat. He offered it to Tukupar, who did not eat it but ate instead the two rabbits he'd hidden. It was dark, so Dakwish did not see that Tukupar had eaten rabbits rather than the meat he'd offered. 'Ha, ha. You ate human flesh,' he said. "Now you are like me."

The storyteller stood, paused, and scanned the faces of the audience. He did a double take when he saw Maggie. He backed up a step, nearly tripping himself on the stump. With his eyes still on Maggie, he sat down hard.

She turned her head from one side to the other looking at the crowd thinking he might be staring at someone else. No. He was looking straight at her.

"I think he likes you," Jimmy whispered.

"I don't get why he's looking at me," Maggie said.

"I'm telling you, the old guy thinks you're hot."

Maggie elbowed her nephew in the ribs. "Knock it off."

The storyteller gathered his composure, and continued.

'I was hungry,' Tukupar said.

'Now you must dance,' Dakwish said.

'I do not dance well,' but he stood.

The storyteller rose from the stump and danced around it, then sat back down, but not before looking directly into Maggie's face again. He tilted his head and wrinkled his brow.

"Looks like he knows you from somewhere and is trying to figure out where he's met you," Jimmy said.

The old man resumed his story.

Dakwish sang a song for Tukupar, who danced even though he said he could not, and while he danced he broke his own arms and legs. Then he rubbed his arms and legs and they healed. Dakwish was impressed. Tukupar said, 'Now it is time for you to dance like I did and show me what you can do.' He thought of his plan to trick Dakwish.

The storyteller tapped his temple with his forefinger.

Dakwish danced into a wild frenzy. He cut off his hair with a knife and threw his hair away, tore off his legs and cast them aside. He flew around with only his body and head, then he broke his head apart. From the middle of his body, feather vine, pewish, grew and twisted around his head and torso and that is how he put himself together again.

Tukupar was unafraid. He threw gnats, sengmalum, into the eyes of Dakwish to blind him. Dakwish went crazy because he could not see. 'Heal me,' Dakwish said. 'I know you can.'

Tukupar thought about it and decided to cure Dakwish because he had a better punishment in mind.

Dakwish was smart, and could sometimes see into men's minds. 'You have bad thoughts about me. Why are you here?" he asked.

'Because I had a son and he is dead now. You know what happened to him.'

Dakwish said, 'What are you going to do to me if it was I who killed him?'

"Can we leave the girls here by themselves if we can see them? I want to talk to you for a sec," Maggie said to Jimmy.

"Sure." He whispered to the twins. "You two stay here for a minute and listen to the rest of the story. We'll be right back."

Jimmy and Maggie rose and walked to a shady spot where they could keep an eye on the twins.

"I'm not trying to tell you how to raise Bird and Flower, so don't get me wrong," Maggie said "But don't you think your little girls are too young to hear about cannibals roasting and eating people? All this stuff about killing and revenge can't be good for them, especially in the wake of those child murders. This is a damned gruesome story for children."

Jimmy put his hand up. "Stop right there. These stories have been told to children for centuries. Bird and Flower need to learn about native culture. You don't even follow the native ways, so why should I care if you approve?"

"Sorry, Jimmy. You're right. Let's go back."

As they made their way to their seats, the storyteller, still sharing the myth, tracked Maggie with his eyes until she took her seat. Several of the children in the front row turned their heads. One said, "What's he looking at?" The old man averted his attention back to the children. He leaned over them.

"...afterwards Tukupar went to the people of his village. 'You have to kill Dakwish for me.' He invited Dakwish back to his village. Right away Dakwish did a terrible thing. He killed a young boy. He pounded him into mush with a pestle and ate him. The boy's father tore at his hair in grief. When Dakwish was not looking, Tukupar signed to a man with a heavy war-club of oak, dadabish, and the man hit Dakwish on the back of the neck and knocked him down. Then the people pounded him with rocks until they killed him, smashing out his brains.'

Flower clamped her hands over her ears. Bird put a comforting arm around her sister.

Two men carried his body to a place near a spring and laid him down, covered him with wood, and burned him. When Dakwish began to burn, the sky thundered. There was a great noise and an explosion. Sparks went everywhere and Dakwish's spirit flew into the air. The people said, 'There he is flying away! The evil one has gone.'

"That is how Tukupar banished evil."

Bird and Flower sat frozen, their mouths open. They uncrossed their legs, leapt from their seats and ran to Jimmy and Maggie who waited a short distance from the circle.

"Daddy, Auntie, that guy actually cooked and ate people. It's so gross. He even killed a little boy," Bird said.

Bird and Flower put their arms around Maggie and clung to her, burying their faces into her chest. She folded them in an embrace and said. "You know none of this is real. It's only a story, a legend."

Jimmy kneeled down and reached for his girls who turned to him for comfort. With his arms around his daughters, Jimmy looked up at his aunt. "I guess you were right about them still being a bit too young for this."

But Maggie didn't hear what Jimmy said because her attention had shifted to the storyteller. After having made a beeline toward her, he stopped a few feet away. Staring at her, the elder tilted his head one way, then the other. He knitted his brows. He took a step back and his eyes shot open in recognition. He snapped his fingers. "I've got it. I *knew* I'd seen you before." He pointed at Maggie. "The Great Father, Cham-na', showed you to me in a dream-vision. You will stop hichakati."

"What is hichakati?"

"Wicked, evil. And, you are not listening to your mother. She has called you for a reason. She's trying to tell you who you are. She asked me to tell you this."

Without another word, the storyteller turned his back to Maggie. A thick knot of children pressed around the elder as the old man pushed back through the crowd to the center of the arena.

"That was weird," Jimmy said.

"Yes, very." An icy chill took hold of Maggie.

CHAPTER 34

Canada, Twenty-Eight Years Ago

From inside the cave, the boy listened to his mother talking to his father, "He's an innocent little boy, Noshi. He's scared. We must be patient with him."

"I'm not inn-o-sense, I'm hungry!" the boy shouted. "Gimme meat now..."

Northern California, Present Time

WINTER DESCENDED ON Wild River County like an angry beast. Heavy wet snow pummeled the roadways, caved in roofs, froze pipes. Jake was busy making coffee when Maggie walked into the office. She stomped her Sorrels on a throw rug, and peeled off her heavy mittens. "That better be French roast."

"Of course. Sit down. I'll bring you a cup."

"Thanks. What's up with you bringing me coffee? You don't do that. What did you do wrong?"

"Nothing. Can't a guy make a pot of coffee? I thought you'd like a cup when you came in," Jake said, pouring brew into a chipped white and blue mug.

"Don't give me that. I know you, remember? Something's up."

He placed the mug on her metal desk and sat down in his own chair. "Mingan didn't show up for trial this morning. No one knows where he is."

"He skipped bail. I wonder what the good Christian folks at his church think now? What's the story?"

"He was scheduled to attend a big revival meeting as one of the featured speakers yesterday at the east end of the county outside of Walnut Grove. He was to board a puddle jumper at the Wicklow Airport, but never made it. Some of the ladies from his church went to his house to check on him. No one home, but his truck's still there." Jake stood and moved close to Maggie's desk. "I know you don't want to hear this, but Mingan still might be around and he's got it in for you. I'm putting a protective detail on you until we find him."

"I don't think so. I'm not..."

"Shut up, Maggie. I'm doing this. We aren't taking any chances and I don't want to hear any crap from you about it."

—

After the violent ghost episode at Mama's, business boomed. Tourists and locals alike crowded in to buy a cup of coffee in hopes of encountering Iggy and Squiggy.

Maggie sat at a stool and talked with Dawn at barista bar. Since Maggie had last seen Dawn a few days before, the girl had dyed her hair Day-Glo orange into which she had tied green plastic beads in the shapes of vampire bats and skulls.

"Halloween was last month," Maggie said.

"Every day is Halloween to me, you know? Sally should post a big spooky sign in the window that reads 'The Only Haunted Bookstore & Coffee House in Northern California.' She held up her hands as though she were framing a marquee. "That's what I'd do if I owned the place."

"Since Mama's up for sale, why don't you buy it?" Maggie said. "Then you can put up any sign you want."

"Are you kidding? I work two jobs and can barely afford the mortgage on my puny condo."

"What's your credit score?"

"Perfect. I paid off my car last year and I pay my VISA balance every month."

"And, you have more than four years of equity in your condo, right?"

"Yeah?"

"You've been working at Mama's since you were a sophomore in high school, Dawn. You're 27-years-old. You could run this business with your eyes closed. Everyone in town knows you, too. I bet if you put your condo and your car as collateral, you could get a loan."

"I still need at least 20k for a down payment. Where would I get that?"

"Maybe I could loan it to you."

Dawn's eyes widened. "Are you joking? It'll take me forever to pay you back."

"I'm not offering you a free loan. I want 10 percent ownership in the business, and I expect 12 percent interest paid back within, say, five years."

"Wow. That would be so cool to own Mama's. I could have open mic nights and poetry readings, and..."

"Whatever you want. I'd only ask that you keep the name to honor Sally, and that you forever offer the same quality coffee at a low price. Oh, and I'd like you to expand your Celtic music offerings. More Chieftains and less Tim McGraw, and no rap."

"Anything else you want?"

"Nope. Run the business as you please as long as you keep the place open so I can get my mug of French roast when I want it."

"Deal." Dawn extended her hand. Her fingernail polish alternated on each nail, neon orange, chartreuse, crimson, silver and plum. She wore enormous silver rings on every finger, and bangle bracelets on her right arm from wrist to elbow. The women shook hands. Dawn's bracelets jangled in rhythm.

—

Sally sliced tomatoes for a salad, while Maggie shredded lettuce. The two women stood hip-to-hip at the kitchen sink making dinner in Maggie's cottage — homemade salmon chowder, garden salad and sourdough toast. "I'm going for another glass of wine. Want a refill?" Maggie asked.

"Naw. I'm already getting a little tipsy. I might burn the toast."

"Suit yourself." Maggie poured the wine. "I was waiting to tell you this until after dinner, but I think I have to tell you now."

"You have to tell me what?"

"I don't know if this is going to work out, but I think you have a buyer for Mama's."

"Really? Since that last deal fell through, I'll believe it when I endorse the final check. So, who is it?"

Maggie took a sip of wine, swished it around in her mouth and swallowed. "Ahhhh. You know? For a $9 bottle of wine from Tippy Top, this isn't half bad."

"C'mon. Tell me who is interested in Mama's."

"Don't you have to stir the chowder?"

"Dammit, Maggie. Who is it?"

"Dawn and me."

Sally spun around and faced Maggie. "What? No kidding?"

"I'll put up the down payment in exchange for 10 percent of the business and 12 percent interest. Dawn will use her condo and her car as collateral. We have an appointment with the bank tomorrow, and I've got a call in to your agent."

"She didn't tell me there were interested buyers."

"That's because I asked her not to say anything. I wanted to tell you myself."

"That's great. Dawn would be perfect, and I'd adore it if you were part of Mama's, too. I love Wicklow, but I'm really ready to get out of town, move down south, and start my new life."

"I know you have to go. I'll miss you, though."

"I'll miss you, too."

Sally folded Maggie into her arms. "With everything that has happened lately, I don't know what I would have done without you. You're a life saver." Sally kissed Maggie's cheek then broke their embrace. "I changed my mind about that wine. I need something in my hand to toast the new owners of Mama Winters' Bookstore and Coffee Shop."

CHAPTER 35

Canada, Twenty-Eight Years Ago

A day later, the liver was gone. Noshi brought in the heart, and with his antler-handled mule skinner, he methodically carved it into small even pieces. That's when Chepi broke down. "No, I can't. I will not eat my child's heart..."

Northern California, Present Time

WHEN JAKE ANNOUNCED his retirement, dozens of letters to the editor in *The Wicklow Daily* begged Jake to run another term. Jake was surprised when Happy said he planned to run. He wasn't sure Happy was best for the job, but he loathed the only opponent, Brock Hanley, the ex-LAPD officer and part-time underwear model who thought himself superior to Jake and Happy, "the country bumpkins," who ran the sheriff's department.

"Brock is an outsider, and doesn't know beans about Wild River County or the needs of its people," Jake told Maggie. "And, he's an arrogant asshole who everyone knows cheats on his wife."

Maggie knew Brock's wife enough to say hello, but other than that, they were hardly friends. The woman was a mousy little thing with freckles and pretty amber-colored eyes who seemed oblivious to her husband's philandering. Maggie referred to her as a 'stand-by-your-man' kind of woman who married for better or worse, in this case, worse.

Maggie entered the office to find Jake reading an article in the paper with the headline, "Choosing the Lesser of Two Evils is Still Choosing Evil." It was about the election.

"I read that, too," Maggie said. The people in this county really want you, not Happy or Brock."

"I'm done. I just want to fish and drink beer. Let's hope it's

206

Happy and not that prick, Brock, who the people elect. I don't know if Happy is up to the job. He's going to need some powerful mojo to pull this off. But, he's definitely better than Brock Hanley. Since I have to choose one evil over the other this election, I'm standing behind Happy."

Wild River County was plastered with campaign signs. "Elect Happy Ortiz for Sheriff, Make Wild River County a Happier Place to Live." "Elect Brock Hanley for Sheriff, A Leader With Proven Experience."

The door opened and Happy appeared. "Folks around here aren't too thrilled about my running for sheriff. Did you read all the letters to the editor?" He held a copy of *The Wicklow Daily*.

"It's not you. It's that everyone loves this curmudgeonly pig-headed guy here," Maggie said rested her hand on Jake's shoulder.

"What about you, Maggie? Do you love me?" Jake winked.

"Oh, shut up," she said taking her hand off his shoulder. She gave him a playful punch in the arm.

"Ouch." He rubbed his wounded bicep. "For a girl, you pack a wallop"

"You haven't seen anything yet, buster. I'll kick your ass." She laughed. "I need to tell you guys I'm working on a new angle for the investigation."

"Oh yeah?" he said.

"What sort of new angle?" Happy asked.

"One that'll bust this case open. We'll have our killer before the election."

"No kidding?" said Happy. "That's great news."

"Tell us about it, Mag," said Jake.

"Not quite yet. I'm figuring out a few things first. We'll have our meeting in a few days with the team and I'll discuss it then." She had no new angle, but the investigative team had become frustrated, was losing hope and with it, momentum. She thought if she lied a little, and word got around she was close to finding the killer, she would invest the team with renewed enthusiasm. Of course, now she had a big problem. Jake and Happy expected her to deliver her grand plan at the next meeting.

"I think I'll go home and spend some time with Rosa and the boys, if it's okay with you, boss." Happy said. "You two closing the office for the night?"

"Soon. We're going to go over a few things and then we'll head out in a couple of hours. Go on. We're not too far behind you, Jake said.

"Are you sure? If you need me, I'll stick around."

"Naw, go on home and have dinner with your family."

Maggie and Jake bid Happy a good night. As Happy walked out the door he tipped his hat in greeting to Sally as she entered.

"I've got a problem and I need a huge favor," Sally said to Maggie.

"What's up?"

"My car's dead."

"Need a jump?" Jake said.

"It's not the battery. Dawn already tried to jump it for me."

"No problem," said Maggie. "Take my truck home. I'll catch a ride with Jake when we're done here, and I'll bring you back in the morning."

"Thanks. It's been a bitch of a day. I feel a migraine coming on. I need to get home and sit in the dark for a couple of hours. Will your bodyguards be outside?"

"I wanted to call 'em off," Maggie said. "But, the sheriff insists I still need babysitters. There'll be a squad car in front of the cabin. I hope the rubes inside of it won't step out to piss on my Shasta daisies."

"Damn it, Maggie. This isn't a joke. Mingan is still out there somewhere."

"Leave it alone, Jake." She nodded at Sally. "Go. Take care of yourself. I'll see you at home later." She pulled her keys from her pocket and handed them over.

"I'm so glad you're my friend," Sally said.

Maggie smiled. "Back at ya."

By the time the two combed over all the evidence once again, and went through every piece of paper they had on the case, it was close to midnight.

"Whatever that new angle you're working out, I hope it's a good one. We need a break." Jake leaned back in his chair and stretched. "I'm beat. Let's get out of here."

"I'm with you. Since you're driving me home, why not come in for a glass of wine before you hit the road?"

"Sounds good."

Maggie put her arm around Jake's shoulders. "I've got a confession to make. I don't think you're going to be too happy about it, either."

"Fess up."

"There's no new angle."

"That's a dirty trick." He shrugged her arm off his shoulders. "What the hell do you think the guys are going to think when they find out?"

"Well, if it works to keep the guys excited about the case, who cares?"

"Yeah, but the team is going to be pissed off big time if you don't come up with it by our next meeting."

"As long as they keep looking for the killer...Let's get on the road. I'm missing my wine time."

The ride home was quiet, Jake and Maggie too exhausted to talk. All Maggie wanted was one or two glasses of wine with Jake, a hot bubble bath, and a good night's sleep.

Jake pulled into Maggie's drive way alongside the squad car. Jake rolled down his window and the driver in the squad car rolled down his and yawned. "Hi, Sheriff. Maggie."

"All quiet?" Jake asked.

"Dead," said the driver, who yawned again. The cop in the passenger seat stretched.

Jake pulled further into the driveway but before he even parked Maggie's heart began to race. Something was amiss.

Maggie surveyed the area. Her truck was parked in its usual place, everything looked normal on the outside. But *something* wasn't right. Ravens circled low overhead.

"I didn't think those birds were out like this at night," Jake said. "These are your ravens, right?"

"Yeah, ravens. Usually, no, not much out at night. Something's worked them up."

Maggie stepped onto the front porch with Jake on her heels. She halted and put her hand up to stop him. She turned to him and put her forefinger to her lips, then pointed to the front door. It was open a crack.

"Sally always locks the door," she whispered. "She's a fanatic about it." She drew her Glock, pushed the door open with her foot and stepped through. It was so dark inside that she didn't see Samantha, who yowled and hissed when Maggie's boot landed on her tail. Jake stayed close behind her, his weapon pulled. The men in the squad car opened their doors and stepped toward the cottage, hands on their holsters. As they approached the open door, Jake signaled for them to stay back.

"Sally?" Maggie called out. She whispered to Jake, "I'm going to her bedroom to see if she's sleeping." She walked down the hallway and tapped on Sally's door. "Sally?" No response. Maggie cracked open the door. The bed was unmade. "She's not here," she called out. "Jake, where are you?"

"The kitchen. Don't come in."

"What do you mean?" Maggie hurried to the kitchen.

Jake blocked her way. "Please, Maggie, don't go in there."

Maggie shoved her way passed him and flipped on the light. In the middle of the floor Maggie saw three things. An overturned chair, a lake of blood, and her best friend on the floor face up. Sally's neck was twisted at an odd angle, her heart cut from her chest.

CHAPTER 36

Canada, Twenty-Eight Years Ago

The boy bolted to his feet, "Daddy? This is rabbit, right? Tell Mommy this is rabbit. Sheshebens is outside in the ground. You'll see." He ran outside and frantically dug with his bare hands into the snow covering the grave. His father pulled him away. The boy kicked at him and screeched. "Lemme alone! I wanna see Sheshebens. I hate you..."

Northern California, Present Time

OTHER THAN MANDATORY counseling after the Bay Area shooting incident, Maggie never had been under the care of a therapist. "Hard work is what takes care of mental issues and trauma, not whining about your problems to some hack Voodoo doctor. What a phenomenal waste of money and time." But Sally's brutal murder dropped Maggie into the open jaws of insanity. When she broke down at the memorial service, she knew she needed help.

Dawn held a Wiccan service and a wake at Mama's. A priestess in a flowing purple garment, wearing a pentagram around her neck the size of a dinner plate, performed a beautiful passage rite. Hundreds of people turned up. Mourners spilled out of the store and into the streets. The fire marshal, who was fond of Sally, and one of her best customers, held back as long as he could, but for public safety, he had to intervene. In a respectful tone, he asked everyone to disburse. The mourners drove to the Trinity Alps. There would be another ceremony, and then the priestess would scatter the ashes. Maggie remained behind. "No, I can't do this. Dumping her ashes is too final," she said to a woman who'd offered to drive her.

Maggie held it together, almost. After the ceremony, she caught up with Jake. "I don't want you to say anything, not to anyone, not to me, but I need the number of that shrink you went to after Shelly died. I feel like I'm bleeding out emotionally, mentally, in every way. I'm losing it, Jake." She leaned into him and sobbed.

He held her, rocking her back in forth in his arms. "Everything is going to be okay."

The therapist, a beautiful soft-spoken woman from Guatemala, Dr. Jessie Ochoa, turned out to be a competent, highly skilled counselor. She recommended a combo of anti-depressants and anti-anxiety meds and scheduled twice-weekly hourly sessions. Maggie did not object.

With Jake's urging, Maggie put in for some time off, and got online to research quiet B&Bs on the Oregon coast. She hired a neighbor to feed the cat and chickens, spread out a bucket of corn for the ravens, packed the Chevy and drove Chester to Bandon. On purpose, she'd left her cell phone at home, and did not share with anyone where she was headed.

It was bloody cold, but every day she bundled up and spent hours walking with Chester on the sand. Every night, she sat in a bubble bath so hot it nearly blistered her skin, downed a full bottle of pinot noir and cried. After, she'd put on a pair of chenille pajamas, curl up on the plush bed with her arms and legs thrown over her bloodhound, the sound of the surf lulling her into blessed, dreamless sleep. She ate very little. She didn't brush her teeth, didn't brush her hair, and didn't care if her clothes were clean or dirty, pressed or wrinkled. All she wanted to do was walk, bathe, drink wine, cry and sleep. It was the first time in Maggie's life that she felt hopeless.

One morning, she climbed out of bed, and flung open the curtains to let the daylight stream into the room. "Okay, Chester. I'm done moping. Let's go home. I gotta catch the sonofabitch who did this to Sally." She packed, then sat on the edge of the bed, and cleaned and oiled her side arm.

She really didn't feel like going anywhere, or doing anything, but she forced herself to shower, and eat a small breakfast of toast and coffee. Chester jumped in the truck and waited while she went inside the office to pay her bill. She walked back out into the thin morning air, and took a deep breath. *Jake's right. It's going to be okay, especially after I kill that murdering psycho.* She and Chester headed south on Highway 101 toward Wicklow, and except for a fuel stop, she drove nonstop to her cabin.

———

The cleaning crew had done their best, but where Sally had bled was a pale pink stain on the plank flooring of Maggie's kitchen. By herself, she pushed and shoved her heavy trestle table, solid wood chairs, the bulky antique buffet and china cabinet out of the room, got down on her hands and knees and scrubbed the floor with every cleaner she could find. Her knuckles and knees turned raw, swollen.

Maggie emptied the spare room where Sally had slept. She put a single piece of jewelry into her pocket, an amethyst and pink tourmaline dragonfly pin she'd given to Sally as a birthday present years before, and stuffed the rest of Sally's belongings into plastic trash bags and threw them into her truck to give to the local Goodwill. She went into the bathroom and unloaded all of Sally's toiletries into a waste basket. First, though, she opened a small cologne bottle. Jasmine perfume filled the room and brought back of flood of memories. Sally had worn this particular cologne since she was a teenager, and used it every day. Maggie allowed herself a moment to inhale the essence of Sally, and to remember better times, then she threw out the cologne, carried the basket outside, dumping it into the larger trash can, slamming the lid shut.

She moved the rest of her furniture out onto the porch and brought in gallons of frost white paint. She painted her entire cabin, the bedrooms, the hallway, living room, bath, and kitchen one coat after another until not one trace of Sally's death remained.

CHAPTER 37

Canada, Twenty-Eight Years Ago

"Time for a walk," Noshi said to his son. He picked up the boy who kicked and snapped at him, growling like a snared badger...

Northern California, Present Time

JAKE ORDERED JOHN Winters' arrest and charged him with murder. The FBI agents questioned him in relation to the child killings. Because of his threats to Sally, and the manner in which she was murdered, he was their prime suspect. When the investigative team wanted to know about Maggie's breakthrough, Jake deflected their questions. "Right now, we are going to stay the course. Any breakthrough that Maggie might have found before Sally Winters' murder no longer applies. We are playing a new ballgame now."

When she showed up at the office, the first thing Jake asked Maggie was, "You up for questioning John?"

"I want to talk to him in the worst way, but Dr. Ochoa doesn't think it's a good idea, and I probably would strangle him anyway. It'd be better for everyone if I stayed away from that piece of trash." She squeezed her eyes shut, and massaged her temples with the fingers of both hands.

"Maggie, you've been under a lot of pressure. I don't think you're ready to come back to work. Take a few more days off."

"I can't sit on my ass and do nothing while kids are dead, while Mingan is out there somewhere, and John Winters is in a warm cell getting three squares a day, and his wife, my dearest friend..." She dropped into a chair and put her head in her hands. *Jesus, I'm a mess.*

Jake extended his hand to comfort her. She moved away from his touch, grabbed a paper napkin off the desk, wiped her face, and stood. "You're right. I'm not ready to come back. I'm outta here. Please don't call me. I need some time to myself."

"Take as much time as you need. I'm here for you."

"I know Jake. You always are here for me. Thanks."

Maggie walked down the street toward The Silverado oblivious to the townspeople's greetings.

She sat on a stool at the end of the bar. The place was empty, cold and dark. No music on the old juke box. The bartender was a young guy with a thick pockmarked nose, one gold hoop earring, and long thin brown hair tied back into a ponytail that looked like an emaciated rat's tail. She didn't recognize him.

"What'll it be?"

"Pint of Harps."

He drew the ale from a tap and placed the full pint before her on a kelly green bar napkin.

"Want to run a tab?"

"Yeah," she said, and downed the Harp in four long gulps. "Another," she said, pushing the empty glass over to the barkeep. "Add a double Jameson back." The guy didn't look old enough to be drinking booze, let alone serving it. Maggie stared at him.

He walked to her, wiping a glass with a bar rag. "Too bad that lady from Mama's was offed."

Maggie responded by draining her whiskey in one mouthful. "Another," she said.

"Another *double*?"

"Got a problem with that?"

"No. No problem at all."

The bartender poured the whiskey and placed it in front of Maggie. "I heard Mama's is haunted, and that lady who owns it is a witch."

Maggie's narrowed her eyes. "Look, you little acne-faced dick. Pour the drinks, and don't talk to me." She downed the second double whiskey and gulped her ale, draining the glass, slamming it hard on the bar.

The kid pointed to a sign behind the bar that read *WE RESERVE THE RIGHT TO REFUSE SERVICE TO ANYONE.* "If you don't want to talk, that's up to you. But either treat me with respect, or pay your tab and go."

Maggie scooted her stool back, stood, and picked up her empty beer mug. She drew back her arm and threw the mug with such force it shattered the mirror behind the bar. The kid's eyes popped open with fear as he reached for his cell phone.

Oh, why did I do that? "Look, I know the owner here. I'll settle the bill and leave a substantial check to pay for the damages, and get out. I promise to make things right."

The kid put his phone down, and leaned over the bar into Maggie. "Give me $200 besides what you owe, and I won't call the sheriff."

"Guess what, asshole? I *work* for the sheriff's office." She pulled aside her jacket to expose her shoulder holster and Glock. She closed her jacket, retrieved her ID, and put it in his face, holding it there while she talked. "Go right ahead and call the sheriff. His name is Jake Lubbock. I'll be happy to tell him you attempted to extort an officer of the law. By the way, my name is Maggie Sloan, and that 'lady' who was murdered in my home has a name, too, Sally Winters, and she was my best friend in the world, you scrawny little weasel." She tucked her ID away, and walked out into the blinding sunlight.

As she climbed into her truck, she smiled...*I can't wait to get home and tell Sally what happened today*...then she remembered.

———

Maggie was pleased Jake had called off her protective detail. She needed alone time, and wanted no one on her property, no one at her door, no one anywhere near. She walked into her cabin to Chester and Samantha's greetings. "You two hungry?" She scratched them both behind their ears. The house still smelled of fresh paint although the walls and floor had long dried. She picked up a small framed photo of Sally and her at a beach in Arcata when they were kids, maybe five years old. After Sally's death, Maggie kept the photo on her fireplace mantle. In the photo, two little girls squatted side-by-side building a castle. Their tiny bodies, one fair and bird-like, one darker, more substantial and taller, were covered in sand. "I'm so sorry about what happened to you." Maggie spoke to Sally's image. She put the frame back on the mantle, lit a small lavender candle, and placed it in front of the photo. It was then, she smelled it. Jasmine. Sally's signature scent. *I must have somehow left a vial or bottle of it somewhere.* She looked everywhere, in the bathrooms, the bedrooms, the kitchen, and living areas. She even overturned the couch cushions. The fragrance eventually faded away.

Her cell rang. She fished the phone out of her pocket, checked the caller ID and pushed the talk button. "Danny, what's up?"

"No, it's not Danny. It's Cathy. Danny is down at the site workin' late. I want to tell you we are havin' a Yurok blessing ceremony for Sally to help her on the boat to the other side of the river. It's on Saturday. You come 'bout one o'clock or so. We are sorry about that girl. We know she was the best friend you ever had. We loved her, too. She was family." Cathy hesitated and lowered her voice. "It must have been mighty awful for you to find her that way right on your floor. You okay, now?"

"Not really, Cathy, but it's nice of you to ask."

"You need me or Danny? We'll be there to your place when Danny's done workin' tonight."

"No, no. Thanks for offering, but it's better that I'm alone right now, I just..."A vehicle's tires sped on her gravel driveway. "Cathy, I gotta go." She clicked off her phone, parted the drapes and looked out as a truck peeled away in the dark. *Mingan Metchitehew, if that's you I'm putting you on notice...come around here again and you're one dead motherfucking Indian.*

—

Danny prepared a salmon feast. A shaman, a Yurok woman with white hair to her knees, showed up in full regalia to perform the ceremony. Traditionally, at death, the Yurok people painted the body with soot and inserted a dentalium shell through the corpse's nasal septum, taking great care to avoid contamination through corpse contact.

Since Sally had been cremated, and her ashes scattered over the Alps, there was no body. The Shaman would not have to deal with a corpse for which she would have charged an exorbitant fee because of the contamination risk. In place of a body, the shaman built an altar on a stump that included Sally's framed image. The photo was adorned with a bit of soot, and in front of the frame, the shaman placed a dentalium shell.

Maggie recalled this photo. It was taken at a Bear Dance a few years back when Sally sat on that same flat rock where she and the twins encountered Mingan alone. So much had changed in such a short time.

Sally was murdered, but since the killer had broken her neck rather than using a war weapon, she was not entitled to go to the willows where she would dance forever. But, because Sally was a good woman, once her spirit went below and crossed the river, it would be released to the sky rather than the dark place.

The Yurok believe when the boat crosses the river, the deceased will never walk the Earth again. If the boat, however, tips over in the river, the deceased will reappear as a ghost.

The shaman sang songs for the dead. Danny and other men manned the drum. There was dancing. No whites were there, only Yurok, Wintu, Modoc, Hoopa, and a few half-breeds, like Danny and Maggie. All knew Sally from around town or the Bear Dances. *She would be pleased to know she was honored in this way.*

The glow of the firelight reflected off the glass covering Sally's photo. Maggie stared at the picture so long her eyes shifted out of focus. Sally's image grew fuzzy. Maggie's heart thumped hard against her ribs. She inhaled sharply when she thought she saw her friend's head move and turn toward her. Sally's smile grew wider, more brilliant. Her eyes closed then opened again. The wraith stood, walked out of the framed photo with her arms outstretched, and leapt off the rock. There she was, as she always had been, petite, bright, with a warm honey smile. *Can't be*. Maggie blinked hard. She scanned the crowd to see if anyone witnessed Sally walking toward her looking so vibrant, so real, and so alive. The fragrance of jasmine filled the air.

Sally came within an inch of Maggie, and whispered, "I love you, my dear friend. And by the way, the boat tipped over."

CHAPTER 38

Canada, Twenty–Eight Years Ago

Noshi tightened his grip and carried his son down the road. He walked until the little boy calmed down.

"A beautiful day, don't you think?" Noshi said, standing the boy on the frozen ground.

"Yes, Daddy..."

Northern California, Present Time

FOR MANY MONTHS, things remained quiet in Wild River County. Other than the standard snow storms, life was smooth, simple even. Mario Panetti's book became an international bestseller, and Warner Bros. planned to make it into a much-hyped movie due out at Christmas. Angelina Jolie contracted to play the part of Maggie Tall Bear Sloan. Mario had become a sensation in Italy. "I'm boycotting that fucking movie it's screened here," Maggie told Dawn one morning over coffee.

Thanksgiving, Christmas, and New Years passed uneventfully. On May 15, Flower and Bird celebrated their birthdays at Danny's place. There were a dozen screaming kids, a piñata in the shape of a star, and a Dora the Explorer cake. Maggie and Jimmy took the children to the creek for a game of hide and seek. They sat on the flat rock to watch them.

"I can't believe the girls will be starting second grade this year," Jimmy said. "Hard to fathom those girls were only six when they rode their bikes all the way out here."

"They were always precocious, Jimmy. I think they'll end up as doctors or captains of industry, or something."

"No news of Mingan's whereabouts?"

"No. The FBI guys are putting in a lackluster effort to find him.

I heard they are following up on a lead in Ontario. Jake's pretty sure he's nowhere around here now, so he pulled his deputies off the search."

"Since the killings in Wicklow started when Mingan arrived, and stopped after he disappeared, do you think he's the monster?"

"Oh he's a monster all right, but I don't know if he's the one who killed all those children, Bobby Jenkins, and...Sally." *God, she missed Sally.*

———

It was planting time again. Maggie decided to double up on her tomatoes and squash this year, and had mapped out a great herb garden. At one time, she'd planned to become an herbologist. She studied with the famous Shannon Flowers from Ashland, Oregon, and wanted to make her own tinctures. She resumed her studies, and with healing balms and tinctures in mind, she planted rue, lemon balm, lavender, clary sage, peppermint, Oregon grape, and bought a Hawthorne sapling. Although the case was not yet solved, her hours working in the sheriff's office with Jake and Happy were cut back to the point where she was overcome with numbing boredom. Gardening, Gaelic lessons, and herbology classes helped fill her days, but she needed something more.

Once or twice each week, Jake or Happy dropped by. She stopped into Mama's to have coffee some mornings, The Dandelion other mornings, and hung out by herself at The Silverado when the Ulster Boys played. She took long walks in the forest with Chester. The dogwood trees were in full bloom, and her tulips, jonquils, and hyacinth created a fragrant color show at her front door steps. She visited Danny, Cathy, Jimmy and the girls on Sundays, and drank...a lot.

Her twice-weekly sessions with Dr. Ochoa seemed to be helping some, at least she dealt with things better. The therapist recommended anger management classes, which Maggie declined.

"I need to be pissed off right now," she said. "I don't want anyone taking away my anger."

Then the dreams started again. She had finished putting in her heirloom tomatoes. It was a sunny afternoon, so she decided on a nap in the hammock. As she rocked herself to sleep, she felt her body lift into the sky, and she was a raven again, among other ravens, flying over the Trinity Alps.

She wondered why she'd never noticed that tiny cabin tucked away in the woods near White Cliffs, well concealed beneath the old growth firs and pines. A narrow deer path led to the cabin and around it, and what looked like a set of human foot tracks ran from between the trees to the back of the cabin. The tracks were almost invisible because the slender trail was overgrown with weeds and forest grasses. She flew closer. The cabin appeared deserted, as though empty for years. Part of the rock chimney had tumbled down, and the windows were broken, some boarded up with plywood, others cracked.

She perched on a window ledge and peered inside. The walls were painted bright red, blue, and yellow. Bunk beds with comforters printed with Mickey and Minnie Mouse characters were on one side of the room. There was a large painted wooden box overflowing with children's toys, and against one wall, in a tidy row, stuffed animals and dolls. A tidy kitchen with a bright red table and three chairs was at the other end of the room.

Someone, a tall man with blonde hair, stocked the cupboards with Spaghetti-O's, Kraft Macaroni and Cheese, Lucky Charms, Oreos and Hershey bars. She cocked her head and watched. Everything so clean inside, so bright, not at all like outside.

The man stopped, and turned toward her. It was not a man, but the monster wearing a blonde wig. She cawed. He pointed a finger at her and said "Catch me if you can, Pukkukwerek," and laughed.

When Maggie awoke, her pulse was out of control. "Oh my God, Chester. He's still here."

For three nights in a row afterward she experienced the exact same dream. Each time the monster said, "Catch me if you can, Pukkukwerek."

The morning after the third dream, she dialed Jake. "He's still around."

"Who is still around?"

"The monster. He never left, he's not behind bars, and he's preparing to kill someone else. Could be Mingan if he's hiding out in the forest, but our guy is not John Winters for certain."

"And, you know this how?"

"Never mind about how I know. I'm asking you to please trust me on this."

"Let me guess. You dreamed it."

"Don't condescend to me, Jake. The guy is somewhere close. The ravens took me to a cabin near White Cliffs where he keeps the kids. We have to reopen the investigation full bore, get those deputies out there to look for Mingan, and find that cabin."

"Maggie, no one has lived in that part of the forest in nearly a century."

"Damn it all to hell, Jake, listen to me. I was right about the Sorenson kids. I knew how to find Flower and Bird when they were missing. Don't shut me down."

"I'll look into it, but I really don't think Mingan is even in the county. He may not even been in the country. The FBI can't find a trace of him. Relax a little, and let me take care of this later."

"Later? Are you fucking kidding me? That monster is going to kill someone else. I know it."

"Nothing has happened since Mingan skipped bail. I'm telling you, it's okay."

"No. It's not okay. There's a lull now, but he's going to slaughter someone, maybe more kids, and you're telling me to...you patronizing jerk!" She clicked off her phone, picked up a cut glass flower vase from her mantel and crashed it to the floor.

She crossed the room to her booze cabinet, opened a bottle, and poured herself a water glass full of Jameson's, downed it, and sat down to her computer to start once again researching information on cannibals, serial killers, and child murders. "I'll find the sonofabitch myself," she said to Chester. "Screw Jake Lubbock."

—

Maggie missed five appointments in a row with Dr. Ochoa, refused to answer phone calls, e-mails, or text messages, and would not open her door even when Dawn and Jake stopped by. When she missed several Sunday family dinners in a row, Cathy, Danny, Jake and Happy all showed up on her front porch.

"Maggie, it's me, Danny. Open up, will you? We're concerned about you."

"Thanks. I'm fine. I've got work to do. I'll see you later."

"I've got homemade blackberry jam and some elk jerky right here for you," Cathy said. "I bet you haven't been eatin' in some long while and I'm mighty worried."

"Thanks. You can leave it on the porch."

"Your nice tomato plants are all dead now, too, and your flowers, all dried up."

"I'll plant new ones later, Cathy."

"Would you open the goddamn door so we know you are okay?" Jake said.

"You bastard. I'm in here doing work you should be doing. I'm finding that child-murdering son-of-a-bitch on my own. I'm figuring out who killed Sally, too. So, if you don't want to help, go back to jackin' off and leave me alone."

"If you don't open the door, Happy and I'll break it in. You've got to the count of ten. One...Two...Three...Four...Five...Don't test me, Maggie. I've had enough of your shit. Six...Seven..."

"All right, all right, dammit." Maggie opened the door.

"Oh my God," Cathy said when she stepped in after Jake. "You have an awful mess in here and you look terrible."

"Jesus H. Christ," Danny said.

CHAPTER 39

Canada, Twenty-Eight Years Ago

"Your brother died so you could see many beautiful days like this." Noshi said to the boy.

"Uh, uh. He fell down and got hurted and he died. That's all."

"No, no. His spirit knew the avalanche would come. Your brother made a big sacrifice so you can grow up to do great things. You will honor him. It is an insult to Sheshebens to refuse his heart." Noshi paused. "Our people tell the story of an ancient legend. Do you want to hear it?"

The boy nodded...

Northern California, Present Time

DISHES WERE PILED so high in Maggie's kitchen sink that some had fallen and broken into pieces on the floor. Ants partied on the stove. Roaches scuttled under the refrigerator. The floor was so filthy it could double as fly paper. Piles of dog feces hardened in the living room, and Samantha's cat box overflowed. Burrito wrappers, dirty glasses, mugs, some with moldy coffee still in them, covered every surface of every piece of furniture in house. The bed had not been slept in for quite some time, but on the couch was a sweat-stained pillow, a wadded up filthy cat hair-covered comforter, and crumbs of stale food. The vase Maggie threw after her last phone call with Jake was still exactly as it was when she threw it, shards of crystal scattered everywhere.

Maggie's hair was matted. Her head looked like it was covered in bad dreadlocks. She stank of sweat and booze, and her clothes were so covered with bits of dried food, coffee stains, and wine spills it was nearly impossible to tell what color she wore. She looked as though she'd lost fifteen pounds, gaunt, vacant eyed, and pale.

Chester whined when everyone entered. He walked out the door, tail between his legs, and lifted his leg on the now dead Hawthorne sapling. Samantha crawled under the couch. There were dozens of ravens perched on every outside sill, and the house siding beneath the windows was covered in bird feces. Maggie didn't care.

She let Cathy lead her to the bathroom and strip off her foul clothing. Cathy ran a hot shower and practically pushed Maggie into it. "Wash your hair real good. I'll find a comb to see if I can't get out those tangles."

When Maggie at last emerged from the bathroom, she looked and smelled better, Happy, Jake and Danny had already grabbed trash bags, brooms, mops, buckets and were busy scrubbing. Happy opened all the windows. "Jesus, it stinks in here."

"Sorry, everybody. I've been so focused on the case, I guess I forgot to take care of a few things."

"Have you even fed Chester and Samantha? What about the chickens?" Danny said.

"I'm not a complete ditz," Maggie said. "Of course they've eaten."

Jake hauled out a huge garbage bag full of trash. When he walked back in he said "Everyone, continue with the clean-up, I'm taking Maggie for a hamburger. She and I need to talk."

Maggie climbed into Jake's truck. "Jake, I'm sorry. I don't mean to be, so, well, you know. I guess I can be difficult."

"Difficult? You are a complete pain in the ass."

Maggie looked the other way, not wanting Jake to witness her shame, her exhaustion.

"The thing is," Jake said. "You've got some sort of sixth sense or women's intuition, some damn thing. I don't know about these spooky dreams and other weird stuff I can't explain going on with you, but there's something to all this. You were right about the Sorenson twins, Bird and Flower, whatever. It doesn't make any sense how that works..."

Maggie turned back to Jake. "I don't know how it works either, and I don't believe in supernatural woo-woo crap. You know that.

But I guess whatever is going on...the dreams...I've learned not to blow it all off."

"What I'm trying to say, I can see that you are determined to solve these cases, and I'm thinking you might have some psychic..."

"No way. I'm not a flaky fortune teller, Jake. This weird stuff has been happening to me since I was a kid, and it's nothing I can control...I want..."

"Would you shut up and let me finish what I'm trying to say?"

"Sorry."

"What I'm getting at is that we all have hunches and feelings, like I got a feeling that Mingan is somehow involved in all this. If he's not our guy, he's part of this, and I want to find him as much as you do. Besides that, I intend to fry the asshole for what he did to you."

"*Tried* to do to me."

"Okay, you're tough, Maggie. We all know that. But the point is..."

"Yeah, about that. What is your point exactly? You've been yammering on for ten minutes and I still don't know. You're worse than a teenage girl talking in circles for half an hour. Why don't you say what you want to?"

"Goddamn it, Mag. The point is I'm going to help you. The other point is...well..."

"Yeah?"

"The other point is...I'm in love with you. Have been for a long time. There. Said it."

"I know."

"Well?"

"Well what?"

"Well, will you go out on a real date with me sometime, like to dinner or whatever?"

"Sure."

"Really?"

"I said 'sure.' Didn't you hear me?"

Jake smiled.

"Let's catch this kid murdering psycho first, though, okay?"

"Okay." Jake's smile grew so big Maggie thought he'd crack his face.

———

Maggie was happy. She still grieved Sally's death, and she was more determined than ever to find the killer and to solve the case, but she felt good. Dr. Ochoa told Maggie she was making great progress and reduced her sessions to once weekly. Dawn worked hard and kept Mama's going full steam. Things were terrific with Danny, Cathy, Jimmy and the girls. Sunday dinners were the highlight of Maggie's week. The raven dreams were a nightly occurrence, and were mostly about the cabin and the blonde haired monster. She recorded them in a journal on Dr. Ochoa's recommendation, and shared them with Jake. The two of them tried to locate the cabin. Maggie sensed it, but after driving around the woods for hours, not even a deer path leading to a cabin. Nothing.

Although they had yet to go on their date, Jake and Maggie met every day at The Dandelion for lunch. Missy reserved a table near the back for them. Since Mingan jumped bail leaving the God-fearing members from Wicklow Christian Church in a lurch, and after the arrest of the two idiots who vandalized Maggie's truck, none of the "good Christian folk" harassed Maggie any longer. Best of all, agents Thompson and Marley left town, and continued work on the lead in Canada. "Good, those jerks can annoy the Mounted Police for a while. I'm so glad they can't be in two countries at the same time," Maggie said to Jake over a bowl of The Dandelion's homemade chili.

Their work on the case progressed at a nice pace. Happy took an active interest in the investigation.

"I guess that boy really wants to win the election," Jake said.

One afternoon, Happy encountered the two hunched over a computer screen, "You two are getting close, eh?"

"Yup," Maggie said.

"How close?"

"Real close."

"I think it's Mingan," Happy said. "It adds up. As soon as he disappeared, no more missing kids."

"Could be," Jake said. "I'm leaning toward Mingan, too, but she's not so sure," Jake pointed his thumb toward Maggie.

"Once you find him, we'll all know, I guess.' Happy said to Maggie. "You're closer to discovering where he ran to?"

"Not really."

"But, good news is we've got a strong lead on where the killer kept the kids," said Jake.

Maggie and Jake decided it was best to keep her dreams about the ravens under their hats. No one would take them seriously. "It'll jeopardize our investigation if it gets out that your dreams are our primary source of clues right now," Jake said to Maggie over one of their Dandelion lunches.

"Let me know how I can help. It would be great if we could catch that bastard before year end," said Happy.

"Keep things going around here until we do catch him, and focus on winning the election. That's all the help you can give to us right now," Jake said.

CHAPTER 40

Canada, Twenty-Eight Years Ago

"The old ones say if anyone eats the heart of a togquos child he will become strong and courageous. Your brother wants that for you. You will eat his heart and grow up to be a powerful and brave man. The more young togquos heart you eat, the stronger you become."

"Togquos? What's that, Daddy?"

"Twin."

"Eating a twin heart will make me strong?"

"Yes. The more togquos heart you eat the bigger and stronger you will get."

"Promise?"

"Promise."

"Gimme twin heart, Daddy. I will eat lots of togquos hearts." The boy smiled. The foul thing inside of him smiled, too...

Northern California, Present Time

MAGGIE AND JAKE pitched in to help with Happy's campaign. Maggie and Dawn held a fundraiser at Mama's. They hired a local band, posted three-colored flyers, and advertised in *The Wicklow Daily*. For $25 a head, dessert bar and unlimited coffee drinks included, the citizens of Wicklow crowded into Mama's. With help from Jake, Danny and Jimmy, they cleared a space in the middle of the store so people could dance. Dawn advertised the event as the "The Happy Dance." Maggie and Jake handed out bright yellow Happy Face buttons superimposed with writing that read "Make Our County a Happy Place." Besides the entry fee, there was a silent auction and a raffle, so the fund raiser netted some decent money, which Happy funneled into local TV advertisements.

Brock Hanley actively campaigned, too. He and his supporters started a letter-writing effort, targeting Happy's comparative youth and inexperience. The editor of *The Wicklow Daily* supported Hanley and published letters saying things like, "Why send a boy to do a man's job? Elect Brock Hanley for Sheriff, a real man with real experience."

"It's going to be a bloody hard race for Happy to win," Maggie said to Jake.

"Yeah, I know. We'll keep our fingers crossed. I'd hoped Happy might score the Latino vote, but other than *hola, cervesa,* and *gracias,* he doesn't speak a word of Spanish, so some of our more culturally engrained Hispanic community members aren't too keen on him. They think he's too Anglo."

"He's married to Rosa, though, won't that help?"

"I wouldn't count on it. He'll need a miracle to pull this off."

———

Maggie decided it was high time to clean out the hen house. "Their droppings and feathers piled so high, I can't find the eggs," she said to Samantha.

She raked with so much vigor and focus that she didn't notice the squad car pull into her driveway, and had no idea Jake and Happy were standing behind her.

"Hi there," said Jake. "Need a hand?"

Maggie jumped and dropped the rake on her foot.

"Ow! Dammit. What are you two doing here?"

"We were checking out a theft call in the neighborhood and thought we'd come by for a cup of coffee."

Maggie peeled off her gloves and put them on a fence post. "Sure," she said. "I'm about ready for a break anyway. What theft?"

"Old lady Brooks again," said Happy.

"Oh, yeah, what is it this time? Did her ninety-year-old neighbor lady climb on her roof and drop through the crawl space to steal a half a bag of almonds from her pantry again?"

"No, this time, she is convinced that a Mexican gardener broke in through a window to steal a box of panty liners and one of her winter boots," Jake said. "I told her all we'd have to do is look for a one-legged Mexican hopping around wearing her boot, and we'd have our man."

"Oh, jeez. We gotta call Social Services. That poor woman needs help," Maggie said.

"She also says she's seen Sally wandering around here. When I told her that Sally's ashes were scattered over the Alps, the old woman insisted she's seen her. She's delusional as hell."

The sky darkened. Maggie looked into the sky thinking a cloud had obscured the sunlight, but no, it was ravens. Hundreds of ravens circled on silent wings. By that time, Jake and Happy were staring upwards, too.

"What the...?" Jake said. "Where'd they all come from?"

The birds descended, cawing, knocking and squawking, more joining in. They flew in from every direction. The sky was black with ravens. Then...the ravens attacked. Swooping down with talons extended, they came within inches of the two men.

"Run for the house," Maggie shouted.

As the three sprinted for the cabin, a large raven swooped down knocking off Jake's hat. Another clawed Happy's shoulder, tearing his uniform, gouging his skin. Maggie and the men ran into the cabin and slammed the door behind them. Jake drew his service weapon, and parting the curtains, looked out the window. "What the goddamn hell was that all about?"

Maggie went to the bathroom and searched her medicine cabinet for some Neosporin and a bandage. By the time she tended to Happy's shoulder, the ravens had gone.

———

That night, the raven dream returned with a vengeance. Maggie flew over her A-Frame, over the river, and into the Trinity Alps, joined by an unkindness of ravens, more than she'd ever seen. "Why are you here?" she asked them.

The one flying closest to her said, "You are not paying attention, Pukkukwerek."

"Pay attention to what?"

"We are trying to tell you."

"I don't understand?"

"You want to find the monster. You need to find his lair."

"Yes?"

"Then pay attention. You must follow us in the forest."

"Follow you? I'm here now. Take me."

"Use your feet."

"What do you mean, my feet?"

Maggie awoke, her head in a fog. *What the hell? First ravens attack me and my guests, then haunt my dreams with riddles?* She recorded the dream in her notebook, and the next day when she arrived to the station, she handed it to Jake.

"What does *this* mean?" he said.

"I guess it means I'm supposed to follow the ravens on foot? Or, I'm supposed to *do* something with my feet? I don't know. Doesn't make any sense to me, either. I'm going to ration their corn if they don't stop messing with me."

CHAPTER 41

JAKE EYED MAGGIE, antsy to get out of the office and embark on her rare two-day weekend. She sighed, fidgeted and paced, nervous as a tick.

"How 'bout we go on our date this Saturday?" Jake asked.

"Not until the case is solved. That's the deal. Besides that, I plan on staying home this weekend alone. I'm locking the door, sleeping, reading, shutting off my cell, and listening to my entire *Chieftain* CD collection...all by myself."

"Sure you don't want company? I can get off early."

"Nope."

"Whatever you say."

"But, if you were to drop by on Sunday evening, and I happened to have a roast in the oven and I invited you to stay for dinner, to be polite, of course...as long as you don't call it a date..."

"What time?"

"Seven."

"What'll I bring?"

"Ice cream. You pick the flavor." She glanced at her wrist watch. "I'm outta here. See you Sunday." Maggie left without waiting for Jake's reply.

Jake's Turn

From the first time he saw Maggie, when they were kids, Jake was smitten. He couldn't talk to her without stuttering. He loved her so much it hurt, but she never seemed to notice. When they were in high school, he asked her to a dance. She said, "I don't go to those things." He was devastated. He sat home in his room all night long listening to his old albums. He played Three Dog Night's, "One is the Loneliest Number" over and over again. He was somewhat encouraged to find out later she'd not gone to the dance either.

He asked her out a few more times, but when she started working on her dad's old truck and John Winters hung around her all the time, he backed off. Still, whenever he masturbated or later, had sex with other girls, it was Maggie he always thought about. Maggie was chummy with Jake, but for sex, she hung out with the older guys from the college, and then she was accepted to UCLA and left. He didn't know if he'd ever see her again.

He met Shelly at The Silverado. They got tipsy and danced until last call. She took him home, and he never left. When they married, he knew he'd made a fine choice. She was cute with a great butt, and she was a decent, gentle woman. They both wanted kids, and he knew she'd be a wonderful mother. He loved Shelly even though Maggie would always be his greatest passion.

He'd been glad Maggie was in Los Angeles, then Washington D.C., and later Oakland, because if she were anywhere in Wild River County, married or not, he might still be pursuing her, hoping. Always hoping.

Less than four years into their marriage, Shelly was diagnosed with virulent inflammatory breast cancer, and within a couple of months she was gone. Once more, Jake Lubbock found himself alone. He missed Shelly. For a long while, he grieved her loss, but when Maggie left the Oakland Police Department, and moved back to Wicklow, he began hoping once again.

A date with Maggie Sloan. I've been waiting for this for over almost thirty years. Jake sat his desk chair and twirled around like a kid on a merry-go-round.

Happy entered the room. "I'm off, boss."

"What you up to this weekend?"

"I'm taking the boys fishing to the lake. They've been looking forward to it for weeks. Rosa and my daughter are going shopping, getting their nails done, girl stuff. How 'bout you? What you got planned for the weekend?"

"I'm working, of course." Jake twirled around in his chair again. "But, I might be having dinner with Maggie on Sunday night."

"No kidding?" Happy laughed. "Way to go, boss!"

—

By a narrow margin, Happy won the election for sheriff.

"He may not have great experience, but at least he has more integrity than that snake, Brock," Jake said. "But, honestly, I don't know how he pulled this off."

"I think it was our great campaign efforts," Maggie said. "I wouldn't worry too much about his lack of experience. As I recall, when you were first elected sheriff, you weren't much older than Happy, and besides, you'll be around to help out when he needs you. Good thing you signed up for the reserves, eh?"

"Someone has to watch out for that kid."

After spending every moment together for months "not dating" Jake invited Maggie out for a special evening. Over a candlelight dinner at Nito's, he proposed.

"You mean as in 'get married?'"

"That's the general idea."

"Hell, no. But maybe I'll let you live with me for a month or two as long as we keep things light and on my terms."

"Everything has always been on your terms, Maggie Tall Bear Sloan. I wouldn't have it any other way."

The following day, he moved into the A-Frame. Having lived since Shelly's death in a dank one-room efficiency apartment behind the sheriff's department, all his possessions, except a few pieces of broken furniture, which he donated to the local Goodwill, fit neatly into the cab of his truck.

—

One night, Maggie had stopped by The Silverado to listen to the Ulster Boys. She'd only meant to stay a little while, enjoy the music and have a beer or two, but by the time she arrived home, it was late. Jake was sound asleep with Chester, the two snoring in dead peace, sprawled out on the bed. Samantha, who was curled up in her favorite spot, the front room window sill, jumped down, stretched, and rubbed against Maggie. "How 'bout we leave the sleeping males alone and you and I cuddle out here tonight?" she said to the cat.

Maggie grabbed a comforter and a pillow, opened the window to let in the cool night air, and with a purring cat on her chest, fell into a bottomless cavern of sleep.

She was startled when she began to shift, black feathers protruding from her arms. The cat leapt off and scooted under the couch. "It's okay, Samantha. It's only me." She reached under the couch. Her fingers were already curling under, transforming. The cat hissed, tucking herself further under the couch until well out of reach.

When Maggie flew through the window, two ravens perched on her roof cawed a greeting to her. She settled near a large male. "Welcome, Sister. We've been waiting for you."

"I don't know why I'm here," Maggie said, hopping nearer to him. She scratched behind her ear and ruffled her feathers.

"Because, Pukkukwerek, you aren't doing your job."

"You do know that I'm not the pukkukwerek or even a raven. My mother is Yurok. My father Irish."

"Jajajaja!" The raven laughed. "You believe you have but one father and one mother only? Jajajaja! You think this is a dream and is not real? Your life is the dream, Pukkukwerek. The joke on you is amusing indeed. Jajajaja! Jajajajajajaaa!" The bird laughed so hard, he choked. He shook his head, composed himself, and then broke into uncontrolled laughing again. At last, spent from so much laughter, the bird coughed and caught his breath. "Now it's time. Fly with us."

In unison, the birds lifted from the roof. In a mass of caws and clicks, and a flurry of feathers, they set off for the Alps, Maggie in the center. As the birds flew, occasionally unable to contain himself, the raven broke into an isolated, "Jajajajaja!"

All became still save the sounds of wings through the air. The night grew cold and crisp. The lights from the town of Wicklow grew smaller and paler until they disappeared entirely.

The Trinity Alps felt different tonight, yet still beautiful, the night air glorious and the gibbous moon luminous.

The ravens soared higher into the starry night sky, then dropped lower skimming the tops of the trees. They circled, then dipped further landing on a tall rocky ledge. Nestled in a thick stand of conifers was...something.

"Pukkukwerek, don't you see it?" one raven said. "He's here."

—

Maggie awoke drenched in sweat. The cat had jumped back onto the couch and settled on her abdomen. "Jesus, Samantha. Holy crap."

She shared her nightmare with Jake, and the two re-doubled their efforts to find the killer but one month followed another, and they came up empty-handed. Although their search lost some intensity, Maggie never gave up. "I know he's out there. We'll find him."

Jake stayed by her side, patient, lending a hand when she asked him to.

—

Six months passed, and another six without incident. No missing twin children. No murders.

Dawn sold her condo and invested her money in Mama's, which had grown from a nice bookstore and coffee shop to the hippest music and poetry venue in all of Wild River County. As a bonus, the lore of the haunting continued to fascinate tourists and locals even though Iggy and Squiggy vacated after they'd last trashed the place. Mama's thrived. Maggie sometimes experienced strange occurrences at Mama's. Sometimes, she'd get a whiff of jasmine scent when no other customers were there. Sometimes, she'd see her coffee mug move a few inches on its own across a bistro table. She never said anything to anyone, and always chalked her experiences up to her imagination.

Once in a while, Jake and Maggie had dinner at Nito's with Rosa and Happy. In spite of the differences in their ages, the four had become tight friends. The more Maggie was around Happy, the more she liked him.

Happy imposed one rule when socializing, that they do not talk about police business, especially about the child killer. "I don't want Rosa and the kids exposed to the grisly details of those child murders. It would traumatize them, and besides that, I need a break from work. No shop talk when we out like this, please."

Jake complied. Maggie had a little more trouble keeping her thoughts on the investigation to herself. "You know," she might say between bites of spumoni ice-cream, "the coroner on the investigation did specify..." That's when Jake would kick her under the table.

"Ouch. Sorry. So, Rosa, how's your dad recovering after his bypass?" That would be it, until next dinner out.

Danny and Cathy lost their house and its sixteen acres to a foreclosure. When Maggie found out they were in trouble, she made an offer to her brother. "I've got a bit of money. Why don't you let me help you? Consider it a long-term loan."

"No. Can't do that. We have to figure this out on our own."

"You hit a rough patch, and your business is folding due to no fault of yours. This economy is kicking everyone's ass."

"That's the problem. Bear and Son's is going under, and in this economically depressed town of only 3,000 people, I'm not likely to find any kind of job that pays a decent wage. Even if I accepted your help, I won't even be able to afford the taxes on this place."

"What about Jimmy and the girls?"

"He'll land on his feet. As a master carpenter, and experienced remodeler, he'll find something down south."

"How far down south? Like Sacramento?"

"Like LA."

"You mean he might move that far away with Flower and Bird?"

"Cathy and I probably will move down with him. There's no work here."

Tears threatened Maggie's eyes. She looked away to compose herself, took a deep breath and turned back to her brother. "I'm so sorry this is happening to you. I don't want you and Cathy to lose your home. If you move away...God...you're my family."

"It'll work out," Danny said. "We'll see plenty of each other. And, thanks for caring. I'm damned lucky to have a sister like you."

Maggie and Danny embraced for the first time in years.

———

Although she remained in the sheriff's reserves so she could more easily continue her work on the investigation, Maggie grew antsy and bitchy after repeatedly hitting the same walls.

"I can't stand this," she said to Jake over a glass of wine on the deck. "We've been looking forever for that sicko child murderer. Maybe I need to step back, take a different approach. In the meantime, I have got to find something else to do before I kill something."

"Good idea. During those times you aren't hunting our psycho, why not volunteer, teach a class, take a class, set up your herbology practice, or join a book club? You can do whatever you want."

"What about you? You're on call for Happy, but as seldom as he needs you, you have to be getting bored, too."

"I'm thinking about writing."

"Writing? Like what? A book?"

"Yeah, I'm thinking of a mystery novel set in Wicklow based on our experiences."

"No kidding?"

"There's a local fiction writing group I might join."

"Okay with me." She grabbed the pinot noir. "More wine?"

"No, thanks."

Maggie shrugged. "More for me." She drained the rest of the bottle into her glass. "You know? I've always wanted to run my own bar."

"A bar? As much as you like to suck up alcohol, sounds right up your alley."

She smacked him in the shoulder. He laughed and folded her into his arms. "Maggie?"

"Yeah?"

"Sure you don't want to get married?"

"Hell no."

———

When The Silverado went up for sale Maggie bought it, and although she had no experience in the restaurant or bar business, she turned it into a profitable venture. Jake joined a writing group and outlined his crime novel. He read pieces of his work every night to Maggie, who considered him an absolute genius. "Grisham has nothing on you," she said.

They donated time to the local food bank, volunteered for Habitat for Humanity, went on double dates with Happy and Rosa, and Maggie, sometimes with Jake or Happy's help, but more often on her own, continued investigating the killings. When short-handed, or working on a difficult case, Happy would call in Jake or Maggie, or both, but as sheriff, he did a fair job on his own.

Although The Silverado was an Irish pub, rather than a western-themed bar as the name suggested, Maggie decided to keep it as is. "This way, I don't have to put out money for new signs, plus the pub is a landmark, familiar to everyone. It's profitable as it is and I don't intend to screw anything up," she said to Jake over coffee one morning.

Jake took a sip of coffee. "What about food?"

"I'm keeping the menu as is, simple Irish peasant chow.

Everyone likes the corned beef and cabbage, lamb stew with soda bread, and shepherd's pie."

"Smart business strategy."

"Of course it is. You wouldn't live with a *stupid* woman, would you?"

———

Diego Juan José Miramar-Sanchez Ramirez, the fine Irish chef, stayed on. Maggie gave him a raise. "As long as you keep up the good work, you'll have a job here forever. The customers love your cooking."

"I was thinking we could add in a beef and leek pasty. What do you think?" Diego asked.

"Sure. Meat pies are great. Go for it."

"How 'bout some salmon dishes, too?"

"Whatever you want, Diego. Pasty and salmon is fine. As long as we offer the favorites, and you keep customers coming through the door, you can put anything on the menu you please."

One slow night she closed the kitchen, and sent Diego home. The last drunken patron slipped off his stool near midnight, and crumpled uninjured to the floor. Maggie helped him to his feet, and sat him down. He'd left a wad of cash on the bar. She counted out what he'd owed her for the drinks and stuffed the rest of the money in his shirt pocket. He mumbled thanks, got up and staggered toward the door.

"I hope you don't live far. You shouldn't drive."

"No worries, dear. My apartment's a block from here. I'm walking."

Maggie escorted him out, locked the front door and hung the "closed" sign in the window. When she returned to clean the bar, a slight built woman with blonde hair was seated at the corner stool with an Irish coffee mug in her hand. *I don't remember anyone ordering a coffee drink tonight.* She walked behind the customer. "Excuse me. I didn't see you here. I'm sorry but we're closed."

The woman turned around and Maggie backed up so fast she nearly fell over a chair. "Oh, my God."

"Maggie, you really do need to listen to those ravens, and to your mother, by the way. But, honestly, shame on you. You should buy better quality beans. I never served crappy coffee like this at Mama's."

———

Maggie opted not to tell Jake about her encounter with Sally's ghost. As always, she was certain she'd hallucinated the entire thing given how tired she'd been and, of course, there were the four shots of Jameson's. After Sally's specter made the remark about the coffee, Maggie squinted her eyes shut. When she opened them, the apparition had vanished. "I really need to slow down on the drinking," she said to the empty bar. Nonetheless, she decided to buy a better brand of coffee.

That night, she slept on the couch with Samantha again. She'd not had the raven dream for a long while, and hoped for a good night's rest, but, no.

"Pukkukwerek. Wake up!" said a large male raven.

"What do you mean? I'm awake. I'm flying with you."

"You are not awake. You do not see."

"I see fine. Trees, mountains, the cliff. I see everything."

"You do not see. Use your feet."

"My feet?"

The ravens flew over the cabin, and for the first time, Maggie was clear on its location.

She *could* see.

When she woke, Jake was still sleeping. She wanted to tell him about her dream, to let him know that she had a lead, but thought better of it. "I don't want to hit him first thing with this," she said to Samantha. "It's Sunday." But, she couldn't push the image of the cabin out of her mind. She knew Happy was an early riser. She sent a text. *"I know where killer hangs out. Remote cabin. Getting close 2 finding the SOB. Can u lend a hand?"*

"Killings stopped. Need u 4 more pressing cases."

"I'll go alone if need be."

"No, not alone. Sounds like u r onto something. Got plans with sons. Lake fishing. Tell me where cabin is, & I'll go after."

"I want 2 go, & I'm sure when I tell him, Jake will want in."

"No prob. Thanks for staying on top of this. I'll text u when/where 2 meet. Stay put 4 now."

"OK. Thanks. Have fun with ur boys."

———

She started a pot of coffee, and while waiting for it to brew, made herself a strong Bloody Mary. Jake padded into the kitchen barefooted, his shorts and hair rumpled. "You didn't make it to bed last night," he said. "Is that a Bloody Mary? How can you drink vodka at 8 a.m.?"

"Don't give me any bull."

"Why didn't you come to bed?"

"Are you my mother now?"

"No need to be so testy. I missed feeling you next to me, that's all."

"Sorry. I don't mean to be a bitch. I guess I didn't get enough rest last night." She took a deep drink from her glass and said, "Tasty. Could use a little more Tabasco, though." Then shook her glass to rattle the ice cubes. "You and Chester were sound asleep when I got in. Didn't want to disturb you, so Samantha and I snoozed on the couch." She told him about her dream. "I finally get what the ravens are telling me. I think the cabin is only accessible by foot."

"So, that's why the birds keep talking about using your feet?"

"Exactly. We've been looking in the right area but only along logging and service roads. It didn't occur to me that we should look where motorized vehicles can't go." She told him about her text to Happy. "He said he'd help later today. He'll contact us when he's ready."

"All right," he said. "Let's meet up with Happy and we'll search one more time and see if the three of us can't find that cabin. Then let's take a break from all this."

"She handed him her Bloody Mary. He took a sip and made a face. "Shit, Maggie. That stuff could melt chrome off a bumper. You sure you're going to be sober enough to tromp through the forest today?"

"Want one?"

"Maybe later, and can you make mine with some tomato juice? Jesus!" He shook his head, and set the glass on the counter. He put his arms around her, pulled her into him and kissed her. "I hope you know how much I love you."

"I know." She kissed him back. When he left the room, she picked up the glass and downed the remainder of her Bloody Mary in hearty gulps. She poured coffee into two mugs and carried them to the deck.

"I'm so damned glad we can almost live a normal life like normal people," Maggie said as they settled on the back porch chairs with their mugs. "Once we find that bastard, we are going to Kauai for a month. Maybe Happy, Rosa and the kids can come with us."

"Deal," said Jake. "We've all been through enough to last a lifetime."

"It's going to be a beautiful week," Maggie said. "I thought maybe..." The phone rang.

"C.O.L.," she said pointing to Samantha curled up on her thighs. The acronym meant, 'Cat on Lap,' which also meant Jake would have to answer the phone.

A few minutes later he emerged. "I hate to do this, but I have to go into the sheriff's office."

"What's up?"

"Happy needs me. He's got long-standing plans to go fishing with his sons and I guess his new deputy, Mike, called in sick."

She sipped her coffee. "Happy did mention something about lake fishing. Well, I think I'll turn off my cell, then, and spend some time working on the case undisturbed. " She grabbed the phone from the top of the side table, and pushed the "off" button. "I'm thinking I might go to White Cliff and nose around for that cabin on my own."

"No, wait, I want to go with you. Besides, if Happy said he'd lend a hand, let's take him up on that. Three of us have a better chance of locating the place, and, once we find it, we don't know what we might run into. Good to have back up."

Happy was at the office when Jake arrived. "Get out of here and enjoy the day. Hope you hook a record breaking bass."

"I'll get back this afternoon. I've got someone to cover while we look for that cabin."

"Good deal. Now, go have some fun with your kids."

"That's all I'm doin' —fishin' and hangin' with my sons, by golly. I'm not going to even think about this darn place for a few hours." Happy moved toward the door, but as he reached for the knob, he hesitated and swung around to Jake. "So, what's Maggie up to while she's waiting for us? Sounds like she's onto something, but I don't want her to get worked up or she'll take off for the Alps to try to find this place on her own. You know how she can be, especially about this case."

"Don't I know it? Catching this killer is her life's mission. But, the way she's sounding, I think she's close to finding out who the psycho is. Good news is she promised to stick around the A-frame, do some research until we all meet. She even shut off her cell, I guess so I won't bug her." Jake laughed. "Now, go. Your boys need time with you."

If it weren't for watching a pair of flies copulating on his desk, Jake would be bored to the edge of madness. He thought he'd examine the old evidence on the serial killer while in the office.

They were missing something obvious, and he was certain if he looked again, he might figure it out, but his mind wasn't on work. He sat on the edge of the desk, banging his heels on the metal side, daydreaming about Maggie. He looked at his watch. *As soon as we're done looking for that cabin, and Maggie and I are finally alone tonight...hot damn.*

As he was about to refill his coffee mug, the phone rang.

"Jake?" Rosa, said. "Where's Happy? I thought he was in the office! God! I've been calling his cell. I've left four messages, and he's not answering or picking up. I need to talk to him right away. It's an emergency."

"What's wrong? Are you all right?

"I told you, I need to talk to Happy right now. I don't have time to chat, Jake. Let me talk to Happy. I am so upset that I can't..."

"Wait. Slow down and tell me what happened."

"One of the boys' has a ruptured appendix. It's bad. Juan's in surgery. I rushed him to the hospital myself. I'm worried sick. I called my parents, and they are on the way, but I can't find Happy anywhere. He must..."

"Hold on. Isn't Happy at the lake with *both* boys?"

Rosa hesitated. "No, of course not. What are you saying?"

"He told me he was going fishing with your sons."

"I thought he might be there at the office. I guess he could be at the cabin. But, there is no cell reception out there. I was hoping he might call in at least. The boys are with me. I don't..."

"What cabin?"

She sighed. "He'll be so angry if I tell you..."

"What cabin, Rosa?"

"He goes to his place near White Cliff to be alone. He says he needs quiet time to escape the stress. Everything gets to him because he's high strung. Always been like that. That's why he goes on so many solo hunting and fishing trips to Oregon and Washington. I wish he would take the boys, but he rarely does anything with them."

"I never knew anything about a cabin. Happy's never mentioned anything to me about it."

"He wants to keep it private. He calls it his 'secret lair.' I know he'll be upset I told you."

Jake drummed his fingers on the desk. "So, how often does Happy go to his cabin?"

"He hasn't been in a long time, but he used to go, oh, several times a year."

"How many times the last two years?"

"Three times," she paused. "No, four."

"Sure it wasn't more?"

"Maybe, why?"

"When was he there last?"

"Why are you asking me all these questions? I don't have time for this. I need to find Happy."

"I'm going personally to look for him, Rosa. If you answer my questions, it'll help me figure out where he is. When did he last go?"

"I need a second to think about it." She was quiet for a moment. "I remember. It was the weekend of Lucille Ortega's wedding. Oh, gosh. That was a long time ago, maybe a year."

"Where exactly is the cabin?"

"I don't know. He never took me there. I used to think he had another woman stashed, but then I realized that wasn't it. He always comes home in a good mood and says that he feels refreshed, his power renewed. He's one of those men who needs time to himself to recharge. That's all it is, really."

"I want you to stay at the hospital with your son. I'll look for Happy. I'm going right now to find that cabin."

"He'll be so upset with me for telling you."

"I think he'll want to know Juan is in surgery given how much he loves those boys."

"You're right. I'll wait for your call, then. If you hear from him, tell him to come directly to the hospital. Thanks, Jake. Bye."

Jake pulled up the investigation archives and crossed-checked the online database and calendar.

Every time sets of twins went missing, Happy was off work.

When Bobby Jenkins turned up murdered, Happy was off work.

When Mingan went missing, Happy was off work.

When Sally's neck was broken and her heart cut out, Happy was off work.

Jake combed his fingers through his hair. *I've known Happy since he was a scrawny kid right out of college. Can't be. Goddamn it! God fucking dammit!*

Jake dialed Maggie. Her phone went to voice mail. *God. That's right...she turned it off.* He locked the office, jumped into his car, and sped toward the Alps.

CHAPTER 42

WHEN JAKE ARRIVED at the fire trail leading to White Cliffs, he stopped his truck and stepped out. As he made his way through the dense brush, ravens gathered in nearby trees. He looked up at them, "I'm here. On foot. See? C'mon lead me. Please."

This is completely insane. Those birds can't do anything. But the ravens lifted from their perches and cawed and rocked at him. They flew a few yards west, settled into low branches and called out to him again.

I'll bite. Lead on.

The ravens flew low and slow, stopping, allowing Jake to catch up. He tromped through the woods, following the ravens. After about twenty-five minutes Jake came across a partial clearing, and there, concealed under a heavy copse of pine was a small, rickety cabin. *No way would I have found this driving an auto.* The ravens circled.

He hunkered down, weapon drawn, and made his way to the cabin, edging along the forest to keep hidden. The ravens landed in the trees surrounding the cabin.

He crouched beneath a window and peered in. Empty. He made his way to the front porch. "Happy, you in there?" He called out several times. No response. "Happy. Open up." No response.

Jake tried the door. Locked. He backed up a few paces and kicked in the door. He was unprepared for what he found inside.

The interior of the cabin looked like a tidy, children's play house. He searched through drawers, shelves. He found all kinds of foods that kids like, mac and cheese, cookies, Goldfish crackers. Everything neat and sorted by date. In a box, he found a blonde wig, and a carton of American Spirit menthol cigarettes. He opened a cabinet and found neat rows of Hershey bars. On the kitchen counter sat a beautiful red stag handled mule skinner adjacent to a well-used whet stone.

An accordion file protruded from a shelf. He pulled it down and placed it on the counter. In it was a ledger. On each page were taped photographs, all of children, twins, dozens of sets of twins, missing and dead including those in Wild River County. There were cataloged newspaper articles from Wild River County, Oregon, Washington and Canada about murdered twins. Some of the articles were dated many years before. *God, Happy started killing when he was only a teenager. How could I not know? Oh, God.*

In a corner, he spied a large brown leather chest secured with a heavy padlock. He searched the kitchen. Under the sink, he found a red tool box and in it a hammer. He squatted in front of the chest and broke off the padlock. He lifted the lid and pulled out all manner of Native American artifacts, feathers, beadwork, leather shirt, and more photos. Native American, Algonquin. *Happy isn't a Mexican. He's Indian. Of course.*

Then a notebook. When he opened it he found a list...a sheet with meticulously penned names of people, some he didn't recognize, others he did, including Bobby Jenkins and Mingan Metchitehew. All the names were crossed out, except one: Maggie Sloan. *He's after Maggie!*

A crackling noise outside the cabin door broke his attention. Jake swung around, dropped to one knee and raised his weapon. "Get in here where I can see you. Hands up."

No response. Jake crept around the perimeter of the cabin under the windows toward the door. He stood, plastered himself against the wall, and peeked through the door. *A rabbit. A damn rabbit.* He holstered his gun, and ran out of the cabin, leaving the door ajar. He sprinted toward his truck. The forest was dense, branches snagged his clothes, tore his skin. He kept running. He tripped over a log, fell, got up and kept running. *Oh, God, Maggie. Oh, God.* While still running, he grabbed for his cell and punched numbers. No reception. He ran and ran.

He reached the truck, jumped in and jammed on the accelerator, leaping over bumps in the road, the vehicle slamming down hard over ruts. He finally got through to the dispatcher and made his request for back-up, although he would make it there before anyone else.

He swerved around corners, missed a logging truck coming in the opposite direction.

Close call. Ravens kept pace with him, flying low. He gritted his teeth and floored the gas pedal so hard his knee popped and his thigh burned. *Oh, God, Maggie.*

CHAPTER 43

"WE'RE GETTING CLOSE to finding the slimy son-of-a-bitch, Chester. The dots are finally connecting." Maggie leaned over and scratched the dog behind the ears. "When we get that shit head, I'm buying the best magnum of champagne I can find and drinking it straight from the bottle." The dog looked at her. "Don't worry. I'll take care of you, too. I'm buying you a steak, and maybe I'll pick up a fresh trout fillet for Samantha. How's that sound?" Chester turned his big head to one side and licked her hand.

Since Jake moved in, Maggie rarely had time to herself like this. She put on her *Inishwen* CD and cranked up the volume. "Maybe, tonight, once I'm done going over these files, and after we find that cabin, I'll get back into my Gaelic lessons," she said. The cat meowed. "Yeah, yeah, I know. I need to take a shower and brush my hair, too. Not everyone is as prissy and neat as a damned Siamese cat."

Meow.

"Don't look at me like that. I never get a full morning to spend in my robe." Maggie sat in the niche by the window at her desk. A raven peered in and cawed. "What are you looking at? Didn't I buy good quality corn last time? "

She booted up her PC and resumed her research into the child murders. "Samantha, I see a clear pattern here." She stroked the cat. "I don't agree with Jake's assessment that we might be dealing with two killers, one a copycat, no offense. Our guy is working alone. No one knew the murderer kept the kids and fed them before he killed them. This sicko doesn't have access to the police records, so, a copycat wouldn't know."

Someone knocked at the door. She stood, closed her robe and crossed the room. She found Happy wearing his lopsided grin standing on her porch.

"Hi, there," she said. "Come on in. I haven't even showered and the place is a bloody mess."

"Oh, I don't care. Hope it's okay I stopped by. I know you were looking forward to the rest of the morning alone."

"Thought you were doing something with your boys. You're still in uniform."

"We had to cancel. Something came up. Since Jake is covering the office, I thought I'd drop in and talk to you about the investigation. It's been a long while since any twins have gone missing. What brought on this sudden interest to go looking in the forest for a cabin?"

The dog lumbered to him for a scratch. "Hi, big guy."

"He didn't even bark when you came in the door. Thanks a lot, Chester. Some ferocious watch dog *you've* turned out to be," Maggie said. "You wouldn't mind letting him out? He probably has to pee. Been in all day sleeping, like the lazy lout he is."

Happy let the dog out the door, closed and locked it, then returned to Maggie.

"You're getting close to finding who the killer is, yeah?" He grinned in a way that reminded Maggie of a little boy.

"I think we'll ID our killer before the week is out." Maggie smiled. "Are we about ready to meet with Jake and go find the cabin? I'll call him." She reached for her cell.

"Let's talk for a few minutes first, and formulate a plan. I could sure use a cup of coffee."

"No problem. By the way, I've been meaning to tell you something."

"Yeah?"

"I have to say I'm impressed with the dedication you've put into this case. You've been more than helpful, even though we haven't had anything to go on for a long while. I know some people were resistant to the idea of you being sheriff, but you always had my vote. Jake and I think you are doing a fine job."

"Thanks. Right now, let's catch this guy. What do you say?"

"I say, 'Hell yeah', and once we get the rotten child-killing prick, we'll invite you and Rosa over for dinner to celebrate."

—

His foot jammed on the accelerator, every muscle in Jake's body tensed. *Sweet God, please, don't let me be too late.* He redoubled his efforts and pushed down even harder on the pedal, swerving to miss rocks.

—

"What else have you got on the investigation besides the whereabouts of the cabin? And...out of curiosity, how did you even know about this place?"

Maggie looked away then back at Happy. "I know you want to know, and I promise I'll tell you the whole story later, but would you trust me for now?"

"Fair enough."

"The important thing is that after all this time, the pieces are fitting together. We are closer now than ever to finding out who this is."

"And who would that be? Not Mingan? I honestly think it is him, and that's where we need to focus our energy...on finding him."

"We know it's not some transient or Sally's husband. But we don't think it's Mingan. Besides, he ran off with his tail between his legs. He may even be dead, for all we know. I'm positive he's not coming back to Wicklow. He doesn't quite fit the profile of our killer, either. I think it's someone local for sure, and someone working alone. Even Jake is beginning to come around to that idea."

"Really? Well, that's fine news. You wouldn't mind if I stepped out back for a quick smoke?" Happy retrieved a pack of menthols from his shirt pocket.

"I thought you quit."

"Nerves." He rolled a cigarette between his fingers and examined it. "Rosa is having a fit about it. I had to promise her I'll quit, but I'm not quite ready."

"Thought you were a Marlboro Red man?"

"Sometimes I like menthol."

"I'm surprised you'd go for American Spirit menthols, though, I mean given...why not Marlboro Green?" She scrunched up her face. "Oh, never mind. Go have your smoke. I'm searching through a few more online articles. I'll put on a pot of coffee. We'll make a plan, and then we can meet Jake." Happy wrinkled his brow and his expression darkened.

"Everything fine with you?" she asked.

"I'm exhausted from working so long on this and coming up empty handed...it's been, what, close to two years? Maggie, really, I should close this case. We've got other pressing matters to attend to, and the taxpayers are not going to be happy to know how many man hours, resources and money we're spending on a dead-end."

Maggie's voice tightened. "You agreed if I stayed on in the reserves that I could continue to work on this. If you don't want to help, or if you have something more important to deal with, I'll do it on my own, but you will keep your promise, dammit."

"It's fine, Maggie." He put his hands up. "Settle down. You can work the case. Well...it's...I guess you really are getting close, right?" His forehead broke out in a sweat.

"Very. Hey, are you coming down with something?" She reached up to feel his forehead. "Maybe you need to get home to Rosa and let her take care of you. Jake and I can go to White Cliff on our own."

"I'm fine," he said moving his head away. "I want to know honestly, how close you are to catching this guy."

"I told you. I'll probably know who the murderer is before the week is over. You don't *look* good."

"I've got a stress headache. That's all." He reached up with one hand to massage the base of his skull.

"Well, I suppose you're entitled. Sheriff's job isn't exactly a piece of cake." When he didn't smile, she added, "There's aspirin in the cupboard where the coffee mugs are. Take a couple, go outside for your smoke, and I'll get the coffee going."

"Yeah, thanks, I think I'll do that." He walked out back without going for aspirin. The screen door slammed behind him.

Maggie ground coffee beans. Through the kitchen door, she watched Happy pace across her deck in hard anxious steps, muttering to himself, flicking his cigarette. *Something is really not right with him today. But...if he doesn't want to talk about it...*

She put on the coffee, then sat down to continue surfing the web. She input for the umpteenth time, "Child murders, Canada." Headlines popped up, and she scrolled through them looking for something she'd not noticed before. After pushing the "page down" button dozens of times, a decades old headline caught her attention. *Algonquin Family Trapped by Avalanche Eats Child to Stay Alive*

"My God," Maggie said after she clicked on the link.

A grainy photo appeared of a native family, a handsome man, a pretty thick-hipped woman, and slight built twin boys, five or six years old. As she read the copy, ravens battered her window with their beaks. "Get away," she pounded on the glass. They fluttered backwards but returned pecking the window even harder, cawing and knocking in a relentless, dissonant chord. "*More* corn? You damned birds are getting to be too expensive. I'm switching you to stale bread crumbs."

———

Each time he hit a bump on the logging road out of the forest, Jake clinched his teeth. His kidneys hurt. His hands, clinched on the wheel, turned from white to purple. He never lost speed. He hit a jack rabbit. He felt the thud of the body under his tires.

———

She returned to the screen, slipped her reading glasses over the bridge of her nose, leaned in and examined the photo. The caption read, *The Megedagik family, one week before their fatal elk hunting trip to the La Cloche range.* She expanded the picture full-page and looked at the boys in the photo, identical twins wearing green baseball caps. There was something about one of them. His smile. A familiar, crooked smile. He was only a little boy, but she knew him.

"I wish you hadn't seen that, Maggie."

She flinched, so engrossed in the article she hadn't noticed Happy standing behind her reading the screen over her shoulder.

"Happy?"

"You don't know how much I wish you hadn't seen that. Why couldn't you just let it be?"

"Happy. I..."

"Shhhhh...you know I can't let you live now. This breaks my heart. I really like you. My idea was to come here today and reason with you. I thought I could get you to back off the case, or try one last time to lead you to Mingan. But you couldn't let it go, could you?"

Maggie's eyes darted around the room in a frantic search for anything she could use as a weapon. She eyed Happy's holstered service revolver.

"You were getting too close, especially that bit about the cabin. But I'd hoped...well now...you know. I can't get caught. Of course you understand, don't you? I'm so sorry."

"Happy, please. I..."

He grabbed her by her shoulders and yanked her to her feet, and as he did, he knocked over her chair. He clutched Maggie's neck with both hands and pressed his thumbs into her throat and shook her. Her reading glasses fell to the floor. She clawed at his face then brought her knee hard into his groin. He grunted, loosened his grip and doubled over.

She reached for his weapon, managing to wrestle it from the holster. He jerked upright, and punched her in the solar plexus knocking the wind out of her. Maggie gasped, and crumpled. With one hand, he grabbed her by the throat and pulled her to her feet, simultaneously grasping her wrist in his other hand. He twisted until she dropped the gun.

She flailed and kicked at him. Her foot connected with his knee, and his shin. With her free hand, she worked at prying his fingers from her neck. She slapped at his face, raked her nails over his cheek, and gouged at his eyes. But he did not react until she brought her boot down hard on the top of his foot. He cried out in pain, relaxed his grip, and she wrenched free. She dashed for the bedroom. Headed for the night stand. Reached for her Glock. He caught up, seized her by the waist and threw her onto the bed. Before she could catch her breath, he was on top of her and had pinned her to the mattress.

The more she fought with ferocity, the more Happy tightened his grip. Blood spotted her arms where his nails dug into her flesh. "Happy, no."

Maggie smelled the acrid stench of a decomposing corpse. Happy's face morphed. His cheek bones protruded from the skin, and putrid skin hung in shreds from his chin and neck. Part of a jaw bone and yellowish teeth jutted through one side where a cheek was meant to be. One eye stared at her, the other empty socket writhed with maggots. Viscous liquid dripped from his face onto hers. The stink overwhelmed her and she gagged...*or was it that he was strangling off her oxygen and that's what caused her to choke? Hallucinating again?* She squeezed her eyes shut and when she opened them, he'd transformed back into what she had once thought was the sweet-looking man with a boyish grin. The ravens battered the window so hard their beaks bled.

Happy crushed her throat with his left hand. He pressed his knee against her abdomen. With his free hand, he reached for the gun. She gasped for breath. Kicked her legs and punched at him with both hands knotted into tight fists. She struggled to wrench out of his arms.

As Happy's thumbs pressed deeper into her throat closing off her air, Maggie relaxed a little. She felt herself sliding away. In the split second between the time Happy stretched for the gun with one hand, and pushed her trachea shut with the other, she slipped into a dream. It was foggy. She was vaguely aware she still struggled although with waning, tepid energy. She felt disembodied, watching him as from a distance choking her, prepared to shoot her in the face with her own gun. In this dream, she saw herself in the reflection of a lake shifting from a woman into a raven, growing black glossy feathers and sprouting wings. Only her eyes remained the same...raven eyes, yes, but the same green color she was born with. She let go.

CHAPTER 44

AS HIS FINGERS made contact with her Glock, Happy softened his grip on Maggie's neck. She gasped as her senses returned. Yanking her head free, she bit down hard on the fleshy part of his left hand. He screamed in pain. Jerked his right hand away from the gun and made a fist. "Bitch! I'll eat your heart while you're still alive."

As he cocked back his fist, she stretched for the weapon and touched it. Without hesitation, she grabbed it, and shoved the barrel in his face. She inhaled and choked. "Get off me."

Happy's eyes widened as he rolled away. He put up one hand. "Take it easy."

Keeping the gun pointed between his eyes, she stood, still choking, her voice raspy. "Stand and get over to the wall. Keep your hands clasped behind your head. You know the drill." She motioned to a bare wall with her gun. "Do it."

He walked over, hands behind his head, and faced the wall. "Turn around."

When he faced her, he was smiling. "I guess everyone's right about you being a bad judge of character when it comes to men, eh?"

"Shut the fuck up. You killed all those babies? Why?"

"Well, since you haven't read my Miranda rights, you and I both know by law you can't use anything I tell you...so...why not? My people have a legend. Want to hear it?" He shook his head. "Silly me, of course you do. The old ones say if anyone eats the heart of a togquos child he will become strong and courageous. The more young togquos hearts you eat, the stronger you become."

"What are you talking about? What in the hell is a togquos?"

"Twin."

"You're a twisted cannibalistic child killer. That story is bullshit."

"No, it's true. I eat the hearts of twin children, and, by golly, good things happen every time. I was the youngest deputy ever in

Wild River County, hired right out of college, brand new in town. How'd you think I got the job? And, now, against all odds, I'm the sheriff. How did you think I managed that?"

"You murdered all those children because of some idiotic superstition and to win an election? What about Bobby, and Sally? What about Mingan? You killed them, didn't you? "

"Be patient." He tilted his head looked at her sideways like a bird might. "By the way, how did you find out about my cabin?"

"Keep talkin', dickhead." She glared at him.

———

Jake's heart pounded so hard he thought it might burst through his chest. Rivulets of sweat dripped into his eyes. Grasping the wheel with one hand, he wiped his face with the other, and as he did, he made a corner too fast almost ending up in a ditch. Yanking the steering wheel, he overcompensated, causing his truck to fishtail. He managed to get the truck back on track, level, straight, and punched the accelerator.

———

"All right, let's start at the beginning." Happy said. "After eating my brother's heart when I was five, I ate the hearts of my first set of twins outside of Ontario when I was fifteen. I'd been having trouble in school. Needed to get my grades up to play baseball. Directly after...holy shit...I had my varsity letter before the end of the semester." He looked to the ceiling. "That was my best year ever in high school.

My second set of twins helped me get laid my first time. She was a beauty. Everyone said she wouldn't put out, but she opened her legs for me. The third helped me ace my SATs so I could get into a decent college. My fourth set scored me the deputy job. The fifth hooked my life's grand prize, Rosa. So on and so on. See what I'm saying? I received exactly what I wanted every time I fed."

"Bobby?"

"Oh, yeah. You did ask about Bobby, didn't you? Sorry. Here's the thing. I'd never killed an adult before, well, unless you count my parents, but that's a different story for a different time. He made a bad mistake. He shouldn't have touched my daughter, should he? You told me you'd feel the same way if it had been Bird or Flower, right?"

"You killed your parents?"

"They were starting to question some things about my... extracurricular habits...made me uncomfortable. I think Dad was onto me. And, speaking of parents, your mother has been calling you, hasn't she? She has been trying to tell you who you are, but you don't get it."

"How did you know?" *How could he know, how?*

"Maggie, neither of us is who we think we are. If you paid attention to the signs, you would have found me out way before now. She did try to tell you that, didn't she? But...oh, yes, we were talking about Bobby, weren't we?"

"When Bobby wound up dead, you were hunting. You weren't even in the state."

"I picked up every one of those calls about what happened to my daughter even though I *said* I didn't have cell reception. Caught a red-eye back. Paid Bobby's cousin in Redding to spring him and, well, you might read they found the cousin's body stuffed in the trunk of his own car, no heart, of course." Happy grinned in that familiar way Maggie had found so endearing at one time. He clucked his tongue. "Corpse is pretty rank by now, I imagine."

"When I made a visit to Douglas Bridge, Lady Luck was on my side. I found Bobby near a dumpster takin' a piss. The guy was so drunk he didn't even notice I was behind him. Such a scrawny, little man. Within a couple of minutes, I had his beating heart in my hands. It was a little more than I could finish. I shared some with a cur dog. Cleaned up at a gas station, slipped back to Oregon for a few days and waited until I was expected back in Wicklow.

All that without getting caught. Pretty damned smart for a guy of 'average intelligence,' wouldn't you say, Maggie?"

"Sally. Why Sally?"

"I feel terrible about that." He shook his head and sniffed in faux remorse. "I liked Sally. She didn't deserve what I did to her."

Maggie was so repulsed by his contrite demeanor she had to suppress an overwhelming urge to punch him in the throat. "What then?"

"You might need a sip of water or a lozenge," he said. "You aren't sounding too good."

"Eat shit. For God's sake, why did you have to kill her?"

"I thought she was you. I knew back then you would dog this case until you found me. I like you a lot but I had to do something, right? I was never quite sure if I should work harder to convince you of Mingan's guilt, or simply get rid of you. I thought I'd play it by ear. I got to your house. Your truck, not Sally's car, was in the driveway, and since her vehicle wasn't around I thought I'd lucked out, and you were alone. I'd been waiting for weeks for an opportunity to find you on your own. I was a little concerned because Jake had a patrol car parked outside your house, but that night, I didn't need to worry in the least. Those losers were snoozing' away. Jake should have fired them, really. Useless pricks."

"Don't play around. Tell me what happened." Maggie thrust the barrel of the gun a couple of inches closer toward Happy's face.

"The house was dark. I couldn't tell with all the lights out who sat at your table. I saw a woman and naturally assumed...I'd broken her neck before I realized my mistake. I wasn't thinking that the woman who I lifted up by her hair was too small, too tiny and delicate, to be you. It happened so fast. Her neck snapped like a cheap toothpick." He lowered his eyes. "God, I feel bad about that. Truly, I do."

"Why did you take her heart?"

"She was dead, and I never believed in wasting anything, especially a fresh, raw heart."

"You sick, sick bastard."

—

Jake pulled onto the highway, then made a sharp right onto a side street, a short cut. The only stop light in the entire county was red. He gunned it, and ran through. The driver of the old Volkswagen Jetta slammed on her breaks so hard her tires smoked as they skidded. She'd come within inches of t-boning him. Jake didn't stop to see if the she was injured. He couldn't. *Maggie, Maggie.*

—

Happy's voice brightened. "Mingan. Let's talk about him. He imagined himself to be a noble Christian vigilante. I couldn't deal with trying to handle you, Jake, the FBI and that Jesus-loving hypocrite, too. I hated him from the get go, and was looking for a reason to kill the prick. His bragging to everyone about getting close to finding the killer...well...you know. Since he tried to rape you, I thought you'd be glad he was dead anyway." He nodded. "You should thank me. I did you a favor."

"Jesus, Happy. You psychotic son-of-a-bitch."

"Can I put my arms down? I'm not going anywhere."

"Put your arms down and I'll splatter your brains against the wall."

"It wasn't difficult. I offered Mingan a ride to the airport on the pretext of making amends. We took a little trip into the forest instead of to Redding. You'll find his body buried out back of my cabin in the woods. You won't be too surprised to hear that his heart was tough, stringy, and tasteless." He made a sucking sound between his teeth, and grimaced as though he'd bitten into a rotten tomato.

"You fed the kids before you killed them, gave them chocolate candy. What's that about?"

"I intended for their last memories to be good ones. I told them we were at my cabin to camp, play games. I told them stories, fed them stuff I know kids like, chicken fingers, pizza, spaghetti. The little tykes were so damned cute." He chuckled. "I wanted them to have fun. I knew what I was planning to do to them could be pretty traumatic." He looked pensive. "The kids all figured I was taking them home while they finished their Hershey bars and I invited them outside. When I broke their necks, I did it quick. Not a single child suffered, honestly. And," he said in a matter-of-fact tone, "I took them one at a time, never in front of one another, no. That would be cruel. When it was over, I treated their bodies with respect, even sang the Algonquin Song for the Dead over them to speed their spirits on their way. See? I'm not as much of a monster as you think I am."

"Oh, yes, you are. You are a much worse monster than anyone could ever imagine."

"I sent them to a better place, and I did my best to give them a little joy, a little happiness beforehand. Would a monster care about such things? Does a shark do his best to avoid undue suffering or pain before he kills his victims?"

"You are no shark. Sharks don't kill for fun. What about Rosa and the kids?"

He punctuated each word. "They...will...be...fine. Rosa comes from a rich family. You know that. Besides, with Rosa's connections and her daddy's money, I'll get one hell of a lawyer who'll get me off with...maybe an insanity plea? I'll do a few years in a locked ward at a country club asylum and be out before my kids graduate high school."

"Don't bet on it, you reprehensible jerk. You'll *never* get out."

"I'll get out. Maybe five, six years of easy, breezy time. I'm a bit thirsty. Can I bother you for a glass of water?"

"Fuck you. When you've answered all my questions, I'm calling this in, and after you're hauled away in handcuffs, you can have water then. I'll make certain someone pisses in it first. I've another question. You had your side arm. Why didn't you shoot me?"

"Guns are not my style. And even though you live in the boonies, a gun blast could alert someone, and there's ballistic tests, traces, evidence. How do you think I've manage to get away for so long? I'm careful. I don't use guns." He paused for a second, "You haven't asked."

"Asked what?"

"Aren't you wondering who leaked info to the press here and to Mario Panetti? If you haven't guessed already, which I know you haven't because you aren't as smart as you think you are, you've got your man." He unlocked his fingers and pointed to the top of his head.

When Maggie's face tightened, he re-laced his fingers and placed his hands back on his head. "Getting that arrogant wop and the national press to print stories took some focus off the case. Pretty smart, eh?" Happy's eyes turned radiant. "You know, Maggie, I've had my sights on another set of twins for quite some time. Remember when you, and everyone were at Danny's house sitting around in the kitchen that time, and you heard something outside?"

"You? I shouldn't be I the least surprised. Go on." She waved the gun.

"What happened was really stupid. I slipped and fell against the window. I know you thought it was Mingan, didn't you?" His voice raspy and shrill, he laughed like a demented clown, like Ed Gein might have after a kill, like Stephen King's Pennywise on crack. "I honestly did my best to point you in the direction of that puss sucking asshole. Everyone else bought that Mingan was the guy." He shook his head and laughed. "Jesus, you are one stubborn bitch, aren't you?"

Maggie tightened her finger on the trigger, then inhaled, and loosened her grip.

"That time, you almost caught me. I got sloppy. Shame on me for being so careless. That whole thing was a little close, you coming out with your Glock." He became quiet, pensive. "You know? I always had a feeling you liked using that thing. Maybe you and I aren't so different. There's a bit of the killer in you, too, like the one in me. Isn't there?"

"You bet. We're far more alike than you can ever imagine."

The window sills were filled with ravens, rocking and cawing, pecking at the panes.

"Oh, I'm not so sure. You're a hard-ass cop first, foremost, and always...but you've got the killer instinct all right." He squinted. "I can see it in your eyes. But, you gotta do everything by the book, don't you?" He shook his head. "Naw. You aren't a real killer, Maggie. Or you would have pulled the trigger by now. You don't have the intestines for it." Maggie fought an urge to smack the smugness off his face.

"Besides, I'm unarmed. You'd never shoot an unarmed man, would you? Anyway, I was waiting, hoping Bird and Flower might come out by themselves to play like they do sometimes. Those little girls would think the blonde wig funny. I'd tell them we were going to play make believe, and with that, it would have been easy enough to get them to take a walk with me into the forest."

———

Jake wasn't big on church going or prayer, but he made a deal with God. *If Maggie is unharmed when I find her, I'll attend services every week. I'll tithe half my paycheck. Please.*

———

"I wanted their hearts, and I still do, really. You know, Maggie, your grandnieces are such sweet, tender little things, Bird and Flower..." He threw back his head and laughed, "but first...*you.*" He unclasped his hands, and lunged toward Maggie.

She fired, hitting his chest. Happy jerked backward. His body smacked hard against the wall. His arms dropped limp to his sides and his face went blank. He slid in a graceful movement down to the floor, leaving a wide smear of blood on the wall. He crumpled to his knees, eyes open, still breathing.

Maggie kneeled beside him. She leaned to his ear and whispered,

"You fucked with the wrong woman. I *do* know who I am. I'm the Pukkukwerek." She stood, aimed her weapon, and emptied her Glock into him, squeezing off one deliberate shot at a time.

There was a loud crash accompanied by the sharp crack of splintering wood and the brittle shatter of glass. Jake, who in his haste had left his house key in the office, had kicked through the front door. He rushed in. Chester, whining, trotted behind. The sheriff entered the bedroom, his service revolver pulled. "Maggie!" He holstered his weapon, ran to her and pulled her into his arms. "Jesus, Maggie. Jesus."

In the distance, sirens. *Jake's backup.*

She let her Glock slip from her hand onto the bed, and leaned into him, folding her arms around him. She allowed him to pull her in close to him. As he buried his face into her neck, Maggie looked over his shoulder, searching.

Chester nuzzled her thigh. Still in Jake's arms, she reached down with one arm and scratched his head. Samantha leapt onto the dresser, tail in the air. Maggie looked through the open bedroom door to the living room beyond. The splintered front door, gaped wide, hung off its hinges. Shattered glass from the inset window, like beads, scattered across the wood floor.

Where are you?

Jake held her tighter. "Thank God you're not hurt."

She craned her neck to look through the parted curtains covering the window. Nothing there but dimming afternoon light pushing in between the dense branches of a red bud bush. *Dusk already? Too early to be this dark.*

Where are you?

She looked to the ceiling.

Where are you?

Then, through the skylight, she saw them, relaxed her shoulders, and smiled.

Oh, there you are.

Quiet as whispers, in a mass so dense they blocked the light of the sun, thousands of ravens circled low over Maggie's cabin.